THE SUMMER I FELL

SONYA LOVEDAY

COPYRIGHT

Cover design by Sonya Loveday
http://www.sonyaloveday.com/
Photo Credit: Pixabay
Formatting by Sonya Loveday
Editor: Editing Services by Cynthia Shepp
http://www.cynthiashepp.com/
Published by Sonya Loveday
First Edition
ISBN: 1499671636
ISBN-13: 978-1499671636

❀ Created with Vellum

CHAPTER 1

The entire south field of the Jacksons property was dotted with the graduating class of 2014. Caps and gowns were shed as the celebration carried over with groups of people, cars, and radio stations all competing to be heard. That was, until the boys rolled up. They had a way of making any social setting gravitate to what they were doing. Radios were lowered or turned off when Aiden Jacobson, Mark Stevens, Josh Howard, Jake Aceton, Jared Jackson, and Eli Benton—the Sexy Six, as every girl in my high school called them, had arrived. The rest of us just called them the Six.

I never understood why everyone was drawn to the sight of them, but it was comical to watch.

Eli was rushed by an already drunk underclassman who had somehow managed to tag along at our last hoorah. He pried her off him and ran his hands down his chest with a laugh, as the others busted his ass at what they'd witnessed. The catcalls were intense as she trailed her hand down his chest. He caught her by the wrist before she got past the button on his jeans. "All right, someone come get jailbait before shit gets outta hand," Eli called out.

She turned her face, and I chuckled when I realized who she was. Kayla Roberts had been trying, unsuccessfully, all year to break into the Six, and they weren't having any of it. Desperate, clingy girls were something they stayed far away from. Kayla's sister, Rachel, marched over, yanked her from Eli, and dipped her head in his direction as she hauled her drunken sister off at a fast clip.

The guys busted out laughing. Aiden yelled above the noise, "Someone put some music on. Damn, this ain't no party!"

It was instantaneous. Luke Bryan's voice belted out of someone's truck, and the party came alive.

I watched all of this from the back of my truck, as I sat on the tailgate and kicked my feet.

Mark broke off from the group first, jingling his keys as he spoke to Jake. They turned in a full circle until Jake looked over to me and pointed with a smile. Mark looked at where he gestured, picking up his hand in a quick wave. I saluted him with my Dr. Pepper can. He shook his head with a smile, turned back to Jake, and then took off across the field.

I wondered what that was about, but knew better than to let my imagination run too wild. Knowing those boys, there was no telling.

I hadn't even planned to come. There really wasn't any reason for me to be there. My circle was a small one. The guys and Paige Holton were my only real friends. It wasn't because I was stuck up. Actually, it was quite the opposite. I'd outgrown this small town long ago. I just didn't feel the need to make any forming or lasting relationships with anyone when I hadn't planned to stick around.

Everything I'd worked so hard for had crashed and burned around me. I couldn't help but feel extremely jaded by the whole experience, but I was a fighter, and I'd keep pushing forward until I made my own way. Whatever way that might be.

I leaned forward and studied my favorite boots. They were worn in all the right places, fitting my feet like a glove. I hardly wore anything else. Tennis shoes were impractical for my day-to-day life. Or rather, they were. What the hell was I supposed to do? I'd counted on the full-ride scholarship, was all but promised it for so long, and it had all been taken away as if I'd only imagined it. And really, hadn't I?

Vet school was the one thing that I hoped would get me out of Opp, and it was gone. It seemed this small town in Alabama had her hold on me.

"Got any more of those?" Jake's voice rumbled into my thoughts about the same time as I heard my cooler slide down the inside of the truck bed. I peered at him over my shoulder, as the cooler creaked open.

"Help yourself," I said, tossing a heavy dose of sarcasm in my reply.

Jake snorted as he pulled an icy can out and slammed the lid closed. He lifted the bottom of his shirt to wipe the top and then hopped up on the tailgate to sit beside me. My breath caught at the sight of his sculpted stomach, and I bit my lip to restrain a groan. It had become harder to hold back my instant reaction to him when he did things like that. "You're supposed to be happy." He quirked his eyebrow at me and popped the can open. His other hand lifted and flicked the icy remains at my face. Cold droplets of water splattered against my heated skin.

Jake, better known as Ace because his last name was Aceton, dodged the sideways punch I aimed at him. He put his hands up in mock surrender and chuckled. "Seriously though, tonight's all about freedom. Taking it all in and having a little fun. School is over, our diplomas are in hand,

and we're one step closer to getting out of here." He flinched when he realized what he said and went to apologize.

"Don't Ace, I didn't take it personal. And I promise that I'll try to have fun." I lifted the hem of my shirt up and rubbed it against my face, feeling the night air touch my side where the material rode up. Swearing I heard a quick intake of breath come from beside me, I darted my eyes over to him, but he wore his usual grin on his face as his eyes twinkled.

He lifted the can to his lips, pulled it down, and glanced sideways at me. "You better, or I swear we'll do what we said we'd do."

I swallowed hard. The Six had pulled rank with me, saying I was to be at the party and I was to have a good time, or they'd carry me off to old man Willis' pond and toss me in without my clothes. I scowled at Ace and crossed my arms. "And how do you propose that's going to go? Because I can assure you that none of y'all will get anywhere near close enough to me to remove a stitch of clothing, let alone throw me into that disgusting ass, bacteria-filled pond."

He wiggled his eyebrows at me, as his lips pulled into a mischievous grin. Suddenly, a hand clamped down on my shoulder. I'd been so focused on Ace that I hadn't seen Jared walk around the other side of my truck. "Already being a party pooper, Riles?"

I grimaced. If anyone would follow through with the threat, it would be Jared. He was the craziest of the Six. I plastered an over-dramatic smile on my face and turned to look at him, even tossing in a little eyelash flutter. "I have no idea what you mean, Jared."

He shook my shoulder and pushed me over so that I sat in between the two of them. I gripped my Dr. Pepper can tighter and tried to stay aloof. It was hard to act that way when threatened by the Six, however. Jared grabbed the can from my hands and finished it off in one swig. "Oh, gross, that was warm as hell."

I leaned back a little to look at him. "I'd say it serves you right for taking my soda when there's a whole cooler full of them back there." I jerked my thumb to the bed of the truck.

His eyes widened, and he leaned back to drag the cooler closer to him. Opening the lid, he hooted with laughter. "See, I knew we kept you around for a reason!" He pulled out the first can his hand touched and held it out to me. I took it from him, as he dug around in the ice. I should have known better. No one kept their back turned to Jared. He was the first one to pull a prank on you. When Ace chuckled, I knew I was in for it. Jared was lightning fast and before I knew it, I had a handful of ice shoved down the back of my shirt. He made sure to catch it between my shirt and my back. A sharp hiss of air escaped my lips, and I bowed forward to get away from the arctic cold melting against my skin. Ace hopped down off the tailgate and caught me before I could jump off to get away.

"Where ya gonna go, Riley?" Ace tormented me with a smile on his face. They meant no harm. If anything, they thought of me as one of their own, so the chances of ever having a boyfriend around the Six were nill.

"That's not fu…" I squealed when Jared rubbed his hand back and forth, spreading the chunk of ice against my lower back. Cold water seeped past the waistband of my jeans and trailed down the center of my backside.

Jared laughed when I all but slammed into Ace to get away from him. "You're a damn jerk, Jared."

His hand shoved at the ice, dragging it across my back, leaving a trail of red-hot pain. I jerked, as I slammed my lips on a howl of pain. Jared snatched his hand away. "Oh shit! Riley, are you okay?"

He yanked his hand back, and the chunk of ice fell to the

truck bed. I grabbed it and went to toss it to the ground, but Ace's hand shot out, catching it before it toppled out of my hand.

"Blood?" He lifted the piece higher to look at it.

Jared bit out a curse beside me. "Damn, Riley. I'm so sorry. Sometimes, I forget you're a girl."

I turned to look at him with complete disbelief etched on my face. "What, the boobs didn't give me away?"

He shook his head and instantly blushed. Leave it to Jared to get embarrassed by the word 'boobs'.

"Here, let me…" He lifted the back of my shirt, but I twisted out of his grip.

"No, Jared. It's bad enough the shit those girls say about me because of you guys. The last thing I need is more gossip about how you got my shirt up at a party."

He flinched away. "Yeah, sorry. But seriously, what do you care what those bitches think? I sure as hell don't."

He grabbed the soda he'd pulled out for me and cracked it open, chugging half the can. When he pulled it away, he covered his mouth on a loud belch.

"You're never gonna change," I said with sigh.

I flicked a glance at Ace, who still stood in front of me, almost wedged between my knees. There was a look on his face that I couldn't quite read. His eyes shifted from mine, and he pegged Jared with a dirty look. "Can you try to control yourself for the rest of the night? I promised her dad I'd take care of her tonight, and we're starting off on the wrong foot already."

Jared brought his hand up and touched his pinky with his thumb. It was their odd symbol for being part of the Six. When you held your hand up in front of you, it sort of looked like one. They used it as a gesture of brotherhood, or some such thing like that. Ace's shoulders slumped into a relaxed position, and he nodded.

"Riley, are you okay? Do you want me to see if one of the girls will look at it for you?" Ace asked as he tossed the ice to the ground.

"I'm fine. I'm sure it's just a scratch. Don't worry about it." I shrugged my shoulders and felt the spot where the ice had dug into my flesh. No way would I let on how bad it hurt.

"Hey jackasses, what's going on over here?" Aiden strutted over and pegged me with a questioning glare. "Hmmm... is Little Miss Riled-up all set for a swim already?" Before I could tell him to keep his ass away from me, Eli strode over.

"Mark's gonna back his truck up over here, so be ready to unload some wood, dickhead." He followed up his statement by punching Aiden in the shoulder. Eli darted out of the way when Aiden lunged at him. Before they could tackle each other, Mark's truck was backed in, and Josh walked over to open the tailgate.

"Hey, knock it off you two and help me get this unloaded." Josh shook his head and pulled an armload of wood out of the back of the truck. The driver's side door slammed shut, and Mark rounded the front and beelined for the bed of mine. The cooler lid creaked open once again as he tossed cans to Aiden, Eli, and Josh. He fished one out for himself and closed the lid with a thump. "Gotta love our Riley. She takes good care of us." He shot a smirk at me, downed the entire can, crushed it in his hands, and tossed it into the back of my truck.

I found myself chuckling at him, as he shot me a wink. "You're a bunch of freakin' animals. I swear!"

The cacophony of noises that came from them could rival a barnyard. Some moo'ed, some oinked, and one of them belted out a rooster crow. I ran my hands down my face. The Six were nothing but a bunch of unruly little boys that never grew up.

Ace moved from his spot in front of me and walked over to help finish unloading the pile of wood in the bed of Mark's truck.

Jared slid off the tailgate and stopped beside me. He tapped my knee and when I looked up at him, he gave me a weary smile. "Sorry about that, Riles. You know I wouldn't intentionally hurt you, right?"

I gave him a smile. "I know, Jared. I'm okay, don't worry about it."

He kicked his shoulder up in a half shrug. "You might think you're tough, but I know I hurt you. If you want one of us to look at it, we can do it where no one can see." There was a glimmer of honesty in his eyes. I knew that all I needed to do was say the word and one of them would do just that. After all, they'd been taking care of me for a long time. Whether I wanted them to or not.

"I'm okay, Jared. Honest."

He dipped his head and left me sitting on the tailgate.

Daylight was slowly waning as the Six unloaded the last of the wood and stacked logs for a bonfire. It was nights like these that made me happy. If only we could minus out the rest of the senior class, it would be perfect.

The guys were pros at building a decent fire, and they all took turns keeping it burning. It was like an unspoken rule between them. Some sort of Six code. They had lots of codes they stuck by, but they never talked about. And I had a feeling one of those had something to do with me.

I slid a glance over to where Ace stood beside the unlit fire. He pulled out a small gas can, poured a stream out on the logs, and walked back over to the truck to put it away. I couldn't tell you who lit the fire, but I heard the gas ignite and saw the outline of the flames dance along the back of Ace's gray T-shirt. I jerked my gaze away from him when he turned, looking back down at my boots. If I didn't stop watching him, someone would catch me, and I'd never live it down.

~

Luke Bryan's voice crooned on about a girl, and how she could crash his party anytime. For a second, I closed my eyes and let the song carry me away to my latest daydream of Ace. His voice broke through my carefully constructed moment.

"Are we boring you?" he asked, sliding back onto my tailgate beside me. I hadn't moved since I'd been shoved to the middle by Jared. When Ace's thigh brushed mine, my eyes popped open, and I shivered from the contact.

He bumped his shoulder into mine. "You okay?"

I bit my cheek and held back a hiss of pain. The ice Jared had tortured me with sure did a number on my skin.

I jerked my head up and down, drawing his attention away from me by pointing to the fire. "I swear if I didn't know better, I'd say you guys were Boy Scouts at one time."

He looked over to where the others stood talking around the fire. "Yeah, well, what can I say? We're all a bunch of fire bugs."

He laughed at what he said, knowing full well that once the summer was over, he'd be stepping into a job with the Forestry Division. That meant he'd be busting people like himself soon. Wherever the Six were, you could guarantee there'd be a bonfire of some sort, and it didn't matter where.

"So what are your plans this summer?" he asked.

Before I could reply, a high-pitched voice interrupted us. Samantha Sloan sauntered over in her skin-tight jeans and cling-wrap shirt that dipped low in the front to give any and all a view of her very ample chest. She batted her heavily mascaraed eyelashes to draw focus to her light blue eyes. When Ace looked at her, she flipped her blonde hair over her shoulder. "She's finally leaving and then maybe one of you lucky boys will look in another direction."

I let the comment slide. At no point had I ever been the reason why none of the Six dated her. She loved saying stupid things like that when they were within earshot.

I waited. One of them was bound to acknowledge her. When they didn't, she turned her focus to me. "So where's your other half?" She must have found her joke funny because she snorted out a squealed sort of laugh.

I arched a brow up at her. "Other half?"

She tossed her hand in the air. "Oh please, we all know you use them," she gestured at the guys, "as a cover to being a lesbo with your girlfriend."

Ace stiffened beside me, and the others stopped talking mid-sentence. I hadn't really looked at her until then and when I did, she backed up a step.

"What bothers you the most, Sam?" She cringed at the nickname. "Is it the fact that none of them will sleep with you? Or that you want to sleep with me?"

Laughter erupted around us, and Samantha fisted her hands at her sides. "You're probably fucking all of them. That's how you keep them close, right? How does that work, Riley? One every night and then a break on Sunday? Or is Sunday the day you sleep with your bestie?"

I flew off the tailgate before Ace could stop me. My fist shot out and slammed into Samantha's eye. She staggered backwards, tripping over her own feet. I hauled her up by her shirt, as the guys circled around me. They weren't letting anyone past them. They knew I'd finally had enough of Samantha's hateful comments and had even asked me when I'd planned to kick her ass.

When I'd straightened her back up, she slapped my hand away. "How dare you?"

"How dare I? You just can't keep your mouth shut, and

I'm done listening to your bullshit." I shoved her, and she stumbled back a step.

Her lip curled, and I knew whatever she was about to say would seal her fate with me. I'd had enough of her snide comments and her bullying ways. I would put an end to it once and for all.

"You are, aren't you? You're sleeping with all of them!" Her shrill voice carried over the quiet night, and I hissed between my teeth when I realized that even the damn radio had been shut off.

The guys had promised that if it ever came to setting Samantha in her place, they'd let me do what needed to be done. By the looks of it, they were having a hard time keeping that promise. Eli had a hold of Josh's arm, and Aiden had his arm out in front of Jared. Mark and Ace kept shooting glances at each other. I waited until they looked at me and shook my head. I was over Samantha dragging my name through the mud because none of them were interested in her.

She shot forward and I dodged her hand, but her intent wasn't to punch me. No, she went for the low-ball move and grabbed my ponytail. I swore under my breath, brought my arm up between us, and pulled my head back with everything I had. When there was enough room between us, I shoved her away. Excited chatter rolled around us. Her friends cheered her on, telling her to 'take care of that whore,' and other hate-filled comments that insinuated my reputation was no better than a hooker's.

Samantha laughed and tossed her hands out to the side. "Look at you. I don't know what I was thinking. Who the hell would sleep with you?" She picked up her hands and swept them in the air from my feet to my chest. "You have nothing there for them to hold on to, and you sure as hell don't look like you could keep up with them." The girls around the circle laughed, as she pointed out all of my flaws to the entire senior class. It hit me wrong, and I let a telltale wince slip across my face.

"Oh, look, she realizes it, too!"

I didn't mean to, but I looked up at Ace. My eyes darted away, but I saw the anger that shimmered there. He was as pissed as I was.

She cocked her hip out and ran her hand down her side to accentuate her voluptuous shape. "Men want something they can hold on to and well, sweetie, you just don't fall into that category, do you?"

I could feel the darkness creeping up on me as anger turned to rage. It consumed me until there was only tunnel vision between her and me. She snickered and pointed past me. "Ah, there she is."

I swung my gaze over to where Paige pushed past Aiden and walked into the circle. Her eyes were wide, and she darted a glance between Samantha and me. A look of complete disbelief was etched across her face.

"Come on, Riley. She's not worth it." She grabbed my arm and pulled me back a step. I tugged myself free of her grasp and looked over to Aiden. He stepped up and pulled Paige back, putting her behind him. I could hear the angry tone in their voices as he whispered a warning that she didn't like.

"Aw, your girlfriend tried to keep you from getting your ass beat. Isn't that cute?" The cooing tone to her voice destroyed the last bit of self-control I had, and I lunged for her. I didn't care if her daddy was the sheriff—that bitch was gonna get it. I'd had enough.

CHAPTER 2

*S*amantha didn't see it coming. She was too busy playing it up to all the onlookers, and it worked in my favor. My fist connected with her jaw, and her head snapped back from the force of the blow. When she staggered backward a few steps, I unclenched my hand and shook my fingers. Her damn jaw had to have been made out of granite because my fist hurt as if I'd punched a damn rock instead of her face.

I let her get her bearings. I didn't want the fight to be over before it started. There was so much more I wanted to take out on her that two punches would never cover it. Her hand went up to her jaw, and she touched it carefully. "You're gonna pay for that, bitch."

I shrugged my shoulders. "I don't see you doing much about it."

Around us, everyone laugh. I wondered if it made her feel just a taste of the hell she'd put me through over the last few years.

She hissed through her teeth. "My daddy…"

"Isn't here," I cut her off. "And even if he were, I'd still whip your ass."

"You bitch!"

"Yes, we've established that already, so are you gonna take a swing or what? 'Cause honestly, I have better things to do tonight."

"Don't you mean people?" she hissed.

"Yeah, well, that too, if I'm lucky." I smirked, which enraged her. Let her think whatever she wanted. I knew the truth. The Six and I had always been friends. Nothing more.

Aiden shouted loud enough for everyone to hear him. "Hot damn boys, this could be our lucky night. Do you think she'll pick me?"

I turned my head and shot him a deadly glare. Samantha took advantage of it. Before Aiden could warn me, Samantha's fist connected with my eye. Her punch hadn't hurt with the little effort she'd put behind it. It was the monstrosity of a ring she wore that really did the damage. The skin under my eye burned, and I knew without even seeing it that she'd ripped a gouge in my skin.

When Samantha stepped back, crying out as she shook her hand, I made my move. I didn't even think about it. I tackled her to the ground and followed through with a punch to her face, not even sure where it landed. I lifted my fist again, but an iron grip caught my wrist and held tight.

I blinked to focus with my good eye and saw Ace leaning in close. "That's enough, Riley. You made your point."

His voice brought me back from the edge of the murderous rage I'd slipped into. He dipped his head in her direction, and I looked at her. My hand was wound tight in her hair, and I'd lifted her upper body off the ground to deliver another blow. I let my body sag, and I felt her shudder underneath me. I'd climbed right on top of her to deliver the next blow and hadn't even realized it. When Ace felt me relax, he let go of my wrist and put his hand out to help me up.

"Let her go, Riley. I think she's learned her lesson."

I wasn't ready to let her go. I had one more thing to say to her, so I leaned in and dropped my voice low enough for only her to hear me. "You're right. I've had them all and let me tell you, they're so good. Too bad you'll never know." I jerked my hand out of her hair and let Ace help me up.

I tilted a little to the side, and he wrapped his arm around me to steady me before he'd let me walk.

A blow to my back took my breath away. I heard Ace cuss as he tried to keep me from face planting into the ground. Even with his help, I fell to my knees. Stars bloomed behind my eyelids, as I struggled to get air into my lungs.

I could hear the other guys shouting, and then Jared hollered over the top of them all. "Get that fuckin' bitch outta here before I forget she's a girl!"

I gasped into the ground, not able to move. Ace hovered over me, talking to me, but nothing made sense. I could feel myself slipping off into the spot where you go when you've been subjected to too much pain and your body shuts down. I swear my mind played tricks on me. The tone in his voice was unsteady. He was scared, and I think he called me baby. My eyes closed, and I let the darkness swallow me. Some graduation day it had turned out to be.

～

"Shit, man. What are we supposed to do?" The fear in Josh's voice made my senses come alert.

"I don't know, but I'm not taking her back to her dad like that." Ace's tone was dead set.

"What if she's got internal bleeding or some shit?" Jared

asked. His voice moved along with him, and I could tell he was pacing the floor.

"I doubt she has internal bleeding. More than likely, the air got knocked out of her. Besides, it's her face that should bother you the most." Paige was there, and she was being the voice of reason. "Boys, just give me a second to look at her without you hovering."

I could hear the tension in her voice, but they listened to her because I heard several sets of feet trekking across the floor, and then a door shut.

Where am I?

Paige's hand came down to rest on my shoulder. "They're gone now. You can open your eyes."

I sighed, and then winced from the pain it caused in my back. "What the hell happened?"

"You finally took on Samantha."

I cracked my eyes open, as Paige squatted down so I could see her. Her hands gripped the edge of the well-worn table that I laid face down on. A sense of relief washed through me. They'd brought me to the cabin.

"The guys made everyone go home, then loaded you up in Ace's truck, and brought you here. They didn't dare take you anywhere else."

I groaned. "A hospital would have been nice."

She gave me a half-hearted laugh. "Yeah right. I can see you coming to in a hospital. You would've decked all of us for that."

I tried to push myself up but couldn't.

"Just lay still for a minute. I haven't had a chance to look at the damage she did to your back with the log she threw at you."

"She threw a log at me?"

"Yep." I felt her lift my shirt up, and then a low hiss

slipped past her lips. "This needs to come off, so I can clean up whatever sliced across your back."

I groaned, knowing I had to not only roll over onto my side, but also force myself upright.

"I got ya, Riles." Paige's hands gripped my shoulder and hip, rolling me onto my side. I stiffened out like a plank, and she smirked at me. "Curl your legs toward the edge of the table and keep yourself locked like this. I'll do the rest."

I clamped my lips together and went completely rigid. Once I pulled my legs up like she wanted, Paige had me sitting upright in one quick move.

"You can loosen up and breathe now," she said, lifting my shirt up my back and over my head. I raised my arms out in front of me, and she peeled it away. Razor-sharp pain exploded across my back with every movement. As soon as I was free, she tossed it behind her. The door creaked open as Ace walked in.

"Ace! Get out!" I crossed my arms in front of my chest, gasping when my skin pulled taut.

"Not gonna happen, Riles. Here, Paige, I brought you the first aid kit."

"Thanks, Ace. I got it from here." Paige walked around me to block his view.

I heard him move around her. The next thing I knew, his fingers touched my shoulder gently. "I swear to God, she's so lucky she's a girl."

I knew he was angry, but I hadn't realized just how much until that spewed out of his mouth. Samantha should thank her lucky stars she was born a girl, 'cause if she were a boy, the Six would have taken her out.

The latches to the first aid kit popped open, and Paige pulled out the items she needed. The room was chilly. No matter how hard I tried, I couldn't fight the shiver that raced up and down my entire body from it. The fact that the AC vent blew down directly on top of me didn't help.

"Paige, can you give me my shirt?" I asked as my teeth chattered together.

"Nu–uh. It's covered in dirt and blood. Just sit tight. I'll get you a blanket when this is cleaned up and bandaged." Paige's hands were as cold as the air blowing down on me, and I shuddered again with a groan.

I heard the slide of fabric and looked over about the same time Ace handed me his shirt.

I greedily accepted it, pulling it close, thankful for the warmth of his skin, which lingered in the material. I looked up at him and caught a flicker of something I'd never seen in his eyes before. It disappeared so fast that it left me wondering if I'd mistaken what I saw. He continued to stare are me, so I gave him a tight-lipped smile of thanks and ducked my head. His scent flooded my nose, and I inhaled the faint hint of cologne as I buried my face in his shirt.

"Hand me another antiseptic wipe, Ace," Paige said.

I heard him move back and whistle through his teeth. "I don't know whose ass I wanna kick first. Jared's or Samantha's."

The cold chill of the antiseptic wipe slid across my back, and a high-pitched whine slipped past my lips.

"Sorry, Riles. I'm trying to be gentle," Paige said as she lightened her touch.

"It's not that. It's frickin' cold." To prove it, my skin broke out in goose bumps that raced along my entire body.

"Hold her hair out of the way, Ace."

He did as she asked, but stopped her before she could continue cleaning my back. I felt my hair slip free, as Ace's fingers run through the length of my hair, collecting it all together and pulling the hair-tie around to wrap it up into a sloppy ponytail.

"You're pretty good at that." I could hear the humor in Paige's voice.

"Yeah, well, don't tell the guys," Ace joked back with her.

He'd done it a few times before when we'd worked together on house calls. The last time had been about a week ago when my hands were covered in blood from rescuing a calf that had gotten itself tangled up in a saggy piece of barbwire fence. We'd been driving down a dirt road that cut between Jared's place and the Willis' when I noticed it. I'd thrown the truck in park, and Ace had followed along beside me to the spooked calf. Not one word was spoken as we worked together to free it. Ace's hands were cleaner than mine were, so he dialed Old Man Willis and Dr. Anderson, our local veterinarian, and we'd spoken to them on speakerphone.

Ace had managed to stay out of the blood when he pulled the fence away from the wounded calf, and I did what I always do. I dove in without a thought to the mess I'd make of myself. I struggled to keep the calf down without hurting it even further. By the time Dr. Anderson made it there, my hair had partially slipped out of the ever-present ponytail I'd kept it up in. I blew the strands out of my face, mostly out of habit. There were just some things I didn't want in my hair. Blood and cow shit were two of them.

Ace had waited until Dr. Anderson had sedated the calf, and we helped him load it up in the back of his truck. Old Man Willis showed up a few seconds later, and we filled him in on what happened. I tossed my keys to Ace and went to bail into Dr. Anderson's truck, but the vet's hand caught the door. He'd tipped his hat back on his forehead and squinted against the harsh afternoon sun. "Isn't today your day off?"

"Yeah, but..."

"No buts, Riley. I swear, you work harder than I do most days. Go, I'll be fine." There was a worn look to Dr. Anderson. A kind one, but tired. He worked around the clock in our town. It didn't matter what time it was. If you called him, he'd be there. He settled his hat back over his shaggy, brown hair and reached out to pat me on the shoulder.

I answered him, as he turned away to walk around the front of his truck. "I don't mind."

"Yeah, but I do. You have plenty of time later to wear yourself out with this job. Right now, you need to enjoy this last bit of freedom and take the day off." He climbed in his truck and fired the engine.

Old Man Willis' truck kicked up a cloud of dust, as he raced down the dirt road and pulled up beside Dr. Anderson's window. They exchanged a few words, and Dr. Anderson drove off with Old Man Willis following behind him. When he passed, the old man stuck his hand out the window with a wave of thanks to us.

"Well, that was… fun," Ace said, as he jingled my keys in his hand.

Turning, I scrunched my face up at him. "Fun?"

He laughed at me and stuffed my keys in his pocket. "Come here, that's driving me crazy."

I tilted my head in question, and my hair bounced off my cheek.

"That." He pointed at my hair.

My eyes cut up to the left, wondering what he meant.

He put his hands on my shoulder, turned me around, and put my hair back to rights.

The first aid kit snapped closed, and I pushed back the latest memory of my time with Ace, pulling his shirt tighter against me. When had he started taking over all of my thoughts?

"Okay, you're all set. It's not as bad as it looks. Bruising from the log she hit you with and a long scrape right under your bra strap, but other than that, you'll live. You'll just be a little sore for a couple of days," Paige said, setting the box on the table beside me. After everything, waking up in the cabin, losing my shirt, Ace walking in on my half nakedness, and still, my biggest worry was how the hell I would get off the table without flashing him.

Embarrassment flooded through me. I knew my cheeks would be a deep shade of red, so I kept my face down. The shirt Ace had taken off and handed to me did little more than cover my face. I hadn't even covered myself up with it. No, I'd been too busy inhaling his scent and replaying the last time we were alone together.

"Did you bring any clothes with you?" Paige asked, as she crossed over to the recliner by the fireplace and sat.

"No. I hadn't planned to stay out tonight." I pulled Ace's shirt lower to cover the plain white bra I had on.

Ace stepped back and leaned against the far wall of the kitchen. "You still have a change of clothes from the last weekend we all stayed out here."

"I do?" How did he remember that, but I couldn't?

"Yeah, I found them in the drawer the other day. Hang on; I'll go see what's there." He walked past me, and my eyes followed him until he disappeared down the hallway.

When I knew he could no longer see me, I carefully slipped his shirt over my head and slid my arms out through the sleeves. I kept looking down the hallway, waiting for him to reappear.

Paige snapped her fingers to get my attention. "You might wanna wipe the drool off your face before he comes back."

I rolled my eyes at her, but I kept my thoughts to myself. Yes, she was my best friend, but that didn't mean I'd said a word about my growing infatuation with Ace.

"Are you staying?" I changed the subject on Paige, in hopes that Ace wouldn't come back down the hallway and hear something I didn't want him to.

"Nah, I have to work in the morning. Hey, what are you gonna tell your dad?" She pointed at my face and winced.

I shifted with a groan. "The truth, which will probably freak him out or piss him off."

My dad was very protective of me since my mom decided that she no longer wanted to live the quiet country life. She left us behind and never looked back. It was probably a good thing too, since I had nothing nice to say to her. How did you just up and leave everything behind? How did you leave your daughter and start over again as if she didn't exist? Dad claimed she had to find herself. My reply was 'good luck with that'. It was a sore subject for both of us.

Paige chuckled as she stood up and stretched her arms. Her hand slapped over her mouth, stifling the yawn that tried to escape.

The front door of the cabin opened, and in trudged the rest of the Six. Each of them carried a bag and a look of concern stretched across their faces.

I picked up my fingers and gave them a half wave. "I'm fine, guys."

"Yeah, well, you don't look fine, so don't try to cover it up to make us feel better," Jared said, dropping his bag on the counter. I jerked around to tell him to shut it and immediately regretted it. Sweat broke along my brow, and a clammy film coated my skin. The next time I saw Samantha, I'd chuck a damn log at her head as payback.

Josh darted in my line of vision and gave me a toothy grin. "You look a little green, Riles."

I swallowed the thickness in my throat and closed my eyes tight, which was a big mistake. "Ow!"

"Damn it, y'all, she's hurt. Stop screwing around with her!" Ace's voice boomed down the hallway before I could even see him.

Josh's hands shot up, palms out, and he backed away from me. "None of us touched her, Ace."

The others ignored Ace's roar of disapproval and set their bags down to put away what they'd brought with them.

"Are y'all moving in?" I asked.

"No, but we figured we'd stay here for a couple of days. Kinda lay low for a little while until you don't look like... that." Jared tossed his head in my direction.

"My dad..."

"I stopped by and talked to your dad. I asked him if he minded if you stayed, and he was cool with it," Josh said. He raked his hands through his hair, telling me there was more to it than that.

I pegged him with the meanest glare I could without howling in pain from it. "What?"

Josh's hands fell to his belt loops and hooked his thumbs. "I told him Paige was gonna stay out here, too." He darted a glance at Paige. I looked over at her about the time she shook her head and threw up her hands.

"Y'all know I can't do that. I'm on shift tomorrow. Besides, I'm on the schedule at the hospital all week. The hours are weird, and I'd planned on crashing in the lounge in between shifts."

Mark crossed his arms and gave Paige a look I couldn't quite decipher. "But Riley's dad doesn't know that. Besides, it's not like you couldn't come out here at least one night. We're not that bad, Paige."

She actually squirmed under his gaze, nodding her head sharply in agreement with what Mark said. When had things got awkward between those two?

Mark's expression changed. He gave Paige a grin that would have melted any of the other girls who competed for his attention. "Good, then it's settled."

"God, you six are so damn bossy. When are you gonna get

it through your thick ass heads that not every female in existence will do what you want when you... ugh, never mind!" Paige slammed her hands on her hips and shook her head. "Make yourselves useful and get her off the damn table. Riley, I'll be by tomorrow with clothes for you." Paige's sentence trailed off as she walked out the door and closed it firmly behind her. The Six thankfully waited until her car started before they broke out in laughter.

Ace shook his head and held his hand out to me. "Come on, Riles, let's get you settled on the couch."

CHAPTER 3

There was no easy way to get off the table. If it didn't hurt so much, it might have been a little humorous. Unfortunately for me, it did hurt, and it was not at all funny. Ace ran his hand down his face. "Riley, I don't know how to help you without hurting you. I can't even put my arm around you and lift you up."

Eli stuck his hand out and gestured for mine. When I stretched it out, he dropped two white pills in my palm. "Take those," he said, as he tried handing me a bottle of water. I went to give the pills back, but he shook his head. "Relax, Riley. They're just ibuprofen with codeine. You need something for the pain, and this will help without being too much. Trust me, you'll want something, and soon, when your back tries to seize up. This is what I took when I tore a ligament a few months back."

I shook my head no and tried again to hand them back, but Ace's hand closed over mine. "Just take them, Riley. Eli's right; you're gonna need something for the pain."

The kitchen went quiet, as if the Six waited for me to give in for once and agree. "Fine."

Eli unscrewed the bottle cap and handed the water to me. Dumping the pills in my mouth, I took a swig to wash them down.

Ace took the water from my hand and handed it off to Eli. "We'll wait a few minutes for the medicine to kick in before you try to get off the table."

I was tolerant up to a certain point. I really was, but sitting on the damn table like a bird on its perch was just as uncomfortable as trying to get off it. I pulled a deep breath in, pushed my hands against the top, and shoved myself off the edge. The slamming stop jarred my body, and Ace grabbed my arm to steady me. His tight hold kept me from falling backwards into the edge and doing further damage to my back.

I huffed deep breaths with each wave of pain that rolled over me, as I chased the black dots in front of my eyes to make them disappear. Ace put a hand under my elbow to help keep me upright.

"Riley, I swear to God, you're gonna be the death of me," Ace muttered under his breath when I swayed against his grip.

Tilting my head to look up at him, I scowled. His eyebrows lifted, and his gaze hardened as if challenging me. His eyes told me everything without saying a word. *"Go ahead and argue with me, you know I'll win,"* they said.

I looked down and groaned at the sight of my pants. "Ace, was there any sweatpants in the clothes I left behind?"

Confusion marred his brow. "You can't even stand up on your own. How the hell are you gonna change by yourself?"

"Y'all shoulda thought about that before you chased Paige off." They had a bad habit of doing that crap. I'd put up with everything they dished out over the years. Paige had only dealt with them since our sophomore year in high school, and she did that for me. The Six made her uncomfortable.

Not because of their looks, but because she was shy and kind of timid. Or was. Ever since she'd started taking loads of college classes in between her high school ones, she'd grown a backbone. It was like her confidence grew when she took on shifts at the hospital and got her foot in the door as an intern. If anything, being around the Six had given her thicker skin. If she could deal with them, she could deal with anyone.

Ace groaned beside me. "How do you want to do this, Riles?"

Josh tossed the last pillow on the couch and walked over to take my arm. "I can help her."

I swear I felt Ace stiffen up beside me. "It's okay, Josh. I can do it myself."

"You're gonna fall on your damn face, which, by the way, would make it worse than it already is." Ace sounded angry. "Josh, hand me those pants," he said, pointing to the clothes he'd laid over the back of one of the recliners in the living room.

Josh grabbed them and handed them to Ace.

My pulse hammered in my neck, and I could feel a cold sweat beading up under my armpits. No way would I let Ace help me undress. "Ace... I got..."

"No. Now stop arguing with me and let's go." His fingers gripped my elbow a little tighter, and we moved down the hallway.

"Huh. Who woulda thought Riley would actually cave in to Ace getting all dominant like that?" Aiden piped up. The guys howled with laughter since it was so unlike him to point something like that out. Out of all of them, Aiden was the one with the least to say.

"Idiots," Ace mumbled under his breath, flipping the bathroom light on.

"They're your friends," I shot back at him.

"They're yours, too. Okay, how do you wanna do this?" I could see the blush creep along his cheeks before he turned and tossed the sweatpants on the counter.

I struggled to sit down on the closed toilet seat. Ace turned just in time to grab my arms and take the weight off my legs. "Thanks," I said, blowing out the breath I'd held. The codeine must have kicked in because the pain had at least dulled, and it was a little easier to move. Leave it to Eli to know just what I'd need. Then again, Eli was constantly getting hurt, so he was experienced with all sorts of injuries.

Before I could ask, Ace knelt down and grabbed the heel of my boot. With a gentle tug, it slipped off my foot, and he set it on the floor beside him. Picking up my other foot, he removed my other boot.

"Riley?" He kept his head bent as he spoke.

"Yeah, Ace?"

"Jake." He whispered his name back at me.

The way he said it was like asking me to call him by his real name, and that was treading dangerous ground for me. Using his nickname kind of put a barrier, a self-created wall up between us. Calling him Jake took it away and made it more. So much more.

He sat back on his feet. Waiting.

"Can you help me up, Jake?" His head snapped up, and he looked at me as his hands came out to mine. I slipped mine over his and felt every ridge, every callous, every single ripple and indent, almost like I'd done it all in slow motion. His hands locked around mine, and he lifted me up until I stood close enough that our chests brushed against one another. I sucked in a sharp breath as my fingers clenched over his. His eyes never left mine until he brought my hand to the sink counter, and I let go to balance myself. He moved the sweatpants over to where I could reach them and turned around. Widening his stance, he put his arm out. "Just grab a hold of me if you feel like you're gonna fall."

"Thanks."

I let go of the counter, unbuttoned my jeans, and then slid the zipper down. The problem was shimmying them past my hips, and not using my upper body to do it. I felt myself falling, and my fingertips slipped off Ace's arm. He spun so fast that I didn't even have time to process that he'd turned. "Riley?"

He cradled my neck in one hand and gripped my hip with the other. He heaved a sigh of relief as his forehead came down to rest on mine. "That. Was. Close."

I could feel his heart beating against my hand and realized in that moment that my hand was splayed over his chest. When he looked down, the corner of his lips kicked up into a half smile. "See, admit it, you need my help."

"Fine. I need you... your help." My admission made Ace's half smile bloom into a full one. He really was devastatingly handsome. And so very, very unattainable.

"What makes you say that, Riles?" His thumb brushed up my neck, as his other hand splayed a little wider along my hip.

"Huh?"

He winked at me. "I've never been unattainable."

I stood there, dumbfounded. "I said that out loud?"

He chuckled and dropped his hand from my neck, as I slumped back into the counter. "Hold on, please." And before I could stop him, he grabbed the sides of my jeans and tugged them down over my hips, all the way to my feet. I couldn't help the blush that bloomed across my cheeks, as I looked down at the top of his head. I could feel the fire of it spreading down my neck to my chest.

Ace reached up past me, grabbing the sweatpants from where he'd set them. He picked up one foot, then the other, sliding the material up my legs and over my hips. When he let go of the waistband, he stood, putting his hands against the countertop, caging me in as his eyes sought mine. I could see his pupils dilate. The vein in his neck stood out, pulsing in time with his heartbeat. His jaw flexed once, and then again, as he stepped forward, lining his body up with mine.

He leaned in, and I closed my eyes on a quick intake of breath. A bolt of electricity zipped through me when I felt his nose brush against mine, and I waited. Would he kiss me? My lips tingled as he drew in a deep breath, making it feel like he'd pulled every bit of oxygen from the air around us. His hand came up, cupping my neck with his fingers. They were warm and rough against my skin. The catch in my breath stalled him, and I found myself reaching out to grab a fistful of his shirt as I trembled. Ace's hand slipped from the counter to my hip. I tilted my lips close enough that they barely touched his. He shuddered as his lips moved lightly against mine with the barest hinted whisper of touch. It wasn't a kiss—it was torture.

"Yo, Ace!" Jared yelled down the hallway. "We got a fire goin'. How many hot dogs y'all want?"

Ace jerked back and dropped his hands. "I'm sorry... I don't know why I did that. I shouldn't have done that." His voice was a hoarse whisper. His words, while apologetic, sent a knife through my heart. Ace didn't want me. He was just being a typical guy.

I turned my back on him and grabbed my jeans, using the excuse of folding them to look away and give him his escape. I cursed myself for being such an idiot. Ace had seen me almost naked. He was only reacting like any other hormone-driven guy and when he realized what he'd started, he'd shut down when reality crashed in on us. Or I should say, when Jared's big-ass mouth opened and reminded us of who we were and where we were. The kick in the ass of it was that we'd left the door wide open. Anyone could have walked in on us while Ace helped me get my pants on.

"Ace, what the hell, man? Is everything okay? Is Riley okay?" The tone in Jared's voice changed as he jogged down the hallway.

I didn't want to face Jared after what had happened, or really, what hadn't happened with Ace, so I grabbed a washcloth from the cabinet behind me and moved around Ace to get to the sink. He backed up to put some room between us and shoved his hands in his pockets, putting his head down so I couldn't see his face. Jared came to sliding halt, as he grabbed the doorframe. His eyes darted between Ace and me, taking in the scene.

"Is everything okay?"

I turned the sink on and wet the washcloth, giving him a smile in the mirror. "Everything's fine. I just wanted to wash my face, Mr. Impatient."

Jared rolled his eyes and stepped into the bathroom. Putting his hand on my shoulder, he forced me to turn around. When I did, he bit back a wince as he grabbed the washcloth from my hand, wiping the cool cloth along the cut under my eye. I hissed at the contact.

Before I could say anything, Ace pushed off the wall. "She can do that herself, ya know."

It sounded harsh coming from him. The Six always joked, argued, and grumbled at each other, but his tone was one I'd never heard him use before on his friends. Jared's eyes darted to look over my shoulder. His mouth kicked up at the corner before he answered, "The rules have changed, brother."

Ace swore under his breath and stormed out of the bathroom.

I caught Jared's wrist and stepped back from him. "What was that about?"

Jared chuckled. "Ace doesn't like his own rules." He

shrugged and handed the washcloth back to me with a wink. "Hurry up. We got a fire rollin' and dogs on."

He walked out before I could reply.

I took a few minutes longer to collect myself. It wasn't very often I had a moment of peace with the Six around. They hovered whether they realized it or not, and all that testosterone at once could be suffocating. I ran the washcloth back under the tap and wrung it out as I assessed my eye. It was swollen, but not as bad as I would have thought, given the expressions on the guys' faces. There was a gash just below my left eye from the ring Samantha wore, but it was more a scratch than anything. Had I not turned my head with her punch, it would have been worse. The bruise would be ugly. The purple in it was almost black, and I knew I'd be sporting it for at least a week. The tightness in my back had lessened, so I was able to lift my shirt to get a look at the damage. A large, red welt ran left to right just under my bra strap, and the beginning of a bruise formed underneath it from the log Samantha had hit me with. I could only hope her bruises were worse than mine. Then again, the bruise to her ego probably went deeper than any mark I could have made on her, so that was at least something.

The guys had made it seem worse than it was. Like always. Sometimes it felt like I had six older brothers, but that wasn't quite right either, because what I felt for Ace was nothing close to brotherly.

His lips had been so close, so soft. His body so hard, so near, and then gone. I let out a watery sigh, as I fought the tears that threatened to spill. Ace would be my undoing if I let him. I needed to come to terms with the fact that he was off-limits, and let it go.

A tear trekked down my face and then another. I didn't have the energy or the want to wipe them away. Besides, it was just me, alone in the bathroom, crying over a boy I couldn't have. Another tear fell as a warm hand landed lightly on my shoulder.

"Oh damn, I should have warned you that you'd probably feel a little out of sorts." Eli's voice was quiet, soft, like he knew if he talked any louder than a whisper, I'd shatter.

A watery laugh slipped past my lips, as I picked up the washcloth and wiped the tears from my face.

"Sorry, Riley." Eli pulled his hand back and leaned against the doorjamb. "If you want, I can help you to bed. It might help if you get some rest. I always took the pain meds before I went to bed, so I could at least sleep through the night."

Eli had become part of the Six when the Bentons adopted him five years ago. He never talked about life before then, and no one asked. Times were a little different back when Eli came into our lives. The Bentons had tried for a long time to have a baby and it never happened, so they decided to try foster parenting. Eli was the first, and only, child the state sent to them. When the state contacted them a year later, informing them that Eli's mother had died from a drug overdose and he had no other family, the Bentons rushed to their lawyer's office. The rest was history.

At first, they homeschooled him, to get him up to grade level, and I think in some ways to protect him from being bullied. Kids were cruel, but parents could be worse. The Bentons knew that bringing in an interracial child to a predominantly white school might be tricky. Their fears were erased when Eli put his foot down and all but demanded to go to school like everyone else.

He went through hell the first week he started eighth grade, but he never let on to his parents about it. At that point, the other five were just a group of friends. Where you saw one, you saw all, and they saw everything. Jared was the first to snap when he watched the class bully, Seth Johns, corner Eli and threaten him. The next day, Seth came to school with a black eye and apologized to Eli, but he wouldn't tell anyone what happened to him. The following month, Ace showed up at Josh's house with Eli in tow, and he'd been one of the Six ever since.

My stomach rumbled, and he snickered. "I guess that means food first, huh?"

The thought of food made my stomach clench. I should have thought of it before I took the pain pills on an empty stomach.

Eli stepped back and jerked his head towards the front of the cabin. "Come on, slugger. I'll walk with you, so you don't fall over your own feet."

"Eli?"

"Yeah?"

I walked past him and ran my hand along the wall to help keep my balance since the next side effect of the pain pills was to make me feel loopy. "The next time you tell me to take medicine, I'm gonna punch you, too."

He cupped my elbow to steady me. "Duly noted, Riles."

The screen door of the cabin opened as I crossed the kitchen, and Aiden stuck his head in. When he noticed me, he grinned. "I was just about to come find out what was taking y'all so long."

"Eli drugged me, and the hallway somehow got longer," I grumbled.

Eli let go of my arm and tossed his hands out at his sides. "I didn't drug you!" The exasperation in his voice made me laugh.

Aiden held the door open for me, and I stepped out into the sultry night air, which did nothing to clear out the fog that had settled in my mind.

"Watch out, guys, Riley's on a bender!" Aiden called out from behind me.

"Shut up, Aiden." I tried to toss him a dirty look over my

shoulder and ended up stumbling into Mark. "Whoa there, Riles." He steadied me and then walked with me to the closest chair.

Josh leaned forward in his chair. "Hey Riles? Do we need to feed you, too? Or do you got that covered?"

I flipped him off, and the six jackasses laughed.

I gave them all a sweeping scowl. "I'm glad y'all are getting a kick outta this."

"Aw, come on, Riled-up, how many times have we seen you like this?" Mark asked as he handed me a doctored-up hot dog. He'd made it just the way I liked it, with mayo and mustard—hold the ketchup.

Josh opened the cooler he had beside him, pulled out a Dr. Pepper, and tossed it to Mark. He cracked it open and handed it to me.

"Thanks. What'd you tell my dad, Josh?" I asked. Sliding the can in between my knees, I bit into my hot dog, hoping the food would absorb the acid rolling in my stomach.

Josh sat down in the chair beside me and held out my phone. "He was worried about you, but I told him you knocked that bitch out and it was long overdue."

"You told him about the fight?" He broke one of the Six's sacred vows? I could feel my one good eye widen and winced at the sting coming from the other.

Josh put his hand up with a snorted laugh. "Uh, negative. You know us better than that, Riles."

"But you just said…"

"I was kidding. Your dad thinks we're hanging out here for a few days. Besides, he was headed out the door for a haul anyway. He said he won't be back for about two weeks since he's headed out to Oregon, and then to Louisiana."

My dad had taken up longer hauls as I got older. When I was younger, he only did runs that got him back home to be with me after school. As I got older, his hauls got longer. Up until last year, I stayed with Paige and her parents. My senior year, I stayed home, and Dad saw to it that the Six kept an eye on me.

I hated that he was gone so much, but I felt selfish saying it to him because up until a few weeks ago, I was supposed to be leaving for college. The Six and Paige knew what happened, but I hadn't told Dad. I didn't want to see the disappointment in his eyes when I told him that the scholarship fell through because he made too much money. No way would I ask him to finance college for me. I'd figure it out.

I put the phone on my lap and finished my hot dog while the Six chatted together.

Jared walked over and slapped Ace on the back, as Mark added another log to the fire. "You know what tonight is, right?"

Jared sounded excited, like a kid who knows what he got for his birthday, but had to wait for his parents to give it to him. The rest of the guys murmured along with him. For whatever reason, they all seemed excited about whatever it was Jared talked about. Well, everyone but Ace. His eyes came up to meet mine, and the look on his face said he dreaded whatever it was.

Jared rubbed his hands together. "Are y'all ready?"

Josh walked over and slugged Jared in the shoulder. "Hold on. Christ, you're like a damn kid on a sugar high."

The guys laughed when Jared dragged his feet over to the nearest chair, slumped into it, and rolled his eyes. "Aren't y'all at least a little excited to open that box?"

I couldn't stop myself from blurting out the question. "The box? The one that's been locked away for how many years?"

A grin split Eli's face. "Yep, the box."

I never in my life thought I'd be privy to the moment when they opened the box they'd locked up four years ago.

The day they got together to fill it was the only day they told me I wasn't allowed to come to the cabin. It had hurt my feelings since they never excluded me from anything. I never brought it up, and neither had they.

Mark cleared his throat and held his soda can up in the air. "To the Seven. May we all find happiness, love, and our way back to each other."

The guys shot up out of their seats and lifted their cans in unison. "To the Seven!" They stood there with their cans hoisted and when they noticed I hadn't lifted mine, they all gave me a dirty look.

"What?" I was confused by not only Mark's toast, but by the fact that they were waiting on me to join in.

"Did you not hear the man?" Jared asked.

"Yeah, he said Seven—not Six... why?"

"Riley, you've been a part of us for how long? It's never been the six of us—it's always been the seven. You've just always excluded yourself, and we're not allowing you to do that anymore," Josh explained.

"Hoist yer can, ya mangy dog!" Jared shouted.

Leave it to Jared to let his love of the *Pirates of the Caribbean* pop out at that moment.

"Now, Riley Ann Clifton!" Mark's deep voice hollered loud enough to reach the next county.

I pulled the can from between my knees and lifted it out in front of me.

"And...?" Mark prodded me.

"To the Seven." I tipped my can at them.

"To the Seven!" they shouted.

Jared shot up out of his seat and ran for the cabin.

Aiden crushed his can, pulling the tab off. "That didn't take him long." He walked over and tossed the tab at me. "Here Riley, something to remember me by."

"Gee, thanks, Aiden."

Ace grumbled from his seat. The word ass-wipe was the only legible thing I heard. Aiden tossed him a smile and cracked his knuckles. "Gotta have a chip in the game, bro. You know the rules, or at least you should anyway, since you made them."

"Shut up, Aiden."

"Oh, come on Ace, you know as well as I do what the outcome of it will be." Aiden shook his head and turned when the screen door slammed shut. Jared strode across the yard with a wooden chest held out in front of him.

"Lookie here, boys! I've waited forever for this!" Jared set the chest down on a large stump they used to split wood. "Ace, where's the key, man? Hurry up! I'm dyin' here!"

Ace rubbed his hand down his face, grumbling, as he stood up from his chair and crossed over to my truck. He walked around to the passenger side and pulled my keys out of the glove box. My heart raced. I'd had the key to the box all these years? Three years ago, Ace had slipped the key on my key ring, telling me that it was the extra key for his garage door. Ace was forever locking himself out of his house or losing his keys, so I didn't think anything about it.

The guys hooted with laughter, confusing me even more.

Ace never lost focus as he walked over to the box, unlocked it, and turned around to face me. His eyes locked with mine as he walked over and held my keys out to me. He mouthed the words, *I'm sorry*, and dropped the keys in my open palm. I wasn't sure what he was apologizing for, unless he meant the almost kiss that never happened earlier in the bathroom. I could feel my eyes watering up, and I cursed myself at my emotion instability.

"Well, what are you waiting for?" Ace called out to Jared, as he walked back over to his chair and sat down. I watched him flinch when the box creaked open and wondered just what was inside that had Ace ready to bolt.

CHAPTER 4

*J*ared's shout of excitement my gaze from Ace, but not before he looked up and saw me watching him. I quickly glanced away, giving my full attention to Jared. In his hand, he held the watch he'd gotten for his fourteenth birthday. He'd worn it all the time and then one day, it was just gone. I'd asked about it, but he said he'd lost it. What he didn't say was that he'd lost it to the box.

"Finally!" he said, raising the watch up at the sky. He slapped it down on his wrist and buckled the strap. "I don't feel naked anymore!"

I laughed along with everyone, remembering what a grouch he'd been for months after he'd 'lost' his watch.

"Who's next?" Jared called out, sticking his hand in the box and pulling out a polished stone. He held it out so that the firelight reflected off the light blue, metal-flaked surface. "Eli, I believe this is yours."

Eli walked over, and Jared dropped it in his hand. Eli rolled it around in his palm as a grin split across his face. He held it up between his thumb and first finger. "This was the first thing the Bentons ever gave me. A gift for no reason other than to see me smile."

My eyes teared up, thinking about it. The fact that we'd all taken our childhoods for granted, knowing at the end of the day that our parents would be there, plucked at my emotions. Eli had spent eight years of his life being moved from place to place, waiting for the moment to have just a slice of the kind of lives the rest of us had.

A tear slipped past the corner of my eye. I brushed it away before the Six could see it.

Jared voice cut through the silence as Eli sat down. "Mark, I believe this belongs to you." In his hands, Jared held a tattered baseball card that Mark plucked from his fingers. "Mickey Mantel, bitches!" He flashed the card around with a smirk on his face."It ain't worth a shit now. Look at it." Jared laughed as he tried to snatch it out of his hand, but Mark darted away before he could.

"Fine, keep your damn card," Jared said as he turned back and, once again, his hand pulled out another item from the box. "Aiden," he called out as he held up a pocketknife. Aiden walked over and put his hand out. Jared slapped the first knife Aiden was given into his waiting palm. It was small, no bigger than two inches. Aiden pulled the blade out, revealing all the chips missing, because he used it on all the things it wasn't meant for. He winced and closed the knife. "Geez, what did I use this on?"

"Everything," the answer came in unison.

I smiled, thinking back on our younger years. The Six would never change. The loud, obnoxious boys had only aged, not grown up.

"Ah ha! Josh, what the hell were you thinking back then, man?" Jared pulled out a guitar pick.

"You boys know that I'm the only rock star around here!"

Josh walked over and snatched the pick out of his hands.

"Yeah, and you'll probably be the first and only one of us to get an STD."

The boys howled with laughter. Jared was a loose cannon, unless he was with the Six. They kept him grounded, but all bets would be called off soon when he left our little town and went on the road. He was hell-bent on being the next Jared Leto and had almost convinced Josh to go along with him. Both weren't just talented, they had the whole package, except for the fact that Jared looked like a rocker and Josh looked like a country singer. They picked on each other relentlessly for it. And they loved to pick up a guitar in front of a group of people. That was probably part of the reason the girls swooned so hard over them. Little did the girls know that all the Six could play, but Aiden, Eli, Mark, and Ace would only play at the cabin. Truth be told, Ace was just as good, if not better, than Jared—to me anyway.

"Ace, get your ass up here, man," Jared called over his shoulder as he pulled out a harmonica. "I'll give this to you on one condition," Jared said, holding it just out of Ace's reach.

Ace put his hands on his hips, his T-shirt stretched out over his shoulders, and shifted from one foot to the other. "Do you know how long it's been?"

"Yeah, right! I heard you not that long ago playing one, so don't try that bullshit," Mark said.

Jared went to hand the harmonica to Ace and pulled it back as he gave him the look that said, *you better do it, if I hand it to you.*

Ace pulled the harmonica from Jared's grip and held it up to his mouth. I closed my eyes just as the first note of a haunting flow of music seeped into the air. When he was done playing, no one spoke until he tucked the harmonica in his pocket and started back to his seat.

"Where you going?" Jared asked. "That's only the sixth piece of seven."

"You can do it," Ace mumbled.

"Ah, no deal, bro. This is all you." Jared pulled out a folded piece of paper and a small, white box.

Ace rubbed his hand down his face and turned back to Jared. "Can I talk to you for a second?"

"You're not backing out. This one was your idea, so you get to be the one to do it," Jared said, shoving the paper and box against Ace's chest.

"Who's idea was it again, Captain Jack?" Ace's comeback made the guys chuckle.

"Whatever! You know what I meant." Jared tossed his hand at us. "Carry on."

Ace looked up at the sky, and he clamped his fingers against the back of his neck. He closed his eyes tight, dropped his hand, and opened the letter as he clutched the box against the lined paper. The sounds of summer were heavy in the air, as we waited for him to read the words written on the page he held.

"Riley,

This is Jared's fault.

I just wanted you to know that before you hear the rest."

Ace's eyes flickered to mine, and then back to the paper.

"I was the one chosen to write this 'cause the rest of them are lazy and their handwriting sucks.

Anyway, the guys and I have something we want to tell you, and I hope you're sitting down for this. You see, we kinda lied to you, like all the time lied to you. And before you get angry, give me a second to explain."

I looked around at all the guys. They wouldn't meet my questioning gaze as they kept their attention on Ace.

"Ever since well, yesterday—or as I'm reading this—ever since four years ago, our plans have changed, unless they've changed

again, and then you won't be mad. You see, we've made a pact. Several of them that you had no idea about. The first thing we decided is that we're each going into a branch of the military. We knew you'd freak out, which is why you think each of us are doing something different."

Ace lowered the paper and looked at me. "Some of this has changed. Jared chose music. Josh is headed to Penn State to be a bonafide Yankee. Eli's headed to a third-world country and will probably end up with Malaria or some shit, and Mark's gonna become a male prostitute."

"Har, har, dickhead. You know I'm headed for a school of the arts in New York, Riley. I've been doing good with my photography, so I want to learn more and open my own studio."

Josh cupped the bill of his Penn State hat. "Why is it you call anyone north of the Mason-Dixon Line a damn Yankee?"

Eli leaned forward and draped his arms over his knees. "And I'm all vaccinated and ready to roll out in two weeks to do a year of volunteer work at a Red Cross station in Haiti." He ended his sentence by flicking Ace off.

I squeezed my hands together, cutting off the flow of blood to my fingers. I knew we'd be separating at one point to head off wherever life took us, but it felt more permanent hearing it. "What about you and Aiden? I thought you were going to be going into the forestry division, and Aiden was going to head out for college in Texas?"

Dread rolled in my stomach when Ace bit his lip before answering. "I'm headed off to boot camp in Georgia two weeks from now. Aiden leaves around the same time for Texas, but not for college. He's going to boot camp, too."

I clasped my hands tighter, willing my mind to slow down. Ace was leaving. He wouldn't be around when everyone left.

Ace lifted the sheet of paper up and continued reading, unaware that my world had spun off its axis.

"When Jared came to us about doing this box, at first it was just supposed to be like a time capsule of sorts, but it didn't feel right without having you here with us. You've always been a part of us— ever since the beginning—and so because we're stubborn and pigheaded—Jared—we decided that we'd add something to the box for you and open it with you, since we didn't let you come when we closed it."

Ace walked over, handed me the white box, and then stepped back. My hand clutched it, feeling the soft leather of the jewelry case.

"This seventh piece of six is something from all of us. You see, you've had a piece of our hearts ever since the beginning. Not one of us have been unaffected by you. At some point over the years, we've each fallen in love with you, so it's only fitting that the combination of that love be shared after all these years. On the day this box is sealed, we will make a promise to each other. It'll be written in our Seven rules, and that's what we are—we're the Seven —and you're at the heart of us all.

Over the years, our feelings might change and our love for you might shift into the kind of love that long friendships are made of, but as of right now, you're kinda driving us all crazy. Or crazier in some cases. By now, I'm sure I've stunned you into silence and you're clutching the box in your hand like a lifeline. So I'll say it for all of us. Open the box, Riley."

Ace dropped the hand holding the sheet of paper to his side. The box was in fact clutched tight in my hand, proving he'd known me so well for so long. I searched his face and flicked my eyes to the box in my hand. I forced myself to look away and opened it.

"We love you, Riley. We always have... we always will."

Ace read the last sentence and folded the paper back up, as I sat in complete shock at what was in the box. It was the most beautiful heart-shaped pendant I'd ever seen. The swirling lines wove around each other, making it look like an intricate pattern.

I brushed a tear away, and then another, but they kept coming when Ace knelt beside me and took the box from my hands. His finger slid down the patterns as he spoke. "We wanted you to have a piece of us, so if you'll notice, all of our initials are inside of the heart. Here's Josh, Jared…" His finger slid along the left and then the right arch in the heart. "Then there's Eli…" His finger went to the top indent and traced the letter E that flowed down. "Aiden… Ace…" To the left of the E was what I always called the fancy A's. "And this is Mark." His finger slid over the M that stretched out at the bottom of the heart and attached to both A's.

It was as complex and amazing as our friendship.

"Well, aren't you gonna say something?" Jared said, leaning over to watch as Ace showed me the secrets my pendant held. I looked up and noticed all of them were around me. I wiped the tears that wouldn't stop falling from my cheeks.

"Thank you. Thank all of you." Before I could recover, they each leaned down and kissed me on the cheek, leaving Ace for last.

"Lay it on 'er, Ace!" Jared hooted.

My eyes popped wide and I snapped my head up to look at Ace, who had turned to scowl at Jared.

Ace took a step in Jared's direction, but I caught his pant leg between my fingers and it brought him to a halt. I held up the box. "Can you help me put it on?"

Ace took the box from my hand and knelt in front of me.

Jared elbowed Eli and said in a mock whisper, "I bet we see this again in the future."

Eli shook his head and pushed Jared. "Shut up, man. Give him a dang break. You know how long he's…you know, and he's leaving. Dude's barely had it together these last few weeks. Don't make him flip on your shit."

I watched their exchange of words. Heard everything as clearly as if they spoke to me instead of each other, even though they whispered. Ace unhooked the rope chain he always wore from around his neck, freed the heart pendant from the box, and slipped it onto the chain. He did all of it without looking at me until the heart slid to a stop, and he held the ends of the chain up. I lifted my hair for him to fasten it around my neck. I could feel the tension coming off him. Could feel his hands trembling as he tried to keep it together and not run over to beat the shit out of his friends. I gripped his wrist before he could snatch his hands away. He looked at some point over my shoulder, and I watched the vein in his neck pulse as his nostrils flared. I squeezed his wrist, and he shifted his gaze to meet mine. "Thank you for the chain, Ace. I'll get one soon and give yours back to you."

I knew what I had to do. I had to break the tension before the night ended up in a brawl instead of the memory they'd all wanted it to be. "But now I have to tell y'all that I kinda feel a little bad. I mean, I only got you T-shirts."

I felt Ace's body tremble and smiled when a laugh broke past the thin line his lips had been set in.

"Oh snap!" Aiden hooted.

"Can you get them for me, Jake?" His hand fell to my knee.

"Sure, Riles. Where are they?"

"Behind the seat of my truck."

Ace stood up, and I lifted my hand to rub my fingers along my very first real piece of jewelry. The chain was warm against my skin and I soaked it in, taking that small piece of heat that Ace had left behind, realizing that twice in one day he'd shared his warmth with me.

I heard my truck door slam shut and turned my head just

as Ace stuck his hand into the bag, pulling out a shirt and looking at the tag. "Size small. Must be Jared's."

The guys laughed as Jared walked over and shoved his hand in the bag. "There is nothing small about me, bro."

I grimaced, realizing I hadn't taken the shirt I'd bought for myself out of the bag. I was just going to put it away since I wasn't one of the Six. I didn't say anything as Ace tucked it under his arm and tossed everyone a shirt. He got to the last shirt, folded the bag, and walked over, dropping the extra shirt tucked under his arm on my lap. "These are cool, Riles." He held his shirt out to me, gesturing for me to hold it. In truth, they were pretty plain. The shirts were royal blue with the number 6 on the right side where a pocket would normally go. On the back, it said *You wish*. No one but the Six would fully understand what it meant, and really, it wouldn't be what anyone thought it meant. It was just what the guys always said to each other when one of them gave the other hell about something they thought they did better.

When I took it from him, he grabbed the bottom of the shirt he'd changed into and pulled it off. The others cheered him on by throwing out comments like, "Take it off," and "Hold me back, cowboy. My nipples are tweakin'." I cracked up at their antics. I'd grown accustomed to the trash they talked. Jared was the worst of the bunch. He always had some sort of odd comeback or comment that flew past his lips before the filter in his brain stopped him.

I folded Ace's discarded shirt and almost dropped it when he'd said that. "Really Jared? Your nipples are tweakin'?"

Jared ripped his shirt off and flexed his arms. "See, look at all this awesomeness. Ace has nothin' on me."

I shook my head, but I didn't say anything back. There was no comparison between Ace and Jared. Ace had the type of body that reflected the work he did outside. Jared was sleeker, defined without being bulky.

Mark shot up from his chair and headed for the cabin. As he walked away, he said, "Everyone put your shirts on. I have an idea!"

Aiden groaned. "You know he's about to do a dang photo shoot, right?"

Jared slipped his shirt over his head, making his words muffled. "Don't worry, Aiden, no one will notice you when they get a load of me."

"Shut up, ass-munch. You know the only drool-worthy one here is me." Eli threw his discarded shirt at Jared, and it hit him in the face.

Jared shook his head at Eli, and then turned to me with a devilish look on his face. "Well, Riles, you're next."

I gripped the T-shirt in my hands. "You pervert, I'm not changing out here in front of you."

"Oh, come on, Riles… Ace got to see…"

The flash of Mark's camera stopped Jared from finishing his sentence. My face burned in embarrassment, and I wished for a place to hide.

"Y'all get your asses over by Riley's truck and stand together," he announced as he walked past the group and jumped in the back of my truck. He set his camera down, fiddling with the settings. When he looked up and no one had done what he asked, he scowled at us. "Seriously, get your asses over here. You too, Riley."

I knew Mark wouldn't stop badgering us until we did what he wanted, so I pushed myself up from the chair and flung my hand out. "You heard him. Let's get this done, so Mark doesn't freak out on us."

The guys grumbled, but they followed me. Mark fired off where he wanted everyone to stand. When they were where he wanted them, he made them turn around, putting their backs to the camera, and then asked me to stand behind everyone a few feet back. I moved so that he could get the shot of the six of them together. The guys stood shoulder to shoulder, leaving a gap in the middle for Mark. But Mark moved to the end beside Aiden. "Riley, move to the center and stand directly in front of the camera. When the flash starts going off, I want you to walk towards us and then stop in the middle. Okay?"

I didn't get a chance to answer him because the flash went off, signaling me to move. I looked over to Mark, and he winked at me. I smiled back at him and took another step. Aiden gave me a smile that kicked up one side of his lips. Josh stuck his tongue out at me, and I laughed. Eli wiggled his eyebrows and darted his eyes to Ace. I forced myself to breathe evenly and not run over to wrap my arms around his neck, pull his lips to mine, and get the kiss I'd been denied.

When I was a few steps away, Ace put his hand out and I slipped mine into his without thinking about it. He pulled me beside him and lifted my hand to his shoulder. The flash of the camera went off and I pulled my gaze from his, slipping my hand up on Jared's shoulder so that it didn't look like I was holding on to Ace, even though I'd done just that.

The flash went off again, as I realized that this night would be one of the last few nights we'd all be together. A tear slipped down my cheek, and I let it fall. Mark broke the silence when he jumped back into the bed of my truck, telling the others to turn around and face the camera. The guys turned around, and we all moved in close. Jared put his hand on my shoulder. Ace's hand rested against my hip, and I felt him grip the hem of the shirt I wore. His shirt.

The camera flashed a few more times and then Mark broke off, jumped into the bed of my truck, and grabbed his camera. "These are gonna be awesome!" He walked away, back to the cabin, as he looked at the screen of his camera. "Yep, these are gonna be perfect," he said to himself as he passed by me.

I could feel the effect of the pain meds, and I didn't like the fuzziness they'd blanketed me with. The worst part was, I wasn't ready to let them pull me down into the clutches of sleep. I wanted to savor every part of the night until my memories were stuffed with these last moments of being with the Six.

I forced myself to walk over to my chair and sit down. When Mark came back out from the cabin, Jared walked over to the box and pulled out a rolled-up piece of paper.

He cleared his throat to get everyone's attention. "Is everyone ready?"

Ready for what? I wanted to ask, but I kept my question to myself. I was eager to know what the paper in Jared's hand said.

CHAPTER 5

*J*ARED'S VOICE RANG OUT, MIXING with the sounds of the crackling fire.

"*The rules of the Six.*

Rule number one: No matter what happens, we will always be friends.

Rule number two: If someone's being an ass-hat, the other five have the right to punch the ass-hat in the face.

Rule number three: At least once a month, we will hang out at the cabin for the weekend.

Rule number four: There will only be the six of us, except for Riley. She's a girl and will be treated as the silent seventh.

Rule number five: We will have each other's backs—no matter what.

Rule number six: No dating clingy girls who get in the way of the Six.

Rule number seven: Riley is off-limits. We will love her from afar until the day we graduate. After graduation, it will be up to Riley to show us how she feels. We will not intimidate her, push her, or even approach her. By now, she's put up with enough of our shit and is probably sick of us.

These are the rules and if not followed, will result in an ass kicking by the other five."

I shot up from my seat. My throat burned with the need to freak out on them. *How dare they make me a part of their stupid rules! How dare they make me seem like their possession!* My chest heaved with the added weight of feeling like a joke to them. Mark tried to steady me, and I shoved him away. "Don't touch me!" I heard the snarl in my voice and wished that it were enough to inflict the pain I felt on them. I'd loved these boys, they'd been my world for so long, and it felt like the floor had been ripped out from under my feet. I clutched at my neck to ease the ache. It felt like I was trying to breathe out of a straw. I needed to get away, so I started searching for my keys. *Ace had given them back to me, right?*

"Riley, what are you doing?" Jared asked as the others sat in silence.

"Where are my keys?" I asked through clenched teeth.

"You're not getting your keys, Riley," Ace said as he approached me.

I held up my hand. "You just stay right there!"

"Come on, Riley. That was written four years ago. We didn't mean anything by it," Aiden said, not moving from his seat.

"Yeah, Riles, it wasn't meant to hurt you." Eli's voice came out more like a plea than a statement.

"Hurt me? Are you kidding me right now? How long have you guys been dictating the way my life would go? Why bother even keeping me around? You make it sound like I was some sort of poison you had to contain! What, were you afraid that if one of you liked me that the whole ship of brotherhood would go down? You know what… don't even answer that. Just give me my keys, so I can go."

"You're not leaving, Riley." Ace's voice had the

commanding tone he always used to make something sound final.

"The hell I'm not. Give me my keys, Ace." I stalked towards him, hell-bent on physically hurting him if he didn't give me what I wanted.

"No. I think you need to sit down before you fall down," he said, shaking his head.

"I don't care what you think, Ace."

Ace waited until I was about a foot away and tossed my keys to Josh. I shoved past him and set my sights on Josh. His eyes rounded, and he looked past me to where Ace stood. I felt my body waver, so I stopped and steadied myself the best I could.

"Give me my keys, Josh."

"Riley, why don't I help you inside? You can get some rest, and we can talk about this in the morning." He talked to me as if trying to calm a spooked wild animal.

"There is nothing left to say. Please give me my keys." The sob I'd been trying to contain broke past my lips, and I clamped my hand over my mouth to keep myself from doing it again.

"If you want to go home so bad, I'll drive you there." Ace brushed past me and gestured for Josh to toss him my keys. "Go get in the truck, Riley."

There was no point in arguing with him. Ace wouldn't take my shit, not like the rest of them did. I think out of all of them, Ace and I knew each other the best. And I knew without even looking at him that he meant what he said. It was either stay there or let him drive me. I turned my back on Josh, Mark, Aiden, and Eli and walked around to the passenger side of my truck and got in, slamming the door hard enough to make the cab of the truck rock in place.

Ace slid in behind the wheel, turned the key, pulled the knob for the headlights, and shifted into drive. I sat with my back to him and watched the side mirror, angry at the five faces that watched us drive away, and hoping that wouldn't be the last time I saw them. I was pissed, sure, but they were like brothers, and that was what hurt the worst.

Ace waited for a few minutes before he spoke. "I know you're hurt…"

A strained laugh was my only reply.

"Come on, Riles. Do you even know how bad we feel for hurting you?"

Ace swerved to miss a dip, which told me that he was paying more attention to me than he was the road.

"If you're gonna drive like that, you should've just let me take myself home." I clutched at the door handle and hissed with the jolt of pain that ran up my back.

"You can't drive with the medication Eli gave you. Even you know better than that." Ace slowed the truck and shifted in his seat, as he rolled his window down. The warm night air felt good as it pushed through the cab and whipped my hair around.

My thoughts cleared a little, as I was hit with the reality that Ace had suckered me into letting him drive me home. "You did this on purpose." I turned on the bench seat and reached out to smack him on the arm.

His hand caught mine, keeping me from snatching my hand back. The truck slowed, and Ace pulled onto the shoulder.

"Riley, can you just stop? Just for tonight, can you try to look at both sides of this? Do you know how long we agonized over you knowing the truth? Do you know how freaked out we've been that you'd find out about it tonight? We've been on pins and fucking needles for days now. We've been tied up in knots over what you'd think or do because of it."

I looked away. I didn't want to see the truth in his eyes,

the raw hurt that was reflected there. I wasn't that important. I was just me, a girl lucky enough to have some really amazing guy friends who were my support system for as long as I could remember. They should have left it alone, left me out of their brotherhood, and just accepted me as Riley, the girl who was a good friend and that was all.

When I didn't turn back and answer, Ace put the truck in drive again and pulled back onto the road.

The worst part was that Ace's words made me think. They made me pick apart everything he said and analyze it for the truth. So what, they decided to protect me? Didn't any brother or best friend do that? And so what, they at one point thought that they loved me. It couldn't have been love, because love, real love, makes you crazy and selfish. You wanted to be with that person so badly that you forsook the consequences. You jumped in with both feet, hoping that you'd find yourself sinking so deep inside the other person that you welcomed drowning with open arms.

Ace's voice broke the silence. "Aiden and Eli were the first to admit how they felt about you the summer between eighth and ninth grade. Do you remember that summer?"

My mind shifted back to those days. Aiden and Eli had started to pick at each other and at one point, they were always trying to show each other up. That didn't mean anything though, right? They were boys. Didn't boys always feel the need to one-up each other like some kind of male dominance thing?

Ace took my silence in stride, giving me a few minutes to process what he'd said. "Then Jared figured out what the deal was when he made a comment about how much you'd grown up that summer, and Mark just about broke his nose."

A flash of Jared popped into my thoughts. He'd said they'd been wrestling before I'd got out to the cabin. Looking back on the memory, I thought about how everyone had acted that day. They'd been broody and snarled a lot at each other. Again, I'd just passed it off.

"And then right before we started school, you and I were out helping Old Man Willis, and there was something about you. I don't know if it was your laugh or the fact that you'd just witnessed a colt being born for the first time, but you turned to me, and the sunlight hit the side of your face, and I swear it was like... You smiled at me. That was all it took. You had me from that damn moment on. None of us have been the same. I knew right then and there that you'd be our undoing if we didn't do something about it. You meant too much to all of us to let our feelings get in the way of the friendship we have with you. You were too important to us. It was my idea and my fault that you're so upset, Riley. Be mad at me, but please, don't turn your back on them."

I gripped the door handle tight and fought to control my voice. "Ace, please tell me that they've gotten over me. Please tell me that I'm not going to have to walk away from them, because I can't hurt them. It would kill me if I hurt them."

"Riley, all of that..." he said, jerking his thumb towards the back window of my truck. "All of it was years ago. They've all come to terms with how they feel. Most of them were over it within the first week of high school. We shoulda never done that... opened that stupid box with you there. It would have saved all of this from coming out. It would have been buried in the past where most of it remains."

"What do you mean by most of it?" I wanted to recall my question back after I asked it. It was like I just wanted to see how far I could dig myself and the situation into the ground. They were all going their separate ways—we were all supposed to be going our separate ways after graduation. How had things got so turned upside down and sideways? How did I allow myself to fall so deep into the feelings I had for Ace? He was supposed to be the one who'd be around the most. He was going to be just up the road, like always, when I came back on college breaks. What the hell was wrong with that? Nothing and everything now.

"…Riley."

I only caught my name. Ace had said something, and I missed it because I was too busy mentally kicking my own ass. Beating myself up on everything that I'd thought was a truth, but ended up being a lie. The last four years had been an illusion.

Ace's hand slid along my jaw, and he stood in front of me. When had he stopped the truck and how did I get out?

"Riley, please baby, you have to breathe." He forced my eyes to meet his, as he cupped my face and looked down at me. My chest tightened and ached, as I heaved to collect a breath that wasn't making it down into my lungs.

"Riley, focus on me, look at me… I'm right here with you. You have to calm down." His face wavered in front of me, and I caught a glimpse of true fear. I blinked once, twice, and static filled the inside of my head—like an antenna TV with its volume turned up as far as it would go.

~

"Riley!" I heard Paige shout as the front door slammed shut. Her footsteps raced up the stairs to my room, and my door flew open. I blinked at the fuzziness that clung to my dreams. I hurt from head to toe and winced as I tried to sit up. A groan escaped from under the covers next to me.

"Go away, Paige." Ace's voice was muffled under the layers of blankets that he'd cocooned himself in.

Paige shot me an, *'I can't freakin' believe you'* look and stormed over to rip the covers from my bed. When she saw Ace fully clothed, she sighed deeply and turned to look at me. "I didn't believe it when Mark called me and said Ace brought you home, but didn't show back up at the cabin. Care to explain why you have one of the Sexy Six in your bed?"

Ace sat up, snatched the covers, and rolled over on his side. "Go yell at someone else. It's been a helluva night, and I don't wanna hear it."

"Shut up, Ace! You have no right to go all assholish on me. I've been worried sick about her all night!"

Ace sat up and ran his hand down his face. He looked over at me, and I watched as his eyes raked me from head to toe. Paige blew out a breath that said she was about to start in again.

Ace held himself upright on one arm and scowled at Paige. "You've been worried? Were you here when she had the mother of all panic attacks? Did you have to calm her down? Did you sit up with her all night when she flipped her shit and cried for half the night?"

I hadn't done that. Had I? I pulled on Ace's arm until he looked down at me. "What happened?"

"The meds Eli gave you kicked in, and you kinda flipped out about everything." His eyes closed and then he sighed deeply when Paige continued yelling.

"Well, excuse me, Mr. I'm-not-in-the-mood! How the hell was I supposed to know what happened? You answered your phone once when Mark called you and you told him to fuck off and leave you alone, that you'd call them in the morning. What were they supposed to think? What was I supposed to think when Mark called me, freaking the hell out, because you didn't answer the phone again and Riley's went right to voice mail?"

My eyes bounced between them, not sure what to even think about the argument they were caught in.

"Mark wanted to know if you'd brought her into the ER when he called me. Do you even know what was running through my mind at that point? You're a real jackass, Ace. And FYI? You're not the only one who cares about her."

Paige crossed her arms and glared at him.

A low rumble came from Ace, like a sinister laugh, and I knew he'd geared up to give her hell. He'd say something he could never take back and the rest of our circle of friendship would burn to the ground if he unleashed the words brewing in his head.

I turned and put my hand on his arm. His eyes snapped to mine, and I flinched at the anger I saw there. "Please, just don't say anything else."

He sighed, shoved himself up, and came around me on the mattress. Stopping in front of me, he blinked slowly, as if to clear the anger from his face while he looked at me. "I'll be downstairs if you need me."

He pushed off the bed and stalked past Paige. She turned to watch him leave. As soon as she heard his footsteps on the stairs, she spun on me. "What the hell is going on, Riley?"

I crisscrossed my legs and put my head in my hands. How could I explain it to Paige? If I told her what happened the night before, it would break the trust of the Six. If I didn't tell her, it would make her angry with me. I had to find some sort of middle ground.

"Please tell me you didn't sleep with Ace." She crossed the room and sat down on the bed beside me. Her hands gripped the side of the mattress, and she waited for me to explain.

I rolled my eyes at her. "Of course I slept with Ace. You just saw it for yourself when you pulled the covers off him in my bed."

She slapped my knee. "You know what I meant, Riley."

"Yeah, I know, but would it really make a difference either way if I had slept with him in the way you're implying?" I was tired of caring what others thought. Who cared if I decided to sleep with Ace? I was an adult, making adult deci-

sions. It was my body, my life, and if I decided to give that to
Ace, it would be between us and no one else. I never got in
the middle of their love lives. Never once said a word when I
knew they were sleeping with different girls and choosing
not to make some sort of commitment. Paige was the only
one out of my group of friends who was anything like me.
Hell, even Ace was guilty of it. The guys never stuck with
someone to see whether the relationship would last. It never
made sense, but it wasn't my business to ask them.

Paige bumped her arm into mine. "Why do you torture
yourself like this, Riley?"

I snorted at her question. "You tell me what I'm supposed
to do, Paige, 'cause right now, I'm scared, I'm frustrated, and I
love him so damn much my insides hurt. He's leaving. And I
don't know when he's coming back. And I'll be stuck here
trying to figure out just what the hell I'm supposed to do
with my life." My words died off with my purge of hurt-filled
words. Paige leaned into me and rested her head against
mine.

"I knew you loved him. Why'd you wait so long to say
something?"

"To who? You?" I asked.

"No, to him. To Ace."

"I didn't tell him, Paige. He doesn't need to know."

"The hell I don't." Ace's voice rolled across the room, and
my head snapped up to where he stood with his fingers
curled around the doorframe. Paige shot up off my bed and
backed up a step when Ace pushed himself off the door and
stalked towards me.

I heard Paige, but I didn't take my eyes off Ace. "I'll call
you later, Riley. Turn on your phone!" Her footsteps
pounded down the stairs, and the front door slammed shut.

I swallowed hard and tried to catch my breath, as my
chest tightened with each step that brought him closer to me.

A fire burned in his eyes. It threatened to engulf me when he stopped in front of me and brought his hands up to cup my face. His eyes snapped like live wires. "You fucking own me, Riley, and there isn't a thing I can do to walk away from you." His lips hovered against mine, and he pulled in a deep breath. When he released it, it bathed my face and sent a shock wave through me from head to toe.

"Tell me this is okay, Riley. Tell me you want me as much as I want you."

I trembled in his hold and licked my lips, as I struggled against how to respond to him. I'd wanted him for what felt like forever, but what happened after he left? Was I supposed to just pick up the pieces and be thankful he gave me a part of himself?

"Riley, you have to tell me, baby. I don't know what you want, and I'm dying here. I need you, Riley. I need you so bad."

I slammed the door shut on my thoughts and sought out Ace's lips. He groaned into my mouth and lowered us to the bed. His body hovered over mine, as he kept one hand along my face and nipped at my lips. His kisses were a slow torture, which he dragged out as he drove me crazy with just his lips and his hands. He rested his weight on me, keeping his chest from pushing against mine. Even lost in the passion he'd created, he'd kept himself in check enough to be cautious of my back. I didn't want him to be careful. I wanted him wild and crazy, and so far past thinking that he was as lost as I was.

He pulled back and I sighed, missing his lips against mine. "Look at me, Riley."

I cracked my eyes open, as heat spread out along my cheeks. I'd never been so open with anyone. Ever.

"You have to tell me to stop, right now, or I might hurt you."

I grabbed his neck and pulled him down against me. He tried to push himself back up, but I moved my legs apart so that he fell into the vee of my hips. I wrapped my legs around him, locking him against me, pressing him against the parts of me that ached for his touch. He groaned, as our lips met in a hungry kiss that had me gasping when he moved against me. Breaking the kiss, he rested his forehead against mine. His heartbeat thundered against my chest, as his hips arched against me. I spoke in a voice so breathless that it seemed to drive him crazy. "I want you, Jake."

My shirt was pulled off in one quick sweep, my bra next, and then he stood me up. His thumbs hooked under the waist of my sweatpants, and he lowered them, trailing his hand down my leg until he pulled them free. His slow path back up my body was trailed with kisses until he stood in front of me. Stepping back, he went to pull his shirt off, but I put my hand over his, pulling the material from his grip. He shivered when my fingers trailed over his skin as I slid it up. As soon as it was over his head, he leaned in and nipped at my lips, reaching for the button of his jeans.

His knuckles slid against my stomach, leaving goose bumps, as his zipper lowered. I stepped back, giving him enough room to slide his pants down. They fell to the ground, and he kicked them away. His chiseled abs quivered with each labored breath, and then he pulled me against him. My world tilted with the feel of the cool sheets under my back, as Ace laid me down, sliding himself on top of me. With one arm braced, he leaned over, grabbed his wallet, flipped it open, and pulled out a condom.

I fought to keep my breathing normal. I didn't want Ace to see what I was feeling and think it was fear. I didn't want him to shut down and walk away from me. Closing my eyes, I ran my hand up his side when I heard the package crinkle.

Ace sat up for a second before lowering himself back

down on top of me, touching me, placing kisses along my jaw and down my neck, along my chest. Before I knew it, I was lost in the storm we'd created. Our bodies fit together like we'd been made for one another, and I hung on when he joined us, making us one. His name rushed past my lips, and he shuddered as he called out mine. The weight of his body pressed me into the mattress as we trembled together.

CHAPTER 6

I woke to Ace trailing his fingers along my arm, as he kissed my forehead. When he noticed me smiling at him, he wrapped his arms around me. My back protested, and I winced. "Sorry, Riles." He blew out a sigh and pulled back to look at me. After all we'd done, the telltale blush of embarrassment couldn't be held back as it flooded my cheeks.

Ace grinned and shifted us so that he leaned over me. He kissed me repeatedly before groaning and pulling away. "Let me get you some aspirin or something. You're gonna be really sore if not." He winced as he ran his hand over my shoulder, pulling me on my side to look at my back. His fingers slipped across my skin so light that it brought on a shiver. Ace pressed a kiss to my shoulder with a low, rumbled laugh that vibrated into me all the way to my core.

My skin prickled in awareness when he pulled back, looking down at me. There was so much that passed between us without words. Too many feelings, which were raw and explosive, brewed in the air. Ace's heavy-lidded gaze made my breath hitch, and he pulled me against him, kissing a path down my neck. We were losing ourselves again, and I melted into the moment—starved for what only he could give me. He leaned into me until his body pressed against mine, quivering as he lost control. The heated silence broke when Ace's phone rang over and over, both of us ignoring it, hoping whoever called would hang up. The phone silenced as Ace settled lengthwise against me and leaned over the bed for his wallet. Shuddering in anticipation, I looked my fill at him. He was my first, and with the way I felt about him, he'd be my only. No one would be as perfect for me as he was. When I ran my fingers over his chest, he groaned and fumbled with his wallet. A sigh rippled through him when he righted himself and ripped the package open. He sat up long enough to slip the condom on, lowering himself onto his elbows and kissing me long and hard.

Ace's phone went off again, the sound mixed with our heavy breathing. He growled against my lips when it continued ringing. Whoever it was, they were adamant about reaching him. Ace lifted himself up slightly and placed light kisses to my lips as his hand blindly sought out the phone. When he found it, he turned it off. I smiled against his lips when he tossed it on the floor. "What if it was important?" I asked when he moved his lips along my jaw and buried his face in my neck.

Ace leaned on his elbow and brought his hand up to my face, brushing my hair away from my cheek. "Right now, nothing is more important than me loving you."

His soft words broke something inside of me—an emotion I'd shoved so far back inside of myself that it rushed out, and tears spilled from the corners of my eyes. Ace leaned in and kissed me. It was tender. A kiss between lovers that went beyond soul deep. I wrapped my hand around his neck and pressed myself against him, telling him with my body how much I needed him.

His tenderness broke, and it was the most intense thing I'd ever felt. The most wild and reckless I'd ever been in my entire life, and I didn't want to be any other way with him.

Ace rocked his body against mine, calling my name out on a growl that rumbled through me. It was the most erotic sound I'd ever heard, and it sent me over the edge with him.

His head leaned against mine, as our bodies stilled. He placed a kiss to my forehead and slid over to lie beside me, placing a kiss over my racing heart before laying his head on my chest. His hand splayed against my stomach, as his labored breaths evened out. Running my fingers through his short, brown hair, warmth spread through me. I felt loved—complete—because of Ace.

"Riley?" Ace's fingers rubbed small circles against my skin.

"Yeah, Ace?"

"Jake," he whispered. "After being so deep inside you, I want you to call me Jake. If only for right now."

I ran my hand through his hair and along his back. He leaned back, propping himself up on one arm and bringing his finger up to trace my bottom lip. "Why did we wait so long, Riley?" His eyes slid closed as he leaned in and kissed me.

I didn't want to think about the fact that he'd leave in two weeks' time. I had to love him in the moment… and worry about everything else later. I'd waited too long for him to see me, love me—the way I loved him. Had always loved him.

"I was just waiting for you," I said, smiling up at him.

He shifted to sit up at the edge of the bed, picked his shirt up off the floor, and handed it to me. Pulling it over my head, I moved my legs slowly to sit on the edge of the bed. He reached out, snagged his jeans up off the floor, stood up, and disappeared into the bathroom. "Be right back," he called out behind him.

I ached pretty much all over, cringing when I rolled my shoulders to stretch. The bathroom door opened, so I smoothed the wince from my face and smiled at Ace when he walked back into my bedroom.

Walking over, he put his hand out. I slipped my hand in his, and he helped me stand. He let go first and ran his fingers up my arm, over my shoulder. His hand stilled at my neck and he stepped forward, wrapping his arms around my waist and pulling me flush against him. Kissing me, he then rested his chin on top of my head. I shifted to lay my head on his shoulder. Tracing an invisible line down his chest, I stopped at the waist of his jeans. His hand found mine and he pulled my fingers up, placing a kiss to the palm of my hand.

"I have no idea what comes next for us, Riley. But I do know one thing. You're it for me. Only you, no matter where I go. I know it's not fair to ask you to wait for me, and I can't say I wouldn't be pissed if you got tired of waiting and moved on, but can we try to make this work?"

"I've waited for you this long. What's a little more time?" I leaned back to look at him and watched the worry slip from his face. "I'm not going anywhere, Jake, unless it's with you."

He leaned back and cupped my face. "I don't know what I did to deserve you, Riley." He brushed his lips against mine about the same time the front door downstairs slammed shut.

"I swear to fuckin' God, one of you better be dead because if you aren't, I plan on killing you both!" Jared shouted as he raced up the stairs.

Ace grumbled as he let go of my face. Jared sounded pissed.

I wondered what smart-ass comment he'd make seeing both of us half dressed. Ace didn't give him a chance to barge in. He crossed the room in three strides and pulled my bedroom door closed behind him just as Jared made it to the top of the stairs.

"What the hell, Ace? I fuckin' call and call, and you don't pick up. Is Riley okay?" He sounded frantic.

"She's fine. My phone died," Ace told him.

I blew out the breath I hadn't realized I'd been holding.

"If she's fine, then you won't mind if I check on her?" There was a tone of challenge in Jared's voice.

"She's getting her stuff together for a shower. You should probably knock first," Ace warned him as my doorknob rattled.

I grabbed the pants I'd had on the night before and slid them on. There was no way I'd be able to put my bra back on. The stiffness in my back made it impossible. I turned to my dresser and pulled out a pair of cut-off shorts when Jared's knuckles wrapped on my door. I called out for him to come in as I pulled my closet doors open and plucked a T-shirt off its hanger. I hugged the clothes against my chest, as Jared looked me from head to toe. "You both suck. All I could think was there was a problem, and we'd spend our last week together keeping vigil over you in a hospital bed." He crossed his arms and gave me his angry eyes.

I chuckled at him and closed my closet. "I'm fine, as you can see. Still standing and everything."

Jared shook his head and snorted. I looked past him to see Ace in the doorway. He'd leaned against the doorjamb, watching us.

Jared saw the direction of my gaze and it was as if everything clicked into place. Understanding dawned on his face, and he turned to look over at my bed. On the floor beside it were the discarded condom wrappers. His eyes snapped to Ace, and I swear I saw a hint of a smile cross his lips. He rubbed his hands together before he spoke. "Get your shit together, both of you. In case you've forgotten, we're staying out at the cabin together before everyone heads out. Now, if you'll excuse me, I have to stop by the hospital and demand Paige's presence for at least a few days, so Mark will stop being an asshole."

I couldn't help but wonder why Jared would think that Paige's presence would make Mark act any different. I'd tuck that question away until I had a chance to talk to Paige.

"What do you want us to bring?" Ace asked.

"Food and contraceptives, people! The basics of life." Jared let a barking laugh out before he stopped in front of Ace. They stared at each other until Ace moved back so he could walk out. Jared put his fist out, and Ace bumped his against it. "'Bout time, bro. I thought you'd never get your shit together." Jared trotted down the stairs and slammed the front door behind him.

"Idiot." Ace shook his head. "I'll run to the store while you get ready, okay?"

"A week with the Six. How could one girl get so lucky?" Crossing over to my bed, I picked up the wrappers Ace had discarded and reached under it to pull out a duffel bag.

"Sorry, Riles. I shoulda picked those up. Now big-mouth Jared knows."

I went for a shrug and stiffened. "I don't care that he knows, Jake. I'm sure by the end of the week, they all would have figured it out."

He smiled and took the wrappers from me. "You're right about that, especially when I carried you off to my room every night."

"Every night, huh?" I bit my lip when I saw his eyes change and desire creep in.

"Multiple times. Are you scared?"

"Of you? Never."

He backed me up against the wall. Groaning against my lips, he forced himself back a step. His chest heaved as he fisted his hands to keep from reaching for me. "I better go, so you can get ready."

I stepped towards him and ran my hand over his shoulder. A heartbeat later, he had me against the wall again. His hungry lips bruised mine in punishing kisses until he went still. "Can't. We can't. No protection. Gotta go. Be back." He spun on his heel, scooped up his T-shirt and shoes, and bolted down the stairs. I heard my keys jingle, and then the kitchen door closed. I rested my head against the wall, sucking in lungfuls of air until I heard my truck start up.

"Oh, Riley, you're in deep, girl," I said aloud to an empty room. My legs shook, as I righted myself and walked to the bathroom.

~

The heat from the water loosened my muscles. I toweled myself off, opened the medicine cabinet for the bottle of ibuprofen, and shook two capsules out into my hand. Tossing them in my mouth, I washed them down with water from the sink. I leaned in and looked at my eye. The purple line underneath it stood out against the coloring of my skin. I wasn't pale, by any means, but I'd started wearing a hat to keep the sun off my face, which also kept me from tanning like I normally did in the summer. It looked bad, but it shouldn't take long to heal. I pulled open the side drawer in the cabinet and took out the little green tin of Res Q Ointment. It was like the miracle of all healing medicines, and I used it on everything. Religiously. The only problem was that I couldn't reach the spot on my back, so I left it out for when Ace returned. A shiver of anticipation rolled through me. He was my very own addiction. I dropped the towel and pulled on my clothes as the front door opened. Ace called out to me.

I stepped out of the bathroom, as he closed the door. I

waited for him at the top of the stairs and held out the green tin. "Can you put this on my back?"

He smirked. "Do you think it's safe to start taking off your clothes again?"

I turned around and pulled my shirt up over my shoulders, but kept in on. Ace opened the lid, smearing the ointment on my back. "It actually looks pretty good, considering."

If Samantha had hurt me any worse, I would have never known what it was like to love Ace. It sort of pissed me off to think about it, so I shook the thought from my mind.

Ace snapped the container together, and I pulled my shirt down.

"I still need to pack," I said as I picked up my comb and brushed my hair. Ace leaned on the doorjamb, watching me. "Did you stop by your house and get your things?"

"I'm all set. And I grabbed some stuff from the store." My eyes snapped up to his reflection in the mirror. A satisfied smile stretched out along his lips. The heat in his eyes rooted me to the spot.

Ace stepped back to let me pass. "Come on, let's get you packed before Jared shows up and does it for you."

I chuckled because he was right. Jared was not a patient person. Ace followed me back to my room and went in search of his phone. He found it under a pillow, turning it back on before slipping it in his back pocket. "Bring a bathing suit. I'm sure we'll end up at the Hole."

The Hole was Mark's term for the man-made pond, big enough to be a small lake. Jared's parents had it dug and then stocked it so the guys could go fishing. Over the last four years, a dock had been added, along with a pair of Jet Skis.

Jared's parents were loaded. No one really knew what they did to make the money they rolled in, but they always doled it out if Jared said it was for the Six. Maybe it was because they felt bad about not being around much.

When Jared's parents concluded that he came with a set of five unruly best friends, they had the cabin built. Calling it a cabin didn't do it justice either. It was massive, with six rooms, one for each of the guys. They spared no expense in building and furnishing it. It was more like a home than a cabin, and the guys loved it. Everyone's parents were happy with it too, since it kept the guys together, out of trouble, and they always knew where their kids were.

I tossed clothes in my bag and an extra pair of shoes in case they wanted to take a walk. Flip-flops sucked in the woods.

I grabbed my phone charger, stuffed it in the bag, and looked around my room for my phone. "It's in your truck," Ace answered my unspoken question.

"Okay, well then, I'm ready," I said, pulling my bag off my bed. Ace took it from me and gestured for me to go first. I stopped by the bathroom, grabbed my overnight case with my toiletries, and added the Res Q Ointment.

When I got to the kitchen, I checked the fridge to make sure nothing in there would go bad before I came back home. There was a gallon of milk so I grabbed it, and then searched the cabinet for the hot chocolate mix. I found a plastic bag and put them in it. Ace had taken my bag out to the truck, and I heard him as his feet scuffed against the step at the front door. I turned with a smile and all but melted. He was leaning on the doorjamb with his arms over his head. He watched me cross the floor until I stopped in front of him. Dropping his arms to his side, he took the plastic bag from my fingers as I tried to form a complete thought. It was impossible, the thought completion, because they all flew out of my head. The only clear thing that came to me was that Ace was so damn hot. Like, lickable hot. The kind of hot that made your toes curl, your mouth water, and your heart race. Pinpricks of awareness jolted along my entire body, and I couldn't move until he nodded his head in the direction of my truck.

Ace opened my door, and I slid in. He put the bag by my feet and closed the door. When he climbed in and started the truck, he reached over and placed his hand on my thigh. Before I knew it, my entire body slid along the bench seat until my hip rested against his. I looked up at him, he shot me a wink, and then put the truck in drive. We'd made it out of the driveway when he slung his arm over the back of the seat and played with the ends of my hair.

I leaned forward, turned the radio on, and slipped into the comfort I'd always had around Ace, before I'd realized how crazy I was about him. Ace's fingers continued playing with my hair. The silence between us was a comfortable one. We'd always been like that though. A smile bloomed on my face, as the morning we'd shared replayed in my thoughts.

"What put that beautiful smile on your face?"

I laid my head on his shoulder and rested my hand on his leg. "You."

He brushed his knuckles against my shoulder and kissed the top of my head. I let a soft sigh slip past my lips, allowing my happiness to beam out of me.

The ride to the cabin didn't take long. When Ace pulled my truck around the back, the guys waved from different spots in the yard. Mark was setting up the horseshoe pit, and Aiden fished around inside a huge cooler. Josh was lying in the hammock stretched out between two large oak trees. His leg hung over the side and pushed him as he munched on an apple.

Eli came out of the cabin and walked over to the truck. When he saw me sitting beside Ace, he smirked and opened the driver's side door. Ace pulled the keys from the ignition and lifted his arm from around me. "Where's Jared?" he asked.

Eli smirked at me. I couldn't help but wonder if Jared had already called them and filled them in. "Not back yet. He said something about stopping by his house to pick up some stuff."

I slid out after Ace, and he put his hand out to help me.

Eli gave me a toothy grin and a wink. "Need help with your stuff?"

"Yeah, grab some of those bags in the back."

Eli reached over the side of the truck and hauled out two handfuls of plastic bags. "Holy crap, half the grocery store is back here!"

Ace snorted. "You guys eat like a bunch of animals."

"True," Eli called out over his shoulder, as he carried the bags to the cabin.

I closed the driver's side door and walked around the truck. Ace grabbed the rest of the grocery bags from the back. "Just get the small stuff, Riley."

I wasn't going to argue, not with the way my back felt.

"Josh, get your ass outta the hammock and come grab our bags."

Josh flipped him off. "Say please, asshole."

"Please, asshole," Ace mimicked as he walked past where Josh pushed himself from the hammock.

Josh pointed his finger at Ace as he walked backwards to the truck. "That's better."

I waited for him as he crossed the yard. "How ya feelin', Riles?"

"A little sore, but not bad considering."

Reaching inside the cab, he pulled out my bag. I closed the door as he slung the strap over his shoulder. He then reached in the back and grabbed Ace's bag.

"Your eye looks better than I thought it would."

"Pretty, right? I hope Samantha's whole face is purple."

"Feelin' a little bloodthirsty today, slugger?" Josh darted out of the way when my hand shot out to slap his arm.

"Nah, she got what she had coming. I just wished she would have refrained from throwing a tree at me."

Josh snorted.

"What?"

"Nothing... well, I mean, it's not nothing, but all I can think of is her turning into like the Hulk or something when you said she threw a tree at you."

I shook my head. "Josh, you have a really weird sense of humor."

"Yeah." He agreed with me because he knew it was true. He always looked at things differently than the rest of us did. However, it did provide us hours of entertainment when he got going.

I pulled the screen door open and let Josh go first.

"Where do you want me to put your bag, Riley?"

Ace replied before I could even form a response. "Just toss both bags on my bed."

Josh whipped his head around and looked at Ace. When Ace gave him a challenging glare, Josh laughed. "This is gonna be an interesting week. I can already tell."

Ace winked at me and went back to putting away the groceries. Eli had remained quiet, pretending that lining up the cereal boxes was the most important job on earth.

I grabbed the milk and put it in the fridge. When Eli stood up, I handed him the box of hot chocolate to put up. "Yes! You never forget, do you?"

Eli had an unhealthy obsession with dark-chocolate, hot chocolate. Secretly, so did I, but he thought I bought it for him. I never corrected him since it gave me hero status in his eyes.

Josh came back into the kitchen and peeked out the front window in the living room. "Jared's back."

As soon as Jared's truck came to a stop, he bailed out and slammed the door. Eli walked over to the kitchen window and opened it, letting in a warm breeze. "He looks pissed."

I looked out the window past Eli and watched Jared holler for Mark. Their conversation drifted along the breeze through the open window. "She's coming, but be ready, 'cause she's pissed at you."

"She can be pissed all she wants, as long as she's here."

I shook my head, wondering what the hell was going on between Mark and Paige.

Ace came up behind me, bracing his arms on either side of me. I leaned against his chest as he ducked his head and rested his chin on my shoulder. "What the hell does Jared have in the back of his truck?"

We watched Jared hand a box over to Mark and then pull another one out. They walked side by side, carrying the boxes to the cabin. Jared stopped and kicked Aiden in the ankle, waking him up.

Ace chuckled when Aiden kicked back at Jared and called him a dickhead. When Aiden saw the boxes, he got up from his seat and limped behind Mark and Jared, his curiosity getting the best of him. Ace moved to lean against the counter, and I turned around as Eli held the screen door open for Jared and Mark.

"Party's here!" Jared set his box down, pulled out several 2-liter bottles of soda, and then opened the box Mark set down. He pulled out two bottles of Crown and a bottle of spiced rum, a smirk spreading across his face. "'Tis a fine thing, rum."

CHAPTER 7

*Y*ou do realize that none of us drink like that, right?" Eli pulled another bottle of rum out of the box and shook his head at Jared.

"That's exactly why we're doing this. And it's like a right of passage for friends. We're all about to go our separate ways, so why not?" Jared snatched the bottle out of Eli's hands.

"I'm not carting your drunk ass to bed, but I'll laugh at you when you pass out," Aiden said as he pulled the bottle from Jared's hands. "Can we hold off on the puke fest until we eat?"

Jared snorted. "Pus—"

"Jared!" Ace's voice stopped Jared from finishing the word.

Jared huffed and set the bottles back inside the box. "Anyway, yabunchapansies," he rushed his insult out so it wouldn't get shut down, "the point is, this week is about us having fun—unsupervised, crazy-ass fun. Things we can look back at and laugh about."

A somber mood hung in the air. Jared was just as affected by everyone moving on, and he wanted to make the most of what little time we had left.

"I think it's a great idea, Jared," I piped up, and they all turned to look at me. "I don't know about you guys, but I think a little fun is in order."

The room seemed to brighten again when they smiled.

I walked over to the fridge, pulled out a package of hamburger, and grabbed a plate. "Can one of you guys go fire up the grill?"

My question put them all in motion. Back to normal. The jokes started, and we moved around each other like we'd always done. I breathed it all in and held it close.

The kitchen cleared out except for Ace. He hadn't moved from his position against the counter. "You're amazing."

I smiled at him. "Why's that?"

"You just have this ability to make it all work out. Like you're the center of our gravity."

I blushed at his admission. I never felt like that. I knew I was a part of them, but a bystander of sorts. "Yeah, well, someone has to keep them in line."

"I'll make those if you want to go put our clothes away," Ace said as he turned to the sink and washed his hands.

Our clothes. A shiver ran down my spine.

"Go get us settled in, Riley. I got this." Ace leaned down and kissed me. My eyes darted to the screen door, waiting for someone to say something.

Ace saw my reaction and smirked at me. "They all know, Riley. You can see it in their faces without them saying a word."

He was right, but it still felt weird. Like we had to sneak around behind their backs, so they didn't find out. But that wasn't the case. They'd seen something change between Ace and me without knowing what had happened. And I damn sure wasn't going to hide how I felt about Ace and be miserable the entire time we were all together, only to be happy in stolen moments when no one was around. I rose up on my tiptoes and pulled him in for a melting kiss. Growling against my lips, he pulled me against him.

"Hey, grab me the... Never mind," Aiden's voice halted, but neither of us turned to acknowledge him.

I broke the kiss. Teasingly, Ace ran his hands down my backside and squeezed. "You'll pay for that later." He nipped at my lips and groaned when I backed out of his arms.

Through the kitchen window, I heard Aiden speak. "I can't get the tinfoil right now 'cause Riley and Ace are practically sucking each other's faces off in there."

My hand flew up to my mouth as a laugh bubbled up. "Well, if they didn't know, they do now."

I left Ace in the kitchen and went to unpack our stuff.

"Hey asshole, come get the tinfoil." I heard Ace holler as the screen door creaked open.

I waited, listening for whatever comment would come next. The screen door closed, and I heard Ace moving around in the kitchen. Maybe they wouldn't say anything at all. The silence was shattered when Mark shouted loud enough for me to hear all the way at the back of the cabin. "Boys, we have a problem. I think Ace ate Riley 'cause she wasn't in the kitchen."

"I bet he did..." Jared's reply was followed by a hoot of laughter.

My cheeks burned and flooded my entire body with heat. It would definitely be a week of good-natured sex jokes at our expense. I had to learn how to shut down the immediate flood of embarrassment. Those boys were like sharks, even the slightest hint of a blush would send them into a frenzy. I'd seen it all too often with them.

I decided to check Ace's closet to see how much room he

had and was shocked to find several of my shirts hung up in between his.

There would be more than enough room in his closet for the shirts I brought. I unpacked my bag and sorted through my stuff, leaving a stack of clothes for the dresser. I carried the shirts over to the closet, hung them up, and turned back to the dresser. I pulled the top drawer open, expecting to find underwear and socks, but found a photo album, receipts, and other stuff shoved inside. I slid it closed, not wanting to intrude on his privacy, even though my fingers itched to move things around to see the rest of the contents.

The drawer below it was where he kept his socks and underwear. Heat spread through me again, and I cursed myself for feeling like a sex-craved lunatic. I rearranged it, stacking my stuff inside. I went to slide the drawer closed, but I stopped myself. If Ace had more socks and stuff, I'd just have to open the drawer again. I turned around and eyed Ace's bag, gathering the courage to open it. *Stop it, it's just clothes. And he asked you to put them away.* I huffed at myself for being an idiot and unzipped it. Pulling everything out, I unzipped the side pocket. I froze. Condoms. A whole brand-new box of them. My cheeks flushed, and I fanned my face with my hand. *Holy meltdown.* I grabbed Ace's socks and underwear, blindly set them in the drawer, closed it, and leaned against it. I eyed the bag and in turn, realized that I'd been staring at the bed as well. A queen-sized bed—a size bigger than mine. Running my hand down my face, I realized I had to get a damn hold of myself.

It was real—all of it was real—and not some dream or fantasy that I'd played out in my mind. Ace and I had shared the most intimate of moments and would do it again. A lot, judging by the size of the box inside his bag. I placed my hand over my heart, as it tried to flutter its way out of my chest. My breaths came out short, and my knees felt weak. The heat of my skin built until I felt it break and leave behind a fine sheen of sweat, like an addict going through withdrawals.

I snatched the box of condoms from the bag, opened the nightstand drawer, and dropped them inside. Closing it, I focused on putting the rest of our clothes away, making quick work of what was left. Shorts went in the third drawer, and my bathing suit got dropped in on top of my underwear. Folding my bag up, I slid it inside Ace's and stuffed them on the top shelf of the closet. His shirts were hung up next, and I tossed my tennis shoes down beside his hiking boots on the floor. I closed the closet, grabbed my toiletries bag, and headed for the bathroom, needing a cold rag to wipe the telltale flush from my face.

I didn't need one of the Six seeing me like that and question me about why I looked like I was about to fall out.

Closing the bathroom door, I set my case on the counter. I grabbed a washcloth and ran it under the tap, wringing it out and bringing it up to my face. The cool cloth slid over my heated skin, making me feel better almost instantly. Setting the washcloth down, I opened the small bag with all my other crap in it and put everything in its place. When I opened the bathroom door and stepped back out into the hallway, I saw Ace walk into his room. The empty bag clenched in my hand as a bout of nervous butterflies attacked my stomach. I pushed my hand against my belly and willed it to settle as I put one foot in front of the other. It was just Ace. The same guy I'd been friends with for most of my life. The same one who had wiped my tears and had my back, and my front and my... I slammed the door on where my thoughts headed and made my way back to his room.

When I stepped into it, he was plugging his cell phone in

and then grabbed my charger. He braced his hand on the nightstand and leaned over to plug it in. The muscles in his arm flexed, and the memories of this morning flooded my mind. His arms braced alongside my shoulders. My hands traveling up them as his muscles tightened and then relaxed with each move against me. I opened the closet, unzipped his bag, and shoved the small bag I'd just emptied inside of it. As I closed the closet, I heard the drawer to his nightstand squeak as he pulled it open and then closed it.

I forced myself to turn around as he crossed the room and closed the bedroom door. Walking over to the dresser, he pulled a pair of shorts out. I chided myself for being nervous to be alone with him.

"You okay, Riley?" Ace's arm came past me as he pulled the closet open and tossed the boots he had been wearing inside with the others, then reached down and grabbed a pair of flip-flops. I moved out of his way and tried to take a breath, but it seemed shallow and forced.

"Riley?" Ace turned around, took one look at my face, and dropped his flip-flops. He stepped closer, and my breath caught on a gasp. "Breathe, Riley." His finger trailed along my lip. He had no idea that it only made it worse when he did things like that.

My eyes fluttered closed, and I melted into his touch.

Ace's hand slid along my hip, sending pinpricks along my skin. "Ah, I think I understand."

I held my breath.

"It's overwhelming to you, isn't it?"

I nodded. To say it was overwhelming put it mildly.

"Riley, open your eyes. Look at me."

I released the breath I'd held, shuddering when my eyes met his.

"Just be my Riley. The one you've always been, only a little wilder when it's just you and me," he said with a wink.

The wilder me was what made me feel like I would combust when we stood with our bodies so close, yet so far apart.

My entire body jittered, flashing hot and then cold. I wanted to melt to the floor. I wanted to attack him. He had me to the point of where I didn't know if I was coming or going.

I stepped back to gather my wits. Ace tilted his head and squinted his eyes as he searched my face.

"I... I can't think with you so close." I clasped my hands together and ducked my head.

He chuckled, and my head snapped up. "It's not funny, Ace."

His eyes crinkled and his mouth kicked up at the corners, creating a devastating smile. I had to get away from him, away from his effect on me, and clear my head.

I made it to the door and turned the knob as Ace's hand shot out, stopping me from pulling it open. His other hand swept my hair off my neck and he leaned in, blowing a warm breath along my skin. Moaning, I tilted my neck to give him better access. He blazed a path of kisses in between the gentle nips he took. I felt myself sinking as his hand came up to my stomach and pulled me into him, holding me upright. His hand fisted in the material of my shirt, and I whimpered. A rumble from his chest vibrated into me, causing my hips to arch back and ground against him. I found myself spun around, his body pressing me into the door. His hands slid down my hips and grabbed my thighs, lifting me up. I wrapped my legs around him and laced my fingers behind his neck, pulling him as close as possible, frustrated with the material between us.

Ace turned us towards his bed and came to an abrupt stop. His eyes changed into slits as he stared at the bedroom window. His grip on my legs loosened until I stood on shaky legs. When I had my footing, he caught my hands up in his and placed them on his chest. His gaze was still on the window, as a sneer crept along the heated flush of his skin.

"Fucking Jared."

I looked over my shoulder at the window and gasped. Jared stood at the window with a crowbar in his hand, shaking it in our direction. "Don't mind me. I was just coming to see if y'all needed me to pry ya apart. Ya know, in case y'all were stuck or something." He hooted with laughter at his own joke. "I see it's not necessary, but it seems the hose might be in order."

His words found their mark, dousing me in an ice-cold bucket of reality. We were outnumbered, surrounded by a bunch of guys who weren't used to us shutting them out.

"I'm gonna hurt him," Ace grumbled.

"Not if I hurt him first," I said, waving my fingers at Jared.

He grinned at me, saluted us with the crowbar, and walked away.

Ace let go of my arms and stepped back. "Sorry, Riley. God, he's such a…"

"Pain in the ass? Mood killer? Dead when I get my hands on him?" I jumped in to finish his sentence.

Ace walked over to his door and pulled it open, gesturing for me to go first. "Yeah, and then some."

We stopped in the kitchen, and Ace pulled a glass from the cupboard. "I need a minute before we go out there."

His movements were jerky. His body stiff as he filled the glass with water, emptying it in one gulp. I leaned against the fridge and watched him fill it again and take slower sips. He kept his eyes focused on the floor, taking even breaths. Slowly, his body relaxed and he set the glass in the sink.

Outside the kitchen window, the guys bickered back and forth. The sound was normal, comforting. Ace snorted when

Mark threatened Jared when he cracked on him about burning the burgers.

Ace pushed off the counter, and his gaze sought me out. "You say the word and we'll leave. We can go back to your house and leave these asshats to themselves for a couple of days."

I wanted to grab my keys and jump in my truck, but I knew I'd kick myself later when we both missed out on being together with everyone. "They're just seeing how far they can push us. So let's give it right back to them." I wiggled my eyebrows at him.

Ace groaned. "You're just as bad as they are. Okay, we'll stay, but I can't promise that I'll keep my hands off you in front of them. I have no control when it comes to you."

"Good." I darted out the door when Ace growled my name and shot towards me. Running across the yard, I squealed when he caught me and slung me over his shoulder. His hand connected with my ass. He kept his hand there as he continued across the yard and set me down in front of a chair.

Silence. The other five stared at us, openmouthed, but only long enough for the dirty jokes to start.

"Watch it," Ace warned them.

The jokes halted when Mark announced the burgers were done. When Jared chimed in that they were way past done, a burger flew through the air and hit him in the shoulder. Jared sprawled on the ground. "Man down! Man down!"

A wave of sadness slid under the humor. *Damn, I'm gonna miss this.*

~

Afternoon gave way to evening and Josh carried over an armful of wood, stacking it by the fire pit. Aiden hauled a cooler closer and grabbed a case of beer, shoving cans down in the ice. It wasn't often they sat around the fire drinking. Mark's camera flashed as he took random pictures. We were so used to him doing it that the flash didn't cause us to turn anymore. He'd captured some awesome pictures of us over the years.

He walked over and sat down beside me. "Hey, check out what I did." He held his phone out to me, showing me the pictures he'd taken from the bed of my truck. "I was able to smooth out the cut on your face and make you look normal."

I smacked his leg with the back of my hand. "I want a copy of that."

"I'll make sure you get one."

Josh walked over and plucked the phone from my hands. "Wow, that came out good, Mark."

"What came out good?" Jared asked, picking up the broken rake handle that served as the official fire poker for the last four years.

Josh held the phone up, and Jared leaned in to look. "Of course it did, I'm in it."

Josh shoved him, and he laughed. "You're so in love with yourself."

"True dat," Eli called out as he cracked his beer open.

"Shut up, Josh. You know I'm the hot one in this group," Jared said, pointing the fire poker's glowing end in Josh's direction.

Josh handed Mark's phone back to him when Jared handed him a beer. "Cheers, asshole."

The guys settled in and bickered. It wasn't long before the 'remember when's' started. I blushed to the roots of my hair when Jared brought up the time we'd all gone swimming in the Hole, and I'd lost my top. Josh thought it would be fun to throw me from the dock. When I hit the water, my bikini top disappeared. I'd been so embarrassed. I crouched in the water with my hands over my chest while they searched for the missing top. Aiden found it and Ace brought me a towel, so I could get out of the water with what was left of my pride.

Ace's hand slid over my leg and squeezed. "I think that's the day I realized there was no way I was getting over you."

I quirked my eyebrow at him. "Why, because I lost my top and you got a peek?"

A slow smile spread across his lips, and his eyes fired with the memory. "I'm a guy, Riley. But that's only part of the reason."

I rolled my eyes and tried pushing his hand away, but he caught mine in his and pulled it up in front of his mouth as he whispered, "You knocked the breath out of me that day. Dripping wet with eyes as big as a does and so innocent. I knew that very second, I'd do everything I could to make you mine one day."

I leaned in the same time as Ace did, lost in his words, not hearing or seeing anything but him.

"Can you two stop making googely eyes at each other and pay attention?" Jared asked.

Ace growled under his breath. I turned my attention to Jared at the same time he chucked a piece of ice, hitting Ace in the chest. He flicked it off his shirt and scowled. "Now I owe you twice, jackass."

Jared crushed his beer can as he got up from his seat and walked over to the cooler. His hand disappeared inside, pulling out a bottle of rum. "I think this calls for a toast!"

He unscrewed the top and held the bottle in the air. "Everyone has to say something. I'll start this off," he said, tipping the neck of the bottle and sweeping it in an arc. "May the memories we've made here last forever." His words faltered at the end of his toast. Putting the bottle to his lips, he took a swig.

I shuddered for him as he hissed through his teeth and handed the bottle over to Josh.

Josh stood, hoisted the bottle in the air, and twisted his mouth like he pondered what to say. The fire snapped and popped in the silence. "To lasting friendships that will span not only across the world, but also the time we're apart."

His eyes glistened when he tilted the bottle back. He handed it off to Eli and wiped his mouth with the back of his hand as he coughed.

Eli sighed and looked at the bottle. "Here's to finding our soul mates like Ace and Riley did." He tipped the bottle towards us and grinned. His whole body shook when he swallowed.

Ace ran his hand along my arm. When I looked at him, he winked.

"My turn!" Aiden shouted as he took the bottle from Eli's outstretched hand. "To the Seven!" Tipping the bottle back above his open mouth, he poured a stream of amber liquid in and swallowed. He pounded his fist against his chest and shouted, "Whooo!"

"Show off," Mark said, grabbing the bottle from Aiden and laughing. "Here's to making this week the best damn one we've had here!" The bottle tilted and sloshed when he brought it back down. He shook it at me, and I stood up to take it from him.

The seriousness of the moment made my chest tighten. It was like saying goodbye before it was time. I pulled a deep breath that came from the tips of my toes, but the tightness wouldn't go away. For whatever reason, I couldn't shake the feeling that it would never really be the same again when the guys went their separate ways.

I hugged the bottle against my chest and trembled. Ace's arms wrapped around me, and the first tear fell. My thoughts weighed heavy on me and for once, I just let them out without worrying what anyone thought. "Promise me this isn't the last time we'll all be together." I searched their faces, looking for something, but I wasn't sure what.

I think they felt it, too. That pull that said, 'This is it—so make the most of it.' I cleared my throat, uncomfortable with the silence. "To the best guy friends a girl could ask for." I brought the bottle up to my lips and took a long swallow, closing my eyes when the alcohol burned a path down my throat. Ace's hand rubbed in soothing strokes against my shoulder. I blinked to clear my watery eyes and handed Ace the bottle, as the rum hit my stomach like a fireball. Warmth bloomed against my skin as Ace's voice rolled over me. "I agree with Riley. We need to make a pact here and now that we'll always make our way back here. But I want to add to that. I want us to keep in touch. I know it won't be easy with where all of our lives are taking us, but it's important. So with that said... here's to us."

Ace didn't make a sound, not even a hiss, when he tipped the bottle back and took a swig.

The moment was broken when a set of headlights cut across the field, and Paige's car came into view.

"Well, it's about damn time," Mark huffed under his breath. I looked over at him and found him watching Paige until her car pulled to a stop, and she got out.

Jared grabbed the bottle from Ace. "To Paige!" The bottle was passed around again until it landed in Mark's hand.

"To you," he said as he stood when she got closer. He handed the bottle over to her, and she didn't even hesitate as she took two long pulls from the bottle. Jared, Aiden, and Eli howled out supporting cheers until Paige handed the bottle back to Mark.

"What a suck-ass day. I needed that, especially having to come out here and deal with y'all too," Paige muttered.

Mark rubbed the spot over his heart. "Been waitin' on you to get here."

"Jesus, Paige, would you just put him out of his misery already?" Jared asked as he walked over and took the bottle from Mark. He screwed the lid on and stuffed it back in the cooler.

CHAPTER 8

*P*aige pegged Mark with a hard look. "Do you know what your idiot friend did when he came to see me today?"

Mark groaned. "No." He looked back at Jared. "What the hell did you do? I asked you to stop in and invite her out here. By the looks of it, you added your own spin on it."

Jared's face split into a grin that threatened to swallow his face. "You mad, bro?"

Paige pushed past Mark and advanced on Jared. "I've put up with a lot of shit over the years from you, Jared. But if you ever show up at my work again and do what you did today, I promise, I will castrate you, so that the chances of ever having a little Jared will be gone."

Aiden lost it. He laughed so hard that he fell out of his chair. Jared's face stayed plastered with his shit-eating grin.

"Aw, come on, Paige. It was funny!"

Paige's arm came back and her fist shot out, but Mark caught her and yanked her backwards at the same time, saving Jared's face.

Jared snapped his teeth together at her and danced further away. "Vicious." He was baiting her... and loving every second of it.

Paige was sputtering mad, trying to get Mark to release her. When Mark realized that she wasn't going to give up, he scooped her in his arms and carried her to the cabin. She struggled and kicked. He stopped when he almost dropped her and set her on her feet. He didn't give her time to steady herself, as he grabbed her by the shoulders and shook her.

"Stop it, Paige!" He sounded angry, but the fight went out of her, and she spun away, all but running into the cabin.

Jared whistled. "That's an orgasmic explosion waiting to happen."

"Why do you always push people so hard?" The question slipped out of me before I could stop it.

"Because some of you are too stupid to see what's in front of you while it's standing right there," he replied.

What did that mean? I couldn't be more in focus of what was in front of me. "Why are you so pissed? It's not like it's your love life we're talking about here. Let it happen on its own, Jared. Forcing something makes it awkward." He had the decency to wince at what I'd said.

Mark and Paige's argument grew louder until we could hear everything they said. Ace shook his head and walked towards the house. As soon as he stepped inside, their voices cut off. Seconds later, he came out holding a radio and plugged it into an extension cord that he dragged behind him. He flipped the power on and turned the volume up enough for us to hear Florida Georgia Line crooning. Ace held his hand out and pulled me up into his arms. Singing along, he spun me in a circle.

The song ended, and the spell broke between us. The guys had ignored us, caught up with giving each other hell. A few minutes later, Mark came back out with Paige. She seemed calmer and a little glassy-eyed. The rum had probably kicked in. Paige wasn't one to explode, but when she did, it didn't last long. It was like a violent storm that blew out just as fast as it blew in, but it could leave devastating destruction in its path.

Falling into a chair across the fire from me, Paige rubbed her head. Mark pulled a beer out of the cooler and handed it to her before he went to sit next to her. Jared walked over and kicked at her shoe, so she'd look at him. Her eyes snapped up, and a frown stretched out over her face. "What, Jared?"

"Sorry, Paige."

"What the hell possessed you to do that? Do you know how many people came up and asked me when I was due?"

Mark's breath hissed between his teeth. His hands clenched on his bouncing knees.

"How the hell was I supposed to know those old biddies would jump to that conclusion? Wait, they seriously asked you that?"

"Yes…" The word dragged out like a hiss.

"What the hell did you say, Jared?" Aiden asked.

Paige kicked him in the ankle, and Jared winced as he stepped back to put a safe distance between them. "This idiot cornered me and asked me when I was going to quit hiding it from everyone."

Jared snorted. "Clearly, I meant something else."

"Yeah, well, did they know that?" Paige shot back at him.

Paige cracked her beer open and lifted it up. "You're a real dickhead, Jared."

Jared swooped in and took it from her hands. "You can't drink that in your condition!"

Paige shot out of her seat and took off after him. He was smart enough to run. Mark groaned and leaned his head back, looking up at the stars. "When will he learn to leave things alone?"

I heard Paige shriek, and then Jared hooted with laughter.

"Put me down, Jared Jackson!" Paige's demand was followed up by a laugh. "You're impossible!"

Jared strode out of the darkness. "Good news! She's not expecting. Aiden, get this woman a beer!"

Josh beat him to it as he grabbed a new can and handed it to Paige when Jared lowered her to her feet.

"Fuckin' Jared. How can he piss you off and make you laugh at the same time?" Paige asked, sliding back into the seat beside Mark.

"We've wondered that for years," Eli said, crushing his can between his hands. Before he could ask, Josh chucked another beer at him.

"Is anyone else glad that Mark and Ace's rooms are at the end of the hallway?" Jared asked.

Ace groaned beside me when everyone else chuckled.

"Jared, go get your guitar." I no sooner had the idea out of my mouth then Jared was halfway across the yard.

"Ace, come help me." Jared didn't wait for a reply as he slipped inside.

"Good call. With his hands and mouth busy, he can't say anymore stupid shit." Ace winked at me and got up to help Jared.

They came out with a guitar in both hands. Jared handed one to Josh, and Ace handed one to Mark. Eli could play, but he was happy to sit and listen. Playing the guitar had never been his thing; he preferred belting out each song as loud as possible.

The hours passed by as the guys plucked away, and we sang along. When the beer ran out, the rum bottle got passed around, until that too, was gone. The fire died out, and the mood mellowed. A yawn passed around the group several times before Aiden called it a night first.

"What's on the agenda tomorrow?" Eli asked.

"The Hole," Mark and Jared answered together.

"Cool. See y'all in the morning," Eli gave a brief wave in our direction and zigzagged his way to the cabin.

"I'm calling it a night, too," Josh said as he got up from his seat and stretched.

Ace stood and put his hand out to help me up. "I think we should all call it a night."

My stomach lurched when I got to my feet and swayed. I'd drunk way more than I ever had before.

Ace helped steady me. "You okay?"

When my mouth opened to answer him, I hiccupped. He shook his head with a soft chuckle. "Yep, you're toast."

I giggled, leaning heavily on him as I stumbled along beside him to the cabin.

"Can y'all get the door?" Mark called out as the door closed behind us.

Jared walked past us. "I got it."

Mark sidestepped Jared with Paige cradled in his arms. "Dang, Paige is passed the fuck out," Jared said, looking down at her.

"Yeah, let's just hope she keeps it all down and doesn't spew everywhere tonight." Mark sighed.

It was like his words triggered my gag reflex. I half stumbled, half ran to the bathroom, barely making it to the toilet when my stomach tried to leave my body.

I begged and pleaded for the volcano in my stomach to stop erupting. Miserable, I was so miserable that I wanted to die. I cursed everything and anything. Ace stayed beside me, holding my hair and wiping my face with a washcloth. He even fed me chips of ice, telling me to suck on them and spit it out. It worked until I swallowed a mouthful of the cold water and retched again.

When my stomach finally decided it was done purging itself, Ace handed me some ibuprofen and a lukewarm glass of water. I eyed them warily, but he told me that if I didn't take them, I'd really hate myself in the morning. Tossing them in my mouth, I swallowed enough water to wash them down. When we were sure they'd stay down, Ace helped me to bed. He peeled me out of my clothes and slid one of his T-shirts over my head.

His lips met mine in a soft whisper of a kiss before he walked around and climbed into bed beside me. I inched closer and curled up against him.

"If you need anything, just wake me up," Ace said as he ran his hand up my arm.

It hit me then. Ace had no intention of doing anything but sleeping. I felt bad, like I'd stolen a night from us that we couldn't get back. "I'm sorry, Ace."

He pulled back to look at me. "For what? Having a good time with our friends? I won't say that I'm not desperate to be with you again, but I'm also glad you let go and had fun, Riley."

I snuggled up against him and felt the weight of my eyelids dipping until I couldn't keep them open any longer.

I woke up, cocooned in a comforter that smelled like Ace, and winced when my head thumped like a bass drum. Never again. Never again would I touch that much liquor.

The bedroom door opened and then closed, carrying in the smell of toast. It wafted across the room, and my stomach clenched. I pulled the comforter up over my head with a groan.

"Uh-uh, Riley. You need food, headache medicine, and to hydrate."

"Go 'way, Ace." I lifted my hand and shooed him.

"Not gonna work."

The comforter was pulled from my death grip, and Ace hauled me into a sitting position. "Trust me. You'll feel better after you get something in your stomach."

I screwed up my face, but took the cup of coffee from him. The first sip tasted good enough that I took another one. Ace took the cup from my hands and handed me a piece of toast.

I grumbled my way through it, but felt relieved when the heavy feeling I'd woken up with receded.

When I finished both pieces of toast and my coffee, Ace took the empty plate to the kitchen as I got our bathing suits out for our day at the Hole.

I could hear the guys in the kitchen; their voices had started out low as they waited for everyone to wake up.

I looked up when Mark's door opened, and he looked at me with bleary eyes. Behind him, I could see Paige's hair spilling over the side of the bed.

"She okay?" I asked.

He turned to look back at her and rubbed his hand against the back of his neck. "Yeah, but it's gonna suck when she wakes up." He tried for a smile that fell flat as he closed the door behind him and made his way to the bathroom.

Ace stuck his head into our room, "Jared said you can use his bathroom if you want."

I nodded, grabbing my bathing suit, shorts, and tank top. Jared's bathroom was attached to his bedroom. His parents added it when they realized that six boys and one bathroom wasn't such a good idea.

I changed, ran a washcloth over my face and arms, and then headed back to Ace's room. My eyes were still sensitive, so I grabbed my sunglasses and a canvas tote bag to stuff some snacks in. When I got to the kitchen, I pulled one strap off my shoulder and held it open as the guys loaded the bag down with snacks. We'd done this so many times that it was like a routine.

Mark came down the hallway, still in the T-shirt and shorts he'd slept in. "I'm gonna stay here in case Paige needs anything. We'll meet you down there in a little bit." He stabbed his fingers through his hair and blew out a long breath.

"If you need anything, just call my cell," Jared said, unplugging his phone and sticking it in the snack bag.

"Thanks," Mark said. He gave a half wave and wandered back down the hallway to his room.

Outside the screen door, I heard the sound of ice being dumped into a cooler. The ice machine had been delivered two years ago during one of our summer stays at the cabin. Having an unlimited supply of ice on hand was nice, especially with the brutal heat of summer. There were days when I wanted to climb inside the opening and lay on the ice just to cool off.

Josh carried the blanket we always used to spread out under the sweeping boughs of the oak tree on the bank of the Hole.

Aiden shoved bottles of water and a few sodas into the cooler, and gestured for Eli to grab one side. Together, they lifted it and carried it across the yard. We always walked to the Hole, since it wasn't that far from the house, maybe a half mile at the most.

Ace pulled the bag from my shoulder and laced his fingers through mine. A lazy day in the sun sounded good.

We were halfway to the Hole when Jared's phone rang. Ace pulled it out of the bag and handed it to him.

"I'll catch up with y'all," he said and then answered the phone as he walked away to talk privately.

Ace and I looked at each other, both not sure what to make of it. Jared never made anything private. He'd always been an open book. Sometimes too much information spilled from him and you wished he had an off button. When I looked back over my shoulder, I could see him rubbing at his neck as he paced. Something wasn't right.

By the time we reached the Hole, Josh already had the blanket spread out. The cooler was placed off to the side of the tree, and the guys were running down the dock. Aiden hit the water first with a splash. Eli and Josh jumped at the same time, sending a wave of water over Aiden's head when he surfaced. All bets were off, and it became a water war for a solid ten minutes.

I still didn't feel a hundred percent, so I opted to sit on the blanket and watch their antics. Ace stretched out beside me and leaned back on his arms, crossing his legs at the ankle. I tilted my head back and inhaled the fresh air as a warm breeze drifted over us. If the temperature of the morning had any indication of what the afternoon would be like, we'd spend the majority of the day in the water. The heat was brutal. Summer had arrived.

"Come on, you guys!" Josh flailed his arms at Ace and me.

Ace stood and put his hand out to help me up. "We better go before they come get us."

I let him pull me up, but stopped him so that I could pull my shorts and tank top off. I watched his jaw clench and his nostrils flare when my shorts slipped past my hips and fell to the blanket below.

Before I could pick them up and fold them, Ace had me in his arms, running for the dock.

"Ace!" I shrieked, but he kept going until his feet left the dock and we were falling into the water.

I shot up to the surface, and Ace reached for me. Kicking backwards, I cupped my hands and attempted to hit him with a wave of water. He laughed and dove down, coming up behind me. When his hand settled on my hip, he pulled me against him and swam us close enough to the bank where I could touch.

I heard Jared's four-wheeler and turned as he backed the double trailer down to unload the Jet Skis. He jumped off the four-wheeler, unhooked one, and shoved it off the trailer. His leg went over the machine, and then he was out on the water like a slingshot.

"What the hell?" Aiden jumped on the four-wheeler as Josh unloaded the other Jet Ski and tried to tie it off to the dock, but Jared's wakes were making it impossible.

Pulling the four-wheeler away from the water, Aiden parked it.

I leaned against Ace, as we watched Jared rip around the Hole like the Devil chased him.

Josh waited until Jared slowed a little bit, and the water calmed to tie up the other Jet Ski. The guys knew when not to mess with Jared. He'd need time and a little space to work through whatever had upset him. It didn't look like it would be something he'd be able to just shake. His shoulders slumped as he rode and there was a set to his jaw. I could see it as clear as if I were right beside him. Jared needed to get whatever it was out of his system before he hurt himself.

"Hey." I turned to Ace. "Can you grab me a water?"

Ace looked down at me and squinted, as if he knew I was up to something.

I batted my eyelashes at him. "Please?"

He wrapped his arms around me and nibbled my neck. "How can I say no to that?"

He released me, and I turned to watch him make his way to the cooler. When he looked back over his shoulder at me, I waved my fingers at him. He shook his head and the second he looked forward again, I lunged for the Jet Ski and took off before anyone could stop me.

My name rolled along the air when Ace hollered for me, but I wasn't turning back around. Jared needed someone, and I was probably the only one he wouldn't deck right about then. I brought the Jet Ski to a stop about five feet from where he passed. His head whipped over in my direction and he made another pass by me, shooting a rooster tail that hit me dead on.

"Oh yeah! Two can play your game, Jared!" I hollered at him.

I cut him off, and he killed the switch on his machine. He cursed me as I looped around him and hit him with a wall of water from the side of the Jet Ski. It sent him bobbing along the choppy surface until he fired his up again and zipped around me in circles. I jumped the wakes he left behind, keeping up with him, until he realized I wasn't going away.

When he finally stopped, I brought mine up beside his, and we bobbed like corks along the surface of the water.

He ripped his sunglasses off and ran his hand down his face, growling when he spoke. "What, Riley?"

"Are you seriously gonna try to pull that shit with me, Jared?"

He heaved a sigh and gave me a look that would terrify any other girl. I just shrugged. "What's going on with you?"

"Can't you just leave it alone, Riley?"

"Uh, no. You don't get a choice with this, so you might as well spill it, Jared."

"Leave me alone."

It felt like a slap. Jared was an ass most days, but he'd never spoken to me like that. And it pissed me off.

I shot up and grabbed his handlebar. My other arm poked him in the chest. "You have a lot of nerve! I just came out

here and risked my freakin' life because you need someone
to talk to. Do you know what the other five are gonna do to
me when I get this parked?" I stabbed my finger at the
machine that rocked under me, threatening to dump me
between where the rubber bumpers kept banging into each
other. My hand slipped off the handlebar and my shoulder
slammed into the front of his Jet Ski. Jared had me back in
my seat before I could understand what happened.

"Damn it, Riley! Alright, Jesus, I'll tell you. Just sit the fuck
down." Jared tipped his head back and let a slew of curses
spew.

"Feel better?"

"Shut up! Ace is gonna have my ass for this," he said.

"I'll give him mine instead." I wiggled my eyebrows at
him. He fell back on his seat and laughed. His hand clutched
at his stomach, and he wiped his eyes.

I waited for him to stop laughing, watching as his body
relaxed and a spark of humor replaced the anger from
earlier.

When he sat up and draped his arms over the handlebars,
I tried again. "Talk to me, Jared. What's going on?"

He pushed himself off the bars, dropped his hands into
his lap, and stretched his foot out to bring our machines
closer. I turned on the seat and hooked my heel on the edge
of his footboard to keep us from floating apart.

When he spoke, he ran his hands down the legs of his
shorts. "The band I signed on with?"

"Destroying Doubt... yeah?"

"Their lead guitar player left earlier than they'd planned
for. They have concerts lined up and can't fulfill their
contracts right now. They need me. They want me to fly out
to California this Friday."

"But... that's in two days." He could be gone in just
two days.

Jared's laugh was laced with frustration. "I told them no."

"You did? But why? That's your dream!"

"Funny that you say that. My manager said the same thing, along with a reminder that the contract I signed clearly stated, in the fine print, that if Kit James didn't stay, I'd be given a forty-eight hour notice. If I failed to uphold my end of the deal, I'd pretty much be blacklisted from the music industry and sued on top of that. Fuck! What the hell am I supposed to tell the guys?"

Hurt. Jared was hurt, and there wasn't a damn thing any of us could do about it, except support him. "Jared?" When he looked up at me, his eyes were swimming in tears. "The guys will understand. This is important to you, which makes it important to them."

He looked away as a tear rolled down his face, and he swatted at it angrily. "What if I've changed my mind? What then?"

"Have you? Have you really changed your mind? Music… being in a band, it's all you've ever wanted. It just came a little sooner than you expected." I gave him a slight shrug and nudged him with my foot. "You have to follow your dreams, Jared. Everyone else is."

"You're not." And just like that, my heart shriveled.

I crossed my arms and felt myself stiffen. "That's not fair. You know that's out of my control."

"Fair or not, it is what it is. I have a deal for you." He slipped his sunglasses back on and gave me his trademark, crooked smile.

"A deal?"

"Yep. I'll follow my dream, if you follow yours. That means you have to accept help, even if you don't want it."

"No, Jared. I won't accept help. I'll figure it out." I waved off his argument, but he barreled on.

"Sorry, Riley, but I'm helping you regardless, so you might

as well just get used to it. Besides, why should you sit here and watch all of us set off to follow our dreams and be left to rot in this place?"

I bit my lip to keep from telling him he could push the issue all he wanted, but it didn't mean I'd accept it. I pulled my leg over the seat, and Jared pushed us apart.

"Race ya back!" He took off before I could catch up with him. Emotional boys were mentally exhausting.

CHAPTER 9

*a*ce was furious when I pulled the Jet Ski up beside the dock. He shot Jared a dirty look and waited for me to climb off. I slid back on the seat and slapped my hand on the open spot. He climbed on in front of me, took us out to the middle of the Hole, and let us drift. I could feel the tension in his body rolling off him. "That was an incredibly stupid idea. I never want you to put yourself in that position again."

I slid back on the seat. If we were gonna have it out, I wanted to see his face. "I wouldn't take that shit from Jared. Why would you think I'd take it from you?"

"Riley..."

"No. Don't you dare try to use that tone of voice with me! I'm not a child. You have no right to tell me what I can and can't do. Jared is our friend, and he needs us right now. I took a chance that he'd talk to me, and I was right."

Ace spoke through clenched teeth. "He could have hurt you!"

"But he didn't." I looked over to where the guys stood on

the dock. They were focused on Jared. I could tell by the jerky movements he made that he was breaking the news about leaving in two days' time.

"What's going on, Riley?" Ace asked me as he watched the scene on the dock.

"Jared's leaving Friday."

"What? Why?"

"The phone call he got was from his manager. Kit James walked and Jared has to go, or he's in breach of his contract."

Ace's chin hit his chest, and I wrapped my arms around him as he soaked in what I'd told him. "We have two more days with him. Let's make the best of it." I ran my hands up his side and kissed the spot between his shoulder blades. Shivering, he rested his hands briefly on mine. His anger deflated, and he took us back to the dock.

～

The fun had been sucked out of the day. We didn't need that. If anything, we should have been making enough crazy memories to last until the next time we were together.

We were sitting on the blanket, spread out, looking out over the water, when Mark shouted behind us. "Y'all look like a bunch of old porch dogs sunnin' themselves, minus the sun."

I looked up, and Paige gave me a *'what the hell is going on'* look.

Josh pulled a leg up and draped his arm over it. He stared at the water but spoke to Mark. "Jared's leaving on Friday."

Mark staggered, bumping into Paige. She steadied him and kept her hand on his arm until they made it to where he half sat, half tossed himself to where he could come to terms with the bad news Josh delivered.

"It's really happening, isn't it? We're all going our separate ways." His words were filled with heartbreaking disbelief.

Paige sat down beside Mark, leaning against him until he looked at her. A look passed between them and Mark shifted, pushing on Paige's legs until he had his head in her lap. He crossed his ankles and closed his eyes.

Paige pulled her fingers through his hair, as she chewed on her lip. I could see a thought brewing, and then she broke the silence.

"I don't know why y'all are sad about Jared leaving. If anything, you should be pissed. He's gonna be getting more ass in one month than all of you will get for the rest of your life."

It went dead quiet for a beat of three seconds when everyone whipped their heads to look at her with eyes widened. She ignored them and shot a toothy grin at Jared. When she winked at him, it broke the spell holding everyone speechless. It took the guys a while to get their laughter under control. They heaved deep breaths and when one would start up again, it set all of them off. They laughed until they clutched at their stomachs. Paige never spoke like that. Sure, she cussed, but she'd never joked or talked like that in the last four years she'd known the Six. Paige was the prim and proper one of the bunch, and she'd just shot the hell out of her perfectly coiffed image. All bets would be off with the Six. She'd sealed her own fate.

"I knew she was one of us!" Jared howled.

Mark reached up, put his hand behind her neck, and pulled her down for a kiss.

It made the guys howl out and try their hardest to embarrass her and Mark.

Ace nudged me with his shoulder. When I looked at him, he wore a goofy grin. "What?"

He shook his head and wrapped his arm around my shoulder. Hugging me against him, he leaned in and spoke against the side of my neck. "Leave it to Paige to snap us back to reality."

The mood around us shifted as everyone accepted that life, no matter how much we didn't want it to, was changing for all of us.

After that, the afternoon was filled with cannonballs, Jet Ski races, and people being tossed in the water. It was perfect.

~

Aiden drove the four-wheeler, loaded with the Jet Skis, back to the shed they'd been stored in. The rest of us collected our stuff and walked back to the cabin. Jared mentioned steak, and we'd hurriedly packed up so we could stuff our faces.

When I made it inside the cabin, Jared had the steaks out on plates and was pulling the spices down to season them. He glanced over at me and spun the lid off the garlic salt. "You can use my shower if you want."

"I planned on it," I said, setting my bag down. There was a handful of empty wrappers and a half-eaten bag of chips. I tossed the bag on the counter, turned the tote upside down over the trash, and shook it.

He spun the lid back on the garlic salt and reached for the pepper as he mumbled, "Saucy wench."

I purposely walked around the table and hip-checked him. He hadn't expected it, and his forehead banged into the top cabinet. I darted away from him before he could touch me with the same hand he'd flipped the raw meat with. I heard him chuckle to himself as I made my way down the hall.

Ace walked into the bedroom and eyed the shorts and underwear I'd tossed on the bed. He leaned against the doorframe as I plucked a T-shirt off the hanger. "I'm gonna grab a shower in Jared's bathroom."

He pushed off the doorframe and dropped a kiss to my lips. "All by yourself?"

"It's how I've done it these last fourteen plus years, so yeah, I think I can handle it." Once the reply left my mouth, I realized what he meant, and the telltale blush of embarrassment tinged my cheeks a bright red. I busied myself by turning away and picking up the clothes I'd set on the bed.

"Yeah, but there's always that one spot that gets missed no matter what angle your arm is bent." His arm shot out in front of me when I went to walk past him. "So really, I'm doing you a favor by coming with you. Ya know—to make sure that one spot gets clean."

I hugged the stack of clothes tighter to my chest. "Oh please, did you honestly think that would work?"

His eyes crinkled at the corner and he brought his hand up, pinching his cheeks to keep his lips from curving into a smile.

"You gotta come up with better lines," I said, pushing his arm down so I could walk past him.

The room swirled around me, and I ended up pressed against the wall. My clothes fell to the floor, and my hands landed against Ace's chest. "How about this…? I'll wash your back, and you can wash mine."

My mouth opened and closed several times as he stood there in front of me, waiting, caging me in as my short breaths pushed my chest against his.

Ace's eyebrow kicked up as he moved back a step, and then bent down to pick up my clothes. When he handed them over, my underwear was hanging from his finger. I went to snatch them, but he pulled them out of my reach. "So what do ya say?

My voice came out a husky whisper when I gathered the nerve to answer him. "I still think you need better lines to get a girl to share her shower."

"Challenge accepted, Riley. I'll work on that later, but right now... shower." He grabbed clean clothes, took my hand, and rushed me down the hallway to Jared's bathroom. When the bedroom door closed behind us, Ace turned the lock in one swift movement.

My feet felt like they were glued to the floor when Ace walked toward me. Prowled was more like it. He pulled at the clothes I clutched tightly to my chest. They fell from my grip, and I wobbled back a step. I wasn't scared, not in the least. No, I was so wound up that the tiniest of touches from Ace would shatter me. He watched me through hooded eyes as he maneuvered around me into the bathroom. The shower turned on and seconds later, steam rose up above the glass doors. I clasped my hands together in front of me, twisting my fingers together as I wondered if I should bolt, chiding myself for being unsure.

Ace twisted at the waist, and I watched the way his skin stretched over his chest, bunching the muscles in his back. His hand came out, inviting me to make the first move—to go to him on my own. I took one step, and then another. Before I knew it, he had a tight grip on the bottom of my shirt, lifting it over my head. His lips found mine and he kissed me, as he tugged the strings holding my bikini top in place. His hands spread out over my back, fingertips digging in as he pulled me close. As he slid his lips along my neck and down to my shoulder, his left hand raked down my side, while his thumb hooked at the waist of my bottoms, dragging the material over my hip. He smoothed his hand up along my ribcage and switched hands, tugging the other side of my bottoms until they puddled at my feet.

I reached out with fingers that shook, ran my hands along his sides, and brought them around, wedging them between us and untying his swimming trunks. Ace sucked in a hiss when I grabbed the top corner of the Velcro and yanked it apart. My hands ran back and forth across the bottom of his stomach until I trailed my fingers under the waist of the shorts, pushing them down and over his nicely shaped backside.

I waited as he took a deep breath and then released it as he stepped back. He held my stare as my top fell to the floor. I stepped out of the tangle of material at my feet and followed him as he walked backwards into the shower. He never broke eye contact once, as he backed me up under the steady pounding of water coming from the showerhead. His touch was light, tracing his fingers up my arms, over my shoulder, until he held his hands at the base of my neck and used his thumbs to tilt my head under the water.

Dropping one of his hands, Ace lifted mine up in between us. My eyes snapped to his when he placed a kiss against my palm and then moved me out from under the shower spray.

He turned away, grabbed the shampoo, squeezed some in his hands, and then stuck his head under the water. Scrubbing the shampoo into his hair, he rinsed it. I had to lean against the shower wall, as I watched Ace turn, lift his arms, and rinse the shampoo from his body. The water ran down over his face, along his neck, over the chiseled perfection of his chest, and...

"Riley?" Ace had been watching me watch him. He had a handful of shampoo that he rubbed between his palms. The shower was huge, but Ace's presence shrunk it down when I turned to stand in front of him. His fingertips against my scalp made me sag against him until he turned me to rinse the shampoo from my hair. Water ran off us and hit the tiled floor in loud splashes with every move. I closed my eyes and soaked in every touch of Ace's body against mine. The creaking sound of a bottle opening snapped me out of the haze he had put me under.

"Ready to get soapy, Riley?" His voice vibrated against my chest. I shuddered when I felt the first slide of soap bubbles run down my chest. Ace's hands roamed my entire body from shoulder to feet. Steadying myself, I held onto his shoulders, feeling his muscles bunch under my hands. I felt the tremors that wracked his entire frame. He was shaking from the arousal he'd built between us. My breath caught in my throat on a gasp.

"Ace…" I moaned when his fingers dug into my hips and he turned me, putting my back against the shower wall.

"No, that's not my name…" He nipped at my neck, and I bucked against him.

"Jake." His name passed my lips on a short gasp. Winding my fingers in his hair, I tilted my face to his until our breaths mingled. His lips sought out mine and placed punishing kisses that didn't slow until my legs threatened to buckle. I fought to stand upright, even with the wall at my back.

"Can't… shit, we can't. No protection," he said with a groan, as he stepped back and turned the faucet over to cold. He closed his eyes as he stood under the spray, shivering as the water ran down over his shoulders. "Riley…" He opened his eyes as he said my name, only my name, but the way he said it, there was so much meaning, so much unsaid, as if he'd stuck everything he felt, everything he wanted to say, and gave it my name.

He shifted in front of me, allowing an ice-cold spray of water to reach me. I scooted out of the way with a loud yelp. "Shit, that's cold, Jake."

He chuckled at me as he reached behind him and turned the shower off.

I collected my hair and twisted it, wringing the water out as Ace opened the shower door. He grabbed a thick, white towel, wrapped it around me, and rubbed his hands up along the outside to help dry my back. When I caught the corners of the towel in my hand, he pulled another one off the shelf and dried himself, leaving me to finish. He watched me as I slipped my clothes on, and I wondered what he found so interesting about me getting dressed. He tossed his towel, grabbed his underwear, and put them on. I totally got it the moment he stood before me in his boxer briefs and then his shorts. I tugged my shirt over my head and picked my towel up just as he unfolded his shirt and tugged it on. Ace had a mouth-watering body, but there was something that just did it for me, seeing him in a graphic T-shirt and a well-worn pair of camo-print cargo shorts. Maybe it was the knowledge that I knew what was underneath his clothing, or maybe I was one of the select few that thought a man being dressed was sexier than a man showing everything. I felt a smile tug at my lips when Ace ran his fingers through his hair and slid his feet into the flip-flops he'd kicked off earlier.

I grabbed our towels, chucked them in the hamper, slid on my shoes, and squeaked when Ace scooped me up in his arms high enough that my feet dangled above the floor. He kissed me and let me slide down his body. "Hungry?"

"Very." My stomach grumbled as I answered him.

"Come on, let's go stuff our faces."

"Go ahead. I'll meet you in the kitchen. I just need to brush my hair."

"Holy hell... did you know that the National Weather Service just issue a drought warning... for this cabin?"

Jared. I sighed and walked down the hallway without replying. Ace could handle it.

"Hey, Ace? Is Riley alright? Did you flush the toilet when she was in the shower? 'Cause dude, she yelped loud enough to wake the damn dead."

Jared wasn't letting up, and I waited to hear the sound of flesh hitting flesh. Nothing... not even a 'shut up, Jared.'

"Aw, come on... how can I give you a hard time if you won't fight back with me?" Jared whined.

"Riley already gave me a hard time... I'm good—yours isn't necessary."

I blushed to the roots of my hair, and Jared howled, literally howled.

The screen door opened and slammed shut. "What the hell are you carrying on about, Jared?" Mark sounded confused.

"I wouldn't even think about saying anything else." Ace's warning was met with silence. The screen door opened, closed, and then I heard Mark say, "What the hell is wrong with Jared? He's so freakin' weird sometimes."

Ace chuckled, and I heard the screen door slam closed once more.

I ran the brush through my hair as quick as I could, pulling it all back into a ponytail. I wasn't going to let Jared's lewd comments keep me cowering in the bedroom. I took a deep breath to calm my nerves. If I went out to join the guys and couldn't control my nerves, it would give them, or I should say, Jared, more ammunition to heckle us. I squared my shoulders and marched down the hallway, not giving myself time to linger in the kitchen and lose my nerve. Slapping at the screen door, I sent it open, and then came to a dead stop as I watched the sheriff's car roll up.

Sheriff Sloan put the car in park and took his sweet ass time getting out of his cruiser. *Fuckin' Samantha*. She had to be the reason he came.

My hand automatically went up to the cut under my eye.

Jerking my hand back down, I walked across the small stretch of space that put me beside Ace.

"Sheriff Sloan, you're just in time. I got steaks on the grill and beer in the cooler." Jared gave the sheriff a cocky grin as he waved the tongs in his hand.

"Wanna go to jail, son?" Sheriff Sloan's face remained devoid of any emotion. His mirrored sunglasses hid his eyes and added that extra bit of cockiness law enforcement tried so hard to flaunt. It was sort of sickening to watch. They weren't all bad, but the ones on a power trip because they held a badge, gave the rest of them a bad name. And Sheriff Sloan was the cockiest person I'd ever known.

I kept my lips pressed into a fine line, as I waited to see what Jared would say.

"Ah, come on now, Sheriff, you know I'd look hideous in orange."

Sheriff Sloan stalked over to the cooler and flipped the lid back, paused for a second, and then closed it.

"Did I say beer?" Jared shook his head and rolled his eyes. "I meant soda. Wonder why I always get those two confused?"

We held our breath. Sheriff Sloan was just as much of an asshole as his daughter was. There was no telling what he'd do or say, and Jared was adamant at poking at him every chance he got.

When the silence stretched out, Jared shrugged his shoulders and turned his back on the sheriff. The sound of grease hitting charcoal was the only noise. But Jared wasn't done. I could see his face from where I stood. He cut his eyes in my direction and winked. *Oh, shit.*

"Aiden, grab the radio. We need tunes. Riley, that macaroni salad ain't gonna make itself. Jesus, do I have to do everything here?" Jared was deliberately ignoring the sheriff, and I had to bite the inside of my cheek to keep from laughing or vomiting.

Paige pushed herself up from the chair she'd been sitting in. As soon as her back was to the sheriff, she mouthed the word '*go*' at me.

Ace gave me a gentle nudge to get me moving.

I felt the tension shift with each step closer to the cabin.

When Paige and I made it inside the kitchen, she spun around on me. "Holy shit, you coulda cut through that with a knife. Guess Samantha decided to be a damn tattletale. Stupid bitch. I can't wait till dear 'ole daddy can't step in for her."

A fine sheen of sweat broke out along my skin. My hands shook, and I pressed them against the material of my shorts to wipe the clammy feeling off.

"What do you think he's gonna do?" I asked.

"There's nothing he can do besides try to bully the information out of the guys. Well, unless he and his daughter decide to press charges against you," Paige said as she moved over to stand in front of the kitchen window, yanking it up.

"What are you *doing*?" I hissed as the window squeaked in protest. The only one that turned to look over at the noise was the sheriff. Paige ignored him and turned on the sink.

She pulled a cabinet door open, took out a box of macaroni, and set it on the counter. "I can't hear shit with the damn window closed. Besides, we need to move around in here so he'll get to the purpose of his visit. Grab me a pan."

I did as she asked and handed it to her. "Grab the fixins and get ta cuttin', Riles." I went on autopilot. Not long after, I heard Jared's voice.

"Well, if you're not here to eat, Sheriff, what are you here for?"

"I'm here to tell you to watch your step."

"My steps are just fine, Sheriff."

"Mr. Jackson, I'm here to remind you that I still hold the law around here, and one of yours has stepped over that line."

"The last time I checked, Sheriff, you either arrest us or leave. Rolling up here and harassing us is against 'your laws' and if you hadn't noticed, this is private property. So I'm going to remind *you*, Sheriff, that unless you have a warrant, you're not welcome here."

My hand shot to my throat when I heard the sound of leather creaking. Paige and I practically pressed our noses to the screen to see outside. The sheriff's hands were clenched along his gun belt. His face pulled into a thin line that said Jared had pushed him too far.

"Would you like me to arrest her now?"

"Try it and see how far you get with that."

"Threatening me will land you in a cell beside her."

"Screw you and screw your cell. I know my rights, Sheriff, and I know a bluff when I see one. But here's something that's not a bluff. If you don't leave right now, I'll be on the phone with my attorney, who will in turn, get a hold of your boss. Guess what happens after that, Sheriff?"

Jared had turned from the grill and took a step towards Sheriff Sloan. "You see, I don't take threats lightly, Sheriff, and you'd do well to remember that."

The sheriff yanked his sunglasses off his face and took a step closer to Jared. "You're just a punk-ass kid who thinks just because his parents are rolling in money, you and your friends can act however you like. Tell Ms. Clifton that I'm watching her. If she so much as steps one more toe out of line, and I hear about it..." He turned on his heel and marched back to his car. When the cruiser door slammed and the sheriff punched the gas to back up, Jared picked his hand up and waved.

"Buh-bye, fucker. God, I hate him. Fuckin' ass-wipe."

I leaned on the counter and let my head fall into the cabinet. The sheriff had thrown down the gauntlet. If his daughter wanted to make my life miserable, all she had to do was run to Daddy and I'd be screwed. I had to get the hell outta our small town, but how?

CHAPTER 10

I volunteered to load the dishwasher, hoping the mundane task helped clear my head. After the sheriff left, Jared made it his mission to carry on and bring some sort of fun back to the atmosphere. No matter how hard I tried to push the sheriff's warning to the back of my mind, it still loomed over my thoughts. Once the guys left, I'd be on my own.

The radio played low outside, the music carrying through the open window. The hot air that drifted in on the night breeze pushed against the cold air rushing through the vents in the ceiling, but I didn't close the window until I finished the dishes.

The screen door opened and Jared walked in, carrying the tongs he'd used earlier. He bumped me with his hip to move me out of the way and grabbed the washrag. "Now, more than ever, you need to listen to me."

I grabbed a cup from the sink and put it in the dishwasher. "Jared…"

"No, Riley. This is important. Okay? You need to figure

out what school you want to go to and let me know." I didn't even get a chance to open my mouth and argue with him.

"Stop. You and I…? We're the only two who will know about this. I don't want to hear a word about it. The sheriff's not bluffing. He'll look for whatever reason to screw with you. And none of us will be here to keep him in check. I don't even want to think about him fucking with you, and you have no one to back you up."

"I can do it on my own, ya know," I grumbled.

"I'm sure you can, but you don't have to. You're gonna take my offer, or I'll take matters into my own hands and toss your ass on my tour bus and force you to live the life of a rock star."

"Well geez, Jared, when you put it that way…" I gave him my back and put the last plate in the dishwasher, held my hand out for the tongs, and waited for him to slap them into my palm. When he did, I wrapped my hand around them, still not paying attention to him, and yanked them. Jared stumbled into me, and I jerked my head to look over my shoulder. He hadn't let them go.

"That's the deal. Take it, or I take you on tour with me."

No way in hell would I travel across country with him and his new bandmates. No. Way. In. Hell.

"Fine!" I snatched the tongs from him, tossed them in the dishwasher, and took the box of soap he handed me.

"Knew you'd see it my way." He left, banging the screen door closed behind him.

I knew he meant well, but at the same time, he'd made me feel like a charity case. I'd take his help, but he'd get every penny back when it was all said and done. I wasn't going to owe anyone for my college education.

∾

The day after the sheriff showed up, we ended up back at the Hole. It was Jared's last day with us before he set off to be some sort of Rock God, and the guys enjoyed giving him a hard time about it.

I ran my hand over the soft material of the comforter I sat on, watching them roughhouse in the water. Paige had stretched out beside me and closed her eyes.

"Are you enjoying the time away from the hospital?" I asked when she laughed at the guys grabbing Aiden's hands and feet, tossing him from the end of the dock.

She sat up, wrapped her arms around her legs, and rested her chin on her knees. "Yeah, I am, but it's back to reality tomorrow."

"So what's up with you and Mark?" She tensed at my question, and straightened herself up. "I could ask the same about you and Ace."

I nodded at her direct jab. Fair was fair, and I had no right poking my nose in her business.

"It doesn't matter anyway. He's leaving for New York soon, and I'm hoping to see myself added to the schedule for rotations so…"

I understood. Life wasn't always fair, and just because what you wanted was right in front of you, it didn't mean you had the ability to reach out and lay claim to it.

I'd pretty much set myself up for heartbreak, knowing Ace was headed out to boot camp and then who knows where. A spark of anger rolled in my gut. I'd gone on so long, thinking he'd be close—right up the street. A Forest Ranger, not an Army Ranger or whatever he'd signed himself up for. He'd never said, and it made me wonder why. I'd never even thought to question it. I'd accepted everything blindly. I pushed that question back, figuring I would ask him when it was just the two of us.

"So have you thought about what you're gonna do now?" I

knew what Paige meant. The scholarship that slipped past my fingers.

"I'm gonna work my ass off, get some loans, and see what happens." I shrugged, inwardly kicking myself for lying to her so easily.

She smiled at me, a large, toothy grin that brightened her whole face. "Now, that's what I like to hear. Good for you, Riley."

I closed my eyes and tipped my head back, inhaling the humid air.

"Oh shit!" Paige scrambled beside me. My eyes snapped open, expecting to find a snake slithering towards us. She darted off the blanket and took off running as Mark came up the embankment. The chase was short-lived when he caught her and put her over his shoulder.

"Riley! Don't just sit there… freakin' help me!" Paige wrestled against Mark's tight hold, receiving a smack on the ass when she almost made him drop her.

Mark's hoots and hollers blended with Paige's shouts of protest as he ran down the dock, jumping off the end with her slung over his shoulder.

They both sputtered to the surface, as Ace sat down beside me.

The air was heavy, like breathing soup, as the afternoon crept on. Dark clouds rolled in, bringing the cooler air that comes before the rain. Thunder rumbled in the distance as we packed up and headed back to the cabin. Before we made it back, lightning split the sky and rain fell in heavy sheets. It was as if even the heavens were angry that our time together was almost over.

Ace followed me down the hallway to his room and closed the door behind me. I grabbed dry clothes and peeled off the wet ones as shivers wracked my body. A loud clap of thunder shook the house and rattled the windows. Outside, lightning ripped across the sky and lit the room up. Ace swore beside me, and we chuckled at our jumpiness.

Across the hall, I heard Paige cry out, followed by the sound of something crashing against the wall.

Ace's voice startled me, as I stared in the direction the noises came from. "Nothin' like a good 'ole thunderstorm to unleash some pent-up feelings."

Confused by what he meant, I turned in his direction. My question died on my lips when I heard Mark call out to Paige, as the thunder shook the cabin again.

"Come on, Riley, before Jared walks down the hall and starts banging on doors to see what's taking everyone so long."

Ace no sooner got the door open than Jared was about to pound his fist against Mark's door. Ace stilled his hand and shook his head. "Leave 'em alone, Jared. They'll be out later."

A knowing grin split across Jared's face before he turned and walked back down the hallway.

The cabin shook again, and lightning forked across the sky. The light in the kitchen dimmed, flickered, and then went out. Jared ran his hand over his face with a groan. "Well, shit. Hope the power comes back on soon, or it's gonna get hot as hell in here."

The rain shifted and blew in through the open windows. The guys scrambled to get them closed, and I grabbed a towel from Jared's bathroom to wipe up the puddles of water.

Aiden grabbed his phone. "Guys, they issued a severe weather alert until midnight tonight."

Eli sprawled out on one of the recliners, while Josh rummaged through the cabinets in search of a snack. I sunk down into the corner of the couch and Ace stretched out, putting his head on my leg. Jared paced the floor. He wasn't a fan of thunderstorms because he hated the lightning. He cringed every time it popped around us, illuminating the darkened room in jagged shadows.

Getting his mind off it would take some doing, but I hated seeing him flinch with every crack that raced across the sky.

"Hey, Jared. When will you have your tour schedule?"

"Why? You gonna come see me play, Riles?"

"Why wouldn't I? Just 'cause you're gonna traipse across the US doesn't mean I'm gonna forget about you."

He rolled his eyes as a bolt of lightning hit yards from the house, and the thunder crashed. Diving towards the couch, he pressed his back against it as he sat on the floor. "Holy fuck, that was close!"

I reached out, putting my hand on his shoulder. "What time does your flight leave tomorrow?"

He turned his head enough to look at me out of the corner of his eye. His face was drawn into hard lines. "Jared… what time is your flight tomorrow?"

He drew in a deep breath through his nose. "Early afternoon."

"Do you need help packing your stuff?" I asked.

The room lit up again, and he pushed harder against the couch. I tightened my grip on his shoulder. "Come on, Jared. Let's go get your stuff together."

There were fewer windows in his room and, with the blackout curtains, it would keep him from seeing the lightning that zigzagged along the sky relentlessly.

Ace propped himself up so I could stand. It wasn't the first time I'd kept Jared's mind busy during a storm. He gave me a wink when I grabbed Jared's hands and helped him up from the floor. I put myself between him and the windows, ushering him down the hallway.

When we made it to his room, I rummaged around his closet, found the battery-operated lantern, and turned it on.

Jared lowered himself to the edge of his bed and braced his elbows on his knees. "Why the hell does it bother me so much?" It was the question he always asked when a nasty storm blew in.

"People just have fears, Jared. There's nothing wrong with it. Mine is snakes and Old Man Willis' pond."

He blew out a shaky breath and ran his hand down his face.

"What bag?" I asked, holding up two different duffel bags for him to choose from.

He pointed at the larger of the two, and I tossed it on the bed. "Are you taking any of your stuff from home?"

"Nah, there's enough here."

"You get underwear duty." That brought a chuckle from him. It also kept his back to the window.

To keep his mind occupied, I grabbed two T-shirts at a time and held them up, making him choose until he had a pile of shirts on the bed. We moved on to his jeans and went through the same process, as the storm outside raged on.

"Start folding those while I get your razor and stuff," I said, pointing at the stack of clothes on the bed.

Jared grabbed a shirt and shook it out in front of him. "I'll get that stuff in the morning after I take a shower." He flinched when the corners of his blackout curtains lit up, and the sky rumbled.

I grabbed a pair of his pants and folded them in half. When he wouldn't stop staring at the window, I smacked him in the arm with them to get his attention. "That shirt's not gonna fold itself."

Keeping his hands busy didn't seem to help. I gave up and snatched the shirt from his hands, tossing it back on the pile. "Play me a song," I told him as I pointed to the guitar in the corner.

He picked the twelve string up off the stand and sat down

against the wall to where he couldn't see the window. His fingers ran over the strings as he tuned it by ear and then ran a few chords as he settled in to play. Song bled into song, and Jared lost himself to the music. I zipped his bag closed and set it down by his dresser. Even when the windows rattled from the thunder, he kept playing, exercising his demons with each strum of the guitar. I curled up and closed my eyes, as the guys trickled in and sat in various spots. When Jared would finish a song, someone would ask him to play something else.

I woke up to Ace running his finger down my nose. "Time for bed, Riley." I sat up, looking around. I'd fallen asleep to the guys singing loud enough to block out the sound of the storm. Jared's bathroom door opened, and he strolled out.

"Aw man, I thought sleeping beauty was staying in my bed tonight," Jared said with wink.

"Not likely," Ace grumbled.

I stretched as I stood, and Ace walked over to wait for me at the door.

Jared leaned against the doorframe to the bathroom. "Can I get a second with Riley, Ace?"

Ace nodded and stepped out into the hallway. "Night, Jared."

"Night, Ace."

Jared waited until he heard the door to Ace's room close. "Thanks for tonight, Riley. I don't know how you do it, but you keep me from the ledge when it gets to be too much."

I waited until he walked over to where I stood. Wrapping my arms around him, I hugged him tight. "That's what friends are for. I'm gonna miss the hell outta you. Promise you'll stay in touch?"

He propped his chin on my head. "I promise. As long as you promise to come see me play."

"It's a deal," I answered him.

He squeezed me tight before releasing me. "Better go before Ace comes back and drags you off."

"You gonna be okay?" The storm had quieted. Thunder rumbled off in the distance. The flash of lightning muted as the wind took the heaviest part of the storm away, leaving a good, soaking rain behind in its wake.

He walked me to the bedroom door. "Yeah, I'm good. Go get some rest, Riley. I'll see ya in the morning."

I nodded sharply and forced myself to reply. "Night, Jared."

It felt like a good-bye. I swallowed the tears as I made my way down the hallway, opening Ace's bedroom door. I kicked off my sweatpants and crawled across the bed. Ace pulled me against his chest. I hugged him tight, refusing to give in and break down. None of them deserved to feel guilty about the futures they chose for themselves. I owed them that much as a friend. My traitorous body rebelled against me. Tears pooled in my eyes, rolling onto Ace's naked chest. He never said a word, just held me as my silent meltdown shook my entire body.

It wasn't all about Jared either. Part of it, but not all. Who would take care of them when they couldn't take care of themselves? Who would know that Aiden was allergic to strawberries, or that Josh couldn't use a certain brand of laundry soap because he'd break out in hives? That Eli had nightmares about his life before the Bentons, and it took hours to bring him around from one? Who would know where Mark kept his inhaler for those random bouts of asthma that kicked up every so often? Who would be there for Ace when the rest of us weren't? Who would keep him from becoming a raging lunatic, one he'd teetered on being for so long—one that we all kept him from being? Out of the Six, Ace was the silent one. The one no one would expect it from. We'd kept it all within our group. There wasn't a soul who knew us, like we knew each other. Jared kept Ace in check, and Ace, in turn, kept the rest of the group in check. It worked… it was a dynamic that had never been split apart. And it scared the shit out of me, knowing that within only a matter of days, it would all fall apart.

It was dark when I woke up. The weight of Ace's body trapped me against the mattress as he bent down to kiss me. "I need you, Riley."

His whispered words rolled through me, and I returned his kiss until he settled over me. We moved together, slowly. Each caress, each roll of his hips, was stretched into the next. He took his time, showing me with his body what he couldn't say with words. It was the single most tender moment I'd ever had in my life.

I stretched, pulling myself from the edge of sleep that beckoned me to roll back over and cover my head. The bedroom door cracked open, and Paige walked in. "The boys are making breakfast. They said to get out of bed, or they'll come get you." Her lips turned up on a smirk. She knew them as well as I did. If they said they'd come and get me, it meant all of them. I huffed and tossed the sheet aside.

Paige stepped into the room and closed the door. "I'm headed out. I just wanted to let you know that you won't be able to get a hold of me for a couple of days."

I rubbed at my blurry eyes and picked out clean clothes. "Okay."

"Riley?" Paige stood in front of me with her arms crossed and her bottom lip between her teeth.

"Yeah?"

"This isn't good-bye. Remember that, okay?"

With my back turned, I gave her a nod and fought the tears that threatened to spill. "I know, Paige."

The door opened, and Paige slipped out. I waited for a minute, and then made my way across the hall to the bathroom. There was no way I'd step foot in the kitchen with puffy red eyes from a night of crying. It was bad enough that Ace had witnessed my breakdown.

The cold cloth helped a lot. My eyes weren't as red as I thought they'd be. A little bloodshot, but nothing that would bring too much attention.

I grabbed my dirty clothes and left the bathroom. After I tossed them on the bed, I made my way to the kitchen as Paige's car started outside.

Jared stood at the stove with his back to the room. "So Aiden's gonna be in Texas, you're gonna be in Georgia, Mark and Josh will be in Yankee land, Eli will be on the other side of the world..." The spatula came up as he turned around. "That, my brothers, is a whole lot of awesome spread out across the globe."

Jared turned back around, slid the spatula under a pancake, and flipped it.

"Yeah, well, I better see some concert tickets, that's all I have to say," Mark said as he got the syrup out of the refrigerator.

Josh dumped a handful of forks on the table, slid out a chair, and sat down. "Me too!"

Jared shut the stove off, grabbed a plate piled high with golden-brown, butter-drenched pancakes, and put it in the center of the table. "Already mooching."

Aiden's fork stabbed into the stack, and Jared brought the spatula down on his hand. "Ouch!"

"Ladies first, jackass," Jared said, raising the spatula again.

Jared eyed me until I stabbed one and put it on my plate. I

moved fast to keep from being in the way of the war of forks that descended onto the diminishing stack of pancakes.

I forced myself to finish what was on my plate. Even though I loved Jared's pancakes, it sat like a brick in my stomach.

It took the Six no time at all to devour every last crumb.

Aiden sat back and rubbed at his stomach, groaning. "I'm so full."

"Fat ass," Mark said, jabbing him in the stomach with his elbow. Aiden bowed forward and kicked at his chair.

"If I didn't feel like I'd puke, I'd take your prissy ass out to the yard and show you a *fat ass*."

I slid my chair back, grabbing the empty plates from the table before they went crashing to the floor. They always cracked on one another, and it usually ended up in some sort of wrestling match in the yard. A few times, it never made it that far, and one of us ended up buying new dishes. I'd be damned if they broke anymore. Mark lunged for Aiden and I snatched up Jared's spatula. It slid down between their faces as I shouted, "Take it outside, you two!"

Aiden and Mark snickered at me but made their way to the door, shoving each other until they were outside. Josh, Eli, Jared, and Ace followed them with shouts that egged the two on. I blew out a breath of relief. The plates were safe.

I plugged the sink, squirted dish soap into the hot water, and grabbed a dish towel. Even though there was a dish-washer, sometimes I liked washing them by hand. It gave me time to think, as I zoned out in front of the window. As I was just about to plunge my hands down into the soapy water, Jared's cell phone rang. There was no way they'd hear me call out to get his attention with the way they carried on outside, so I grabbed his phone and saw it was his dad.

"Hey Mr. Jackson."

"Riley?"

"Yep."

"How's everything going? We haven't seen you in a while."

"Good, just tryin' to keep these boys in line."

"Either you have the patience of a saint, or you're just as insane as they are," he said with a low chuckle.

"Probably a little of both."

I liked Jared's parents. Out of all the mismatched parental units, Jared's were probably the coolest.

"Is my son right there, by chance?"

I laughed. "Yeah, let me see if I can get his attention."

Shouts came from the yard loud enough that Jared's dad could hear them over the phone. "Is everything all right, Riley?"

"The norm, sir, the norm."

"Ah, I see." He knew how they all acted, but hearing it was far different than seeing it. If I were on the other end of the phone, I'd be worried at what I heard too.

"Hang on, I gotta go get loud."

"Give 'em hell, Riley Girl."

I have no idea why, but Jared's dad always tossed that nickname in at some point in our conversations.

"You know it." I set Jared's phone down and walked out to where I'd be close enough to be heard, but far enough away to not get hit, and let out an ear-piercing whistle. The guys stopped long enough to wince as they looked in my direction.

"Jared, phone."

I walked away as they started up again with Jared right behind me. I pointed to his cell phone when we got inside the cabin. "It's your dad."

He snatched up the phone from the counter, sticking it between his shoulder and ear as he snatched the dish towel out of my hands. "Hey, Pops. What's up?"

Jared's dad hated it when he called him Pops. I winced

and shoved my hand into the sink, dragging the soapy rag over a sticky plate.

"I figured I wouldn't see you until you popped into one of my shows... Yeah, I'll stop by before I go to the airport. Okay. Bye."

He pulled the phone away, shut it off, and set it down on the counter.

"How long are they in town for?" I asked as I handed him another plate to dry.

"Not sure. It's weird though... them being in town right now. They weren't supposed to be back for another week or so." Jared hitched his shoulder and opened the cabinet to slide the plate in.

"Are they still working for the same company?"

"Cole Enterprise? Yeah, I doubt they'll ever leave. The money's too good. Ya know?"

"What do they do there?"

Jared took the glass I held out to him. "Right now, they're working on a second location, but it's all hush-hush. Dad slipped up and told me it was in Scotland the last time he was home. Weird, right? What the hell is so important you can't even talk about it?"

It was sort of odd, but then again, the military had all sorts of things they didn't talk about. Maybe his parents were more than they let on. "Do you think your parents are spies?"

He laughed at me. "Yeah right! Have you seen my mom? She's tinier than you!"

"Whatever, Jared." I shot him shut-up look and handed him another plate.

"So they came back to see you off?"

"I guess so... maybe. It's weird, though. Ever since they hooked me up with getting my demo out, and I landed a manager, they've kinda been off the grid."

It was no secret that his parents weren't exactly happy

with his choice of career, but they did step in and help him when they realized he was going to do it with, or without, their help.

"Hey, do you think you can do me a favor while I'm away?"

His question took me by surprise. "What?"

"My car. Do you think you can drive it sometimes? That way it doesn't sit for too long."

"You want me to drive your car?"

"I'd appreciate it. That way it doesn't sit for too long without being driven. You'd be doing me a solid."

"I guess so."

"Good, but no cow pastures… okay?"

I rolled my eyes. "Black top only. Got it."

He put the last plate away, and I pulled the plug in the sink.

"I guess I better get my stuff together, so I can head home and see the 'rents before I head out."

He was back with his bag in hand as the others strolled in. "I'm headed out. Gotta stop at my parents. They wanna see me before I leave."

A somber mood rolled in and heads dipped. Deep breaths were pulled in and let out as one by one they hugged Jared, wishing him luck. He sauntered over to me, lifting me off the floor in a bone-crushing hug. When he stepped back, his car keys were dangling off his finger. "No cow pastures." He tapped my nose and walked out.

"Josh, come fire up your piece of shit and give me ride home!" Jared shouted as the screen door closed. Josh grabbed his keys from the hook by the door, clenched his hand around them, and then squared his shoulders as he walked out of the cabin. Seconds later, we trailed out behind them, waving as Josh and Jared drove away.

CHAPTER 11

I don't think the guys realized that Jared and all his quirks were what kept the Six such a tight-knit group of friends. Sure, they would all still be friends, but Jared was that one friend that kept the insanity rampant in the group, and every one gravitated to his crazy ass, including myself.

The afternoon Jared left, we moved around the cabin like zombies, meandering around, not quite sure what to do with ourselves. I kept myself busy by cleaning the living room. Eli grabbed the vacuum, and Aiden cleaned the windows. Outside, Ace started the lawn mower and slipped his sunglasses over his eyes. Mark grabbed his keys and shouted over the sound of the vacuum. "I'm headed out to the store. Need anything?"

I couldn't take it anymore. The sound of the lawn mower outside, the vacuum inside—it was static noise, the kind you filled the silence with when you were so far inside of your head that it was deafening. I walked over to the stereo and turned it on, needing something—anything—to stop the sadness that crushed against us. Harvey Danger's voice rolled out of the speakers, singing about paranoia, and I found myself smiling. Jared would crank that song and belt it out at the top of his lungs. There was enough of Jared around the cabin. We could either chose to accept that life was moving forward or slink off and sulk about it.

I grabbed a dust rag and furniture polish, happy that I'd found a way to cope with the fact that no matter what, we had memories. Good memories. Happiness. Enough of it that, no matter where life took us, we'd always be able to recall all the fun we'd shared over the years.

I could see Eli and Aiden out of the corner of my eye. I watched smiles slip across their faces, as their heads bobbed along with the music. Song by song, the mood lightened.

Mark returned with enough junk food to last for days. I opened the door and let him in. As soon as the bags were on the table, he unloaded them. "I ran into Josh at the store. His mom wants him home for dinner tonight. He said he'd be back tomorrow."

Eli rolled the vacuum back in the closet and walked over to help us put away Mark's junk food haul. "Dang, son. Got enough sugar there?"

"You better eat up, Eli. I don't think they sell honey buns in Haiti," Mark said as he tossed one to him.

"I got that all worked out. Don't you worry about that."

"Oh yeah?" Mark chuckled.

"My girl Riley will be my sugar connection," Eli said, ripping open the cellophane wrapper and taking a huge bite.

"Whose girl?" Ace said from the other side of the screen door as he passed by.

Eli rolled his eyes. "You know what I mean."

Ace used the T-shirt he'd been wearing to wipe the sweat from his face as he continued on to the hose on the side of the house and sprayed the grass cuttings off his feet.

I walked past Eli and got a cup down from the cupboard.

"So let me get this straight. You expect me to send you boxes of junk food?"

"Yep." He smirked and shoved the rest of the honey bun in his mouth.

I filled the glass with ice and ran it under the tap. "You're lucky I like you, Eli. It'll probably cost me an arm and a leg to ship you junk food."

"But think of the happiness it will bring the kids!"

I smacked Eli in the shoulder when I walked past him. "That's just a dirty trick. Now I have to do it."

When the screen door slammed behind me, I heard Eli's smart-ass comeback. "See, plenty of ways to get a sugar momma. Ouch! Why'd you hit me?"

"You're an idiot," Mark replied.

They busted out laughing.

~

Ace rinsed his sunglasses, slid them on top of his head as he turned the water off, and held the nozzle in to relieve the pressure. When the water slowed to a trickle, he held the hose over his head, then dropped it and ran his hand down his face to sluice it off. I walked up beside him and handed him the glass of ice water. He took it from me and leaned down to give me a quick kiss. "Thanks."

He drained it in three swallows as he looked over the yard. "It's funny how you take it all for granted sometimes."

I shrugged, looking out over the freshly mowed yard and inhaling the sweet smell of cut grass. "It'll always be here. The same way a piece of us will too."

Ace smiled as he bounced the ice in his glass and then tipped it back against his lips. He crunched his way through a piece of ice and then wiped his shirt across his forehead. "So I have a question for you…"

My insides clenched as my nerves bounced inside of me like a super ball on concrete. What kind of question? He sounded very serious, and I had no idea where he was headed with his thoughts. "I might have an answer."

Ace smiled and turned his gaze out to the yard as he spoke. "My mom's planning on driving to Georgia for my graduation. Will you come with her?"

"And watch you graduate boot camp? Of course!" I took the glass from his hands, but he caught my wrist before I could take a step back.

"Yeah?" His eyes crinkled at the corners.

"Yeah, I'll be there."

"Good. Now go get your bathing suit on and come swimming with me." He gave me a heated look and let my wrist go.

I walked back inside, dazed. Ace wanted me to be at his graduation. He wanted me to go with his mom. Giddiness rolled through me, and I almost bumped into Mark, not paying attention to where I walked. "Whoa, what 'cha doing, space cadet?" He laughed as he jumped back.

"Me?"

"No, the other Riley."

Eli walked over to stand beside Mark, waving his hand in my face. "Oh yeah. She has it bad."

My eyes darted between the two of them. "What?"

They looked at each other and busted out laughing.

"Where ya headed, Riley?" Mark asked.

"To get my bathing suit on. What's with all the questions?" I sidestepped them and went to change.

Neither one of them lowered their voices as they spoke.

"Ace is a lucky bastard," Mark said.

"I hope one day I can put that same kinda look in a girl's eyes." Eli sounded odd. They both did.

I passed by Aiden's door as he opened it, startling me. "Oh, sorry, Riles. Didn't mean to scare ya."

He walked past me, heading for the kitchen. I continued on to Ace's room as his voice carried down the hallway. "What's up with Riley?"

Mark and Eli cracked up. "Dude… that girl's in love with a capital Ace," Eli sputtered.

"What the hell does that even mean?" I could hear the confusion in Aiden's voice.

"Never mind, bro. Just go with it," Mark answered.

"But I don't understand. There's no 'ace' in love…"

"Oh, I wouldn't be so sure about that," Eli all but sang.

I closed the door and changed into my bathing suit on something close to autopilot. Could he be in love with me? There was no doubt about how I felt for him. He all but consumed me. I didn't just love him—I worshiped him.

Blindly, I grabbed the closest shirt to me, pulled it on, and made my way back to Ace.

He was still standing where I'd left him, except he wasn't alone. Aiden, Mark, and Eli all stood there waiting for me, too.

"Well, are we swimming or what?" Aiden asked.

Ace took my hand when I stepped up beside him. "You okay, Riley?" His question snapped me out of whatever it was that had me in its grips.

I flashed him a quick smile and looked ahead as Aiden looked back over his shoulder at me. "I'm fine."

Aiden looked from me to Ace, and his hand came up to cover his mouth. His words were mumbled, yet still clear. "I totally get it now. Ace is in love with Riley. And Riley's in love with Ace!"

My hand clenched against Ace's. He knew how I felt about him. He'd heard it straight from my mouth when I'd admitted it to Paige. But he'd never said anything in return, and I hoped that Aiden's comment didn't make him take a huge step back.

I took another step and jerked to a stop. Ace's feet were planted firmly as he tugged me against him. I put my hand on his chest to steady myself. Ace waited until the others were out of hearing distance before he spoke.

"Riley?" His finger slipped under my chin, and he forced my head up to look at him. "What's wrong?"

"You're the fourth person to ask me that in less than ten minutes, and I'm not sure why."

"You have this look on your face. Like you're here, but you're not here."

I scrunched my face at him, not sure what he meant by that. "I don't understand."

"You're off in your own little world. What's up?"

"I am?"

"You should see your face," he said, running his knuckles down my cheek.

My eyes fluttered closed, and my breath caught on a soft gasp.

"Hey! Lovebirds! Can you two stop mooning over each other for five minutes and go get the Jet Skis?" Mark shouted, waving his hands at us when we turned to look at him.

"We're busy. Get 'em yourself," Ace said as he splayed his hand against my back and pulled me close. He leaned down, placing a kiss on my neck. My head tilted without me even thinking about it, and I held on to him tighter when my knees threatened to buckle.

"You two have it bad," Mark said as he jogged past us.

Ace's laugh broke the line of kisses he trailed up to my chin. "Very, very bad."

"The worst." I tipped my head back and pulled Ace down for a kiss.

The sound of the four-wheeler approaching broke us apart.

"Later, Riley. Later, I'm gonna show you just how bad."

I trembled. Not out of fear, but anticipation. It set off a current that zipped through me and made me ache. He hadn't said he loved me, but he had showed me instead. Loving someone didn't mean just saying the words. It was the feeling behind it. The knowing that you affected them just as much as they affected you.

Hearing someone say I love you brought a sense of joy.

Feeling someone tell you that they loved you? It was deep. Soul deep. It filled you with a sense of completeness and contentment. It was bliss and wonder. Raw and honest. It was everything and anything with no room for questions or second-guessing.

And the sad part? I was setting myself up for heartbreak when Ace left. What if he realized that I was nothing more than a crush to him? What if he found someone new? Someone more like him? I bit down on the inside of my cheek hard enough that my eyes watered. I had to stop thinking like that. It wouldn't do me any good. Things were brand new with Ace. I had to accept that in just a few days, he'd be gone, and we'd either be doing the long-distance relationship thing… or moving on with our own lives. My chest constricted with the thought. Losing Ace… no, I didn't even want to think about it.

I tugged on his hand, moving him towards the Hole. I'd enjoy every single second, until there were no more left.

When we got down to the dock, Aiden and Mark were already out on the water, jumping each other's wakes.

Eli sat on the edge of the dock, laughing when Mark caught enough air that he lost his seat. The Jet Ski went one way, and he went the other. "My turn!" he shouted at Mark.

He flipped him off, climbed back on, and took off across the water.

"Jackass," Eli said, watching him jump another wake. "I hope he falls off again."

"Ten buck says I can make a bigger splash than you," Ace said as he ran up behind Eli and jumped off the edge.

Eli shot to his feet. "Oh, you are so on!"

Ace hit the water, and they didn't stop until I declared a tie.

Mark and Aiden cruised across the water, killed the engines, and drifted towards us.

Eli hung off the ladder on the dock and when Mark got close enough, he tackled him off the Jet Ski. Eli's head broke the water first. He climbed on the Jet Ski and took off, laughing at Mark when he sputtered to the surface.

"I think he took guerrilla warfare classes or some shit. Jesus, he about broke my damn back," Mark said as he pulled himself up the ladder.

"Maybe you shouldn't have flipped him off?" I covered the laugh that escaped, but Mark heard me. I flew off the end of the dock and hit the water.

Water went up my nose, and I came up coughing. Mark sailed over my head and hit the water with the biggest splash I'd ever seen. I swam over to the ladder, and Ace helped me back up on the dock. I didn't give him a chance to freak out, as I held my hand up to silence him. "I changed my mind. Mark wins!"

Ace took step back, confusion written all over his face. "Mark wins what?"

"Yeah, what do I win?" Mark said as he hauled himself up the ladder.

"That was the biggest splash I've ever seen. And you caught some pretty good air time too. So you win. Pay the man, Ace!"

"Yeah, pay me, Ace... Wait, why is Ace paying me?" Mark said, shaking his head to get the water out of his ear.

My smile died on my lips when I looked over at Ace. He was silent. Deadly silent. The muscle in his jaw clenched, and his nostrils flared. Ace was seconds away from snapping, and I had no idea how to stop it from happening. Jared always talked him down when he got like that. But Jared wasn't there. Mark noticed the same thing I did and took a few steps back. Ace's hands fisted at his sides. They were so tight, his knuckles turned white.

Aiden tied off the Jet Ski he'd been floating on and shot up the ladder. "Ace, think about it, man. He was only playing around."

Ace's eyes snapped to Aiden, and he sneered. "He could have hurt her. She could have drowned."

"Riley? Ace, she's a better swimmer than all six of us put together. You know that. Why don't you and Riley head up to the cabin? The Jet Skis are almost out of fuel and I don't know about you, but I could go for some food."

Ace's eyes slipped closed for a second, and he took a deep breath. When he released his breath, his fists unclenched.

I shot Aiden a quick nod of thanks and curled my pinkie around Ace's. "I'm hungry, too."

Ace moved with me as I walked. I didn't try to talk to him about what happened. I knew enough to let him cool down when he got that angry. By the time we'd made it to the cabin, he was more relaxed. His steps were more fluid, less marching, and I knew he'd be all right once we made it inside.

He hated getting angry like that. It always left him in a bad mood when it happened. And eventually, he'd apologize. Mark had only been joking around when he pushed me off the dock. They'd all done it before, even Ace had.

We worked at the counter side by side, making sandwiches and stacking them on a plate.

"I'm sorry, Riley," Ace said, breaking the silence.

"For what?"

"You know what for."

"Ace, how many times have I been thrown off that dock?"

"Yeah, but this time it was different. This time…"

I smiled up at him. "This time it pissed you off. I get it. But Mark wouldn't do anything to intentionally hurt me."

"I know." He paused as he reached for me. I leaned into him as he ran his hands down my bare shoulders. "You're important to me, Riley. I wouldn't just hurt someone for hurting you. I'd kill them."

"Yeah, well, I don't think orange is a good color for you so…"

Ace's body shook when he laughed at me. "I can't even have one serious conversation with you before the smart-ass comments come out of your mouth."

I batted my eyelashes at him. "Yes, and you love me regardless."

My hand shot to my mouth, and I gasped. *Shit!* I said it without even thinking about it. I couldn't look away from Ace, but I wanted to. I wanted to take several large steps backwards and run down the hallway.

Ace pulled my hand away from my mouth and brought my palm up to his lips. His eyes never broke contact with mine when he placed my hand against his face. "Riley, I love you so fucking much it hurts."

My knees gave and he lifted me up in his arms, holding me close as he stared into my eyes. Both of us were caught up in what he'd admitted. The screen door squeaked open, but neither of us turned to look at whoever it was that came in. Ace's arms bunched around me, and then carried me down the hallway, never once looking away from me to watch where he was going.

"There they go again," I heard Aiden say as Ace caught his foot on the bedroom door, shoving it closed.

He set me down on my feet and put my hands on his shoulders. I shivered with every lingering touch he placed on my skin. My bathing suit landed in a pile on the floor with Ace's shorts. His chest heaved into mine as we fought to control our erratic breathing. His hand flexed against my hip, and he walked me backwards to the bed.

As Ace stretched out beside me and leaned over to place a kiss on my waiting lips, his cell phone rang. I jumped. Ace ignored it and ran his fingers along the side of my face, down my neck, as if tracing every detail and absorbing it. His phone quieted, and then rang again. He huffed out an impatient sigh. "That has to be Jared."

He sat up, grabbed his phone off the nightstand, and shook his head as he put the phone up to his ear. "Your timing sucks, bro."

I pulled the covers down and scooted over on the bed, giving Ace enough room to lie down beside me. When he settled in, I pulled the sheet up over the both of us and rolled over to lay my head on his chest as Jared's voice vibrated through Ace's phone.

"The fuck, man? I'm sitting here twiddling my damn thumbs, and this is a bad time for you? Whatever."

Ace sighed and settled in for one of Jared's long-winded conversations. "Did you just say twiddling?"

"Yeah, fuckin' twiddling. My ticket wasn't at the counter, and now I have to wait another three hours to get on the next flight out. Can you believe that shit? So I called my band manager to find out what the damn deal was and get this, he says 'it happens, buy the ticket and I'll get the money back to you'. I already hate him. The fuck am I gonna do, Ace? I signed my name on the damn line, and now he's being a douche."

Ace shifted to get more comfortable and ran his hands over my hair. When he got to the hairband, he tugged it free so he could run his fingers through it as he tried reasoning with Jared. "It was probably just a mix up. Don't freak out yet. If the guy is a real dick, then tell him to shove his contract up his ass."

Jared's laugh rattled through the speaker, and I knew Ace had somewhat talked him out of going into a full freak out.

With Ace's fingers running through my hair, and the low rumble of his voice as he talked to Jared, it made my eyes heavy. I closed them and just listened as the two of them talked. Jared needed someone to talk to as he sat alone, waiting for his flight. It occurred to me then that Jared wasn't as independent as I'd thought. He needed us just as much as we needed him. It made me wonder how we'd all move forward, feeling so severed off from each other.

The moment between Ace and I had cooled off, and it gave me time to think about what had happened in the kitchen. Ace loved me. I loved him. Where would that lead us when he left? Would he get through boot camp and then ask me to go wherever he went? Would he stay in the US or be shipped out to another country? Could I leave my dad behind? My dad was hardly ever around, but that was because of his job. We had a great relationship. I knew the only reason he worked so hard was because he wanted to support us the best way he knew how. Leaving him to go out of state wouldn't be bad since he traveled all over and would find a way to see me on his hauls. But overseas? I'd only see him if he decided to take a vacation, or if I did. And really, wasn't I getting ahead of myself? Sure, Ace said he loved me, but that didn't mean he was committing himself to me.

I wouldn't ask. He needed to tell me what he wanted. I

wouldn't be able to live with myself if he made me a bunch of promises he had no intentions of keeping, just to make me happy before he left.

As they wrapped up their conversation, I heard Jared tell Ace to call him when he could. That he was sorry he'd miss his graduation, but he hoped to see him when Ace was on leave.

When Ace hung up, he took a deep breath and blew it out. "Am I doing the right thing, Riley?"

His question caught me off guard, and I pushed up from his chest to look at him. "What do you mean?"

"Leaving. I don't even know if it's what I want anymore."

"What brought this on?"

"Everything. You, my mom… I dunno. I feel like I'm leaving everything behind to start over, and I can't help but feel… hollow. I'm not ready to say good-bye to you yet. Not now. Not when we're… this."

I braced myself up on one arm and trailed my finger along the lines between his brows. "Jake, everything will be fine. Besides, it's not like you're gonna be gone forever, and neither will the others."

His eyes closed, and he pulled me back to his chest. Rubbing small circles against my back with his hand, he kissed my forehead. "So you'll wait for me?"

"I've waited a long time for you, Jake Aceton. I can wait a little longer."

He pulled me on top of him and lifted his head to meet me in a kiss that set us on fire.

CHAPTER 12

It seemed like all I did was blink, and the time flew past before I could call it back. Time didn't care that you wanted to savor every second of it. It marched on like always and left me scrambling to make the most of what little of it I had left with Ace before he headed off to boot camp.

Josh and Eli decided to go home first so that they could pack up their rooms. Josh needed to sort out what he'd be taking with him to college, and Eli needed to figure out how much he could live without while going to Haiti. Both were torn over leaving until I told them I'd be stopping by to oversee their shitty packing skills.

Ace's mom, Mary, had taken a couple of vacation days to spend time with him before he left, and they extended the invite to me since Ace knew I'd be sitting all by myself at home. I loved Ace's mom. She was probably the sweetest person I'd ever met, and she loved Ace more than anything else in the world.

I pulled up in his driveway as his mom opened the door

with a smile on her face when I got out of my truck. "We were wondering when you'd get here."

I notice Ace standing behind her and couldn't help the hunger that crept through me at seeing him. "Hi."

Ace's mom turned to look behind her and chuckled. "I'm gonna go throw a load of wash in."

I think she said it as more of a reason to give us a minute alone, and we didn't waste it. I launched myself into Ace's arms and kissed him soundly.

When I pulled back, Ace's eyes smoldered. "I want to do so many inappropriate things to you right now."

The door to the laundry room opened, and Ace's grip on me loosened. I slid down the front of his body until my feet touched the floor. He growled in response and shifted me in front of him so his mom couldn't see the evident desire I'd sparked in him.

"Will you be staying for dinner?" Mary asked as she set down a rounded basket of laundry.

"Yes," Ace answered for me, sliding himself into a chair.

I scowled at him. "If that's all right with you?"

"Of course it is. I see the way he looks at you. He's happy and for that, I'm happy. I just wonder what took him so long to figure out he loved you when the rest of us could see it from a mile away." Mary shot a wink at him and grabbed a towel from the basket.

Ace smirked and pulled me down into his lap, which didn't help his situation any, since I couldn't keep still.

I elbowed him and stood up to help his mom fold the basket of clothes. "Behave," I whispered to him.

By the time the basket of towels was folded, the flush on his cheeks had dimmed and he'd tampered the wild look in his eyes.

"I'm gonna stay at Riley's tonight. Is that okay with you?" Ace sprung the question on his mom out of the blue, and I all but choked on the gasp of surprise that shot through me.

Mary didn't miss a beat. She turned around and pegged him with a serious look as she pointed her finger at him. "If you make me a grandmother before you're settled down with your career, I'll castrate you myself."

My cheeks blazed, and I couldn't look up from the floor.

Ace took it in stride with a laugh. "Momma, when have I ever been irresponsible?"

I darted a quick glance in their direction when she answered, "Never. But as your mom, the woman who's been through it all with you, I'm asking you... both of you, to be careful and use protection."

I wanted the floor to swallow me whole.

"We've got that covered." Ace chewed his lip to keep the smirk off his face when he looked at me.

"Good. Now, let's go finish packing up your bag so you don't have to worry about doing it later." His mom walked out of the kitchen. I ran my hands over my face, trying to get it to stop burning.

Ace's arms wrapped around me, and he pulled me into a tight hug. "That is the most interesting shade of red I've ever seen on you."

I buried my face in his chest. "That's not funny."

He pulled back and lifted my chin up. "Riley, look at me."

I squeezed my eyes tighter. "I can't. Just give me a minute, Ace."

"Jake."

"Give me a minute, Jake."

"Riley, I know you're embarrassed, but think about it. What's so wrong with the way we feel? It's not like we were caught in the act. My mom gets it, she gets us, and I'm glad. I don't want to feel like I have to sneak around to be with you."

A groan slipped from me. "Ace, she knows we're sleeping

together. And you're her son... She probably thinks I'm some loose girl with no morals and..."

He pinched my lips together. "And you're talking a bunch of shit about the woman I love, who happens to have the best morals of any girl I've ever known, and is far from being 'loose'. She's funny, smart, and so beautiful that I want to lock her away from the rest of the men in the world. You're my everything, Riley. I don't care who knows it, and I damn sure don't care what they think about it. I'd shout it from the rooftops for everyone to hear, but this is a small town, so everyone probably already knows it by now."

He'd made me feel a little better, but by no means ready to face his mom. I ran my hand down his chest and pushed myself back a step. "Jake, I can't face her right now. Can I come back in a little while?"

He blocked me from the door and crossed his arms. "Hey, Mom!"

Oh no! "Stop it! What are you doing?" I hissed at him.

"Yes?" she called out from the other side of the house.

"Can you please tell Riley that it's perfectly normal for a mom to know that their son is intimate with the girl he loves, so she won't freak out and leave?"

"What?" She was almost to the kitchen. "Is everything all right?"

I tried to shove him out of the way so I could run out the door, but he was immovable. "Please move," I whispered.

"No, I only have a short amount of time left with you and I'm not giving any of it up, so deal with it."

Anger burned through me, and I fought the tears of embarrassment that flooded my eyes.

"Oh, no. Riley, I'm so sorry. I shouldn't have said that with you here." Her arms came around me, and she hugged me. "I didn't mean to upset or embarrass you. I was just being a mom and didn't think about how it sounded other than a warning to my son."

I sobbed against her shoulder. She squeezed me tight and then pulled me back. "There is nothing wrong with your relationship with my son. From here on out, my lips are sealed." Her finger ran across her lips on an imaginary zipper, and then she broke into a smile. "Now, let's go get him packed. Okay?"

She didn't give me a chance to say no as she put her arm around me and walked me to Ace's room. I could hear Ace following along behind us. When we got to his room, his mom let me go as Ace blocked his bedroom doorway with his arms, as if I'd take the opportunity to bolt. I wanted to, but decided to stick it out and make the most of the time we had left.

After a few seconds of holding his ground, Ace walked over to me and dropped a kiss to my forehead. His mom handed him a stack of clothes, and he shoved them into a duffel bag. He had to stop his mom from packing every single piece of clothing he owned with a reminder that he wouldn't be wearing them much since he'd be in uniform most of the time. Her eyes watered, and she wiped away a tear that escaped with a chuckle. "I suppose you're right."

When Ace zipped the duffel bag up, his mom walked over to his bedroom door, stopping just shy of the hall. "I'm gonna go start dinner. I'll call for you to come and set the table when it's time." When she stepped out, she pulled the door, but left it cracked. She didn't have to say anything more.

Ace pulled me down to sit beside him on the bed. "Sorry about earlier. I hope you're not angry with me."

I'd wanted to be angry. He'd outmaneuvered me in my embarrassment and forced me to stew in it until I relented. "You're lucky I don't hold grudges."

He pulled me closer and moved my legs over his. "When I

come back, on leave, we need to sit down and talk about what's next for us. I really don't want to do it now and rush things, but I want you to know how I feel."

I leaned back on one arm, willing the nervous roll of my stomach to settle. Ace wanted more, and it made me deliriously happy. "Do you have any idea where you'll be going after boot camp?"

"Not yet. I have an idea, but I'm waiting to see what happens." His muscles bunched along his shoulders when he shrugged. "Will it matter to you? I mean… with where we'll live?"

In a swift move, I was on his lap, facing him. "I just want to be wherever you are. I don't care where or how, or even why." I cringed after admitting it, hoping it didn't make me sound as clingy as I felt.

He smiled at me. A smile that crinkled at the corners of his eyes, telling me it was what he wanted to hear.

"I can't wait to get you home, Riley." He kissed my lips and stood up with me in his arms. "Now, let's head downstairs before I shock my mother and really embarrass you."

My feet hit the floor, and I staggered out of his arms. "That's probably a good idea."

∿

We made it through dinner. The mood was light, as we talked about everything except for Ace leaving. He stood next to his mom and helped her with the dishes, as I cleared the table and wiped it down. When the last dish was put away, Ace's mom put her hand on his arm. "I think I'll be heading to bed early, maybe even read a book for a little while."

Ace pulled her in for a hug. "I'll see you in the morning?"

Stepping back, she put her hand on his cheek. She smiled,

the same smile that crinkled at the corners of her eyes like Ace's. "Have fun. Behave."

Ace lifted her off her feet. "Yes, Mom. I promise, no kids."

She slapped at his arm, and he set her down. She turned to me with a wink. "Keep him in line, Riley."

I rolled my eyes and chuckled. "You know that's next to impossible."

"Yes, but doable." She pulled me in for a quick hug. "See you tomorrow?"

I swallowed the lump in my throat when she stepped back. We'd be each other's support when Ace left. I nodded, not trusting my voice, and put a fake smile on my face. I'd fall apart on my own, because it would be messy and heartbreaking, and there was no way I'd allow anyone that close to see it.

She turned away with a wave of her fingers over her shoulder. "Good night, you two. Don't forget to lock the door when you leave."

Ace snatched my keys from where I'd left them on the hook by the door. "Night, Mom," he called out to her as he swung the front door open and ushered me out of the house.

He opened the passenger side door, and I climbed in the truck. When the door closed behind me, he darted around the back and jumped into the driver's seat as the door swung open.

"In a hurry, Ace?" I turned in my seat, not able to hide the smirk on my face as I watched him jam the key in the ignition and start the truck. We were rolling out of his driveway before he answered.

"You. Me. The rest of this night. I'm gonna make the most of it. Every. Single. Second."

I shivered at the husky tone in his voice. His hands clenched the steering wheel as he drove. When he passed my street, I turned my head and watched the street sign disappear in the distance. "Uh, you missed my street."

"I know. I'm not taking you home. Not just yet."

"Where are you taking me, exactly?"

"You'll see." He never once looked over at me when he spoke. If anything, he leaned closer to the steering wheel like it would make us get to wherever we were going faster.

Whatever it was, it had him on edge, more than I'd ever witnessed before with him.

He drove us out to the cabin and brought the truck to a stop by the front door. I went to open my door, but he put his hand up, silently gesturing for me to stay put. I gave him a confused look, but he didn't stop to explain as he disappeared inside. When he came back out, he had an armful of blankets and a couple of pillows.

He dumped them in the back of the truck, got back behind the wheel, and drove across the yard to the Hole. When he stopped the truck and pulled the keys out, tossing them on the seat, I knew we'd made it to his intended destination.

"Why here?" He gestured for me to slide across the seat to where he stood just outside the door.

Curiosity had me across the bench seat and inches from where he stood, as I waited for what he had to say.

He put his hand out and helped me from the truck. When I stood in front of him, he reached into the truck bed, pulled out the pillows, and handed them to me. I hugged them against me as he pulled the blankets from the back. He held them with one arm and then led me out to the dock. When we got to the end, he dropped the blankets and spread them out, gesturing for the pillows in my hands. I gave them to him, and he dumped them on the makeshift bed he'd made.

Not a word passed between us, as the sounds of the night

filled the silence. I opened my mouth to say something, but he placed his finger against my lips. "Shhh. Look up, Riley."

I tilted my head, seeking out the night sky. It was beautiful. The stars shimmered against the inky blackness like a blanket over us. I knew then that Ace wanted to make this night something special. Something we could both call back to us when we were apart. I would always remember it as the night he covered me with stars. My eyes blurred. I could feel the threat of tears and couldn't stop them. Ace's hands came up to cup the back of my neck, using his thumbs to tilt my face. The first tear rolled down my cheek. Brushing it aside, he leaned in to kiss me. He didn't have to ask me what was wrong. I didn't want him to either. I just wanted—needed—him more than I ever had, and somehow he knew it.

Every touch was slow. Every kiss was drawn out, slipping into another one. A deeper one. Shoes were kicked off. Clothes were peeled away until the night air touched our skin, doing nothing to cool us down. Together we moved until we were lying on the blanket. Reaching for each other, we sighed with every touch our bodies made. We moved as one under the stars, as the night came alive around us.

Ace kissed me, wrapping the blanket around us to fend off the mosquitos that tried feasting on us. When there was no reprieve from them, we packed up the blankets and pillows, stowed them behind the seat of my truck, and Ace drove us to my house. Our conversation was light as we joked about all the places we'd be itching at in the morning.

When he pulled into my driveway, our eyes met again, and it was a race to see who could get upstairs first. The entire night was a continuation of us loving each other. Slow, fast, tender, reckless. When the morning sun slipped across the horizon, our chests heaved against each other.

I trailed my hand through his hair. "You're gonna be exhausted on the drive to Georgia."

He pulled my fingers to his lips and kissed them. "I love you, Riley."

"I love you, too."

Ace forced himself to get out of bed, and then strode across the hall with his clothes from the day before. The shower turned on, and I let the tears fall. The pressure of holding them back had become too much, and I didn't want Ace to be left with the memory of me crying before he left.

When he got out of the shower, he found me downstairs making a pot of coffee. We both needed a little caffeine boost after spending all night wide-awake. I decided it would be best if I stayed home and let him have a few minutes with his mom before he left. While he was in the shower, I called Aiden, Eli, Mark, and Josh. They wanted to see him before he took off. It would be easier on everyone if they came to my house and said their good-byes on neutral territory.

Josh strolled in first. "Oh, good, you have coffee." He walked past me and pulled down a cup. The spoon clinked against the glass as Aiden knocked on the door and then let himself in, Eli behind him. Mark showed up a couple minutes later and plopped down in a chair.

"I'd have been here sooner, but I had to stop by the hospital for a minute," he said, tugging his hands through his hair.

"Everything okay?" I asked.

"It will be as soon as Paige stops being so damn hard-headed," he answered with a scowl that pinched his eyebrows together.

Ace pulled out a chair at the kitchen table and tugged me into his lap as he replied to Mark. "The good ones are always worth the wait."

Mark sighed and slumped in his seat. "I'm tired of wait-ing." He waved away what he said, letting his hand drop in his lap. "So you're driving up there alone, huh?"

"Yeah, there's no reason to have my mom come with me, only to have her turn around and drive back. Besides, I'll see her and Riley at graduation, and then I'll be coming home for a few days of leave." Ace's fingers linked with mine, and he lightly squeezed them.

"I guess this is kinda it for all of us. Come tomorrow, we're all headed out in opposite directions," Aiden said. He chuckled, but it came out sounding uneasy and forced.

"How the hell are we supposed to keep in touch with you?" Josh kicked Eli's chair.

Eli wiggled his eyebrows and pulled a phone from his pocket. "SAT phone, baby! Now there's no excuse not to call me. And I better get some damn texts with pictures, too. And not no damn pictures of all the food you assholes are eating either."

Aiden yanked the phone from him with a hoot of laughter. "Why? You're the one who signed up to go to a third-world country that eats bugs and shit."

"You're an idiot," Eli said, snatching the phone from Aiden.

"Kidding, man. Just kidding. It's cool you're doing this. Not many people wanna give up the time or their comfort to go where you're headed. Props, man. Got nothin' but love for ya, bro," Aiden said as he fist-bumped Eli.

"Sorry to cut it short, but I still have to finish going through my room," Josh said as he stood up to leave.

I moved from Ace's lap and steeled myself for the round of good-byes happening. Eli swept me up in a hug and put me back down after he made me promise to call him. Josh swept in, gave me a loud, smacking kiss on the cheek, and darted out of Ace's reach.

Aiden bumped his shoulder into mine. I wrapped my arms around him and squeezed. "Will you be coming back on leave after boot camp?"

He smiled down at me and tapped me on the end of the nose. "Nah, after boot camp, I'm off to see the world."

"The world? As in another country?" I asked.

"Probably several other countries. Don't worry; I'll pick you up souvenirs." He winked at me, turning around to shake Ace's hand. "Good luck. I'll be seeing you around."

Ace kept a hold of his hand as he pulled him in for a one-armed hug. "Take care, Aiden. Keep in touch."

Aiden's arm tightened around Ace. "Let us know when the wedding is so we can all be here. Okay?"

Ace looked over at me with a wink. "Don't worry; you guys will be the first to know."

I could feel my eyes bulging, but I kept my mouth shut.

The guys shuffled out the door with Ace trailing along behind them. I stood firmly rooted to the kitchen floor until I heard the sound of truck doors closing. I darted out the door, slipped my arm around Ace, and held myself firmly against him, not wanting to miss the chance at waving to them as they left.

Eli was the last one to back out of the driveway. He honked his horn and waved out the window.

My hand dropped to my side, and my chest hitched. Ace put his arms around me and held me against him as he dropped his chin on top of my head. "My mom's on her way to pick me up."

That one small sentence crushed me from the inside out. It took everything in me not to cry. My body trembled against his as it sought out a way to release the over-whelming emotions that had taken over.

Ace's mom pulled in the driveway, and I felt him stiffen beside me. He tipped my head back to look down at me. "This isn't good-bye. It's just a see ya soon."

I forced my lips to give him a smile as I nodded.

"It's only for a little while, and then we'll have..." his

words died off, and I watched his throat work up and down before he continued, "...and then we'll have forever." His words were strained, and I knew he fought for every one of them.

I lifted myself up on my tiptoes and kissed him. His breath hissed between us and he pulled me roughly against him, kissing me with a fierceness that stole my breath. When he broke the kiss, he pulled away from me, trailed his finger down my cheek, and closed his eyes. He kept his eyes closed as he stepped back and turned towards where his mom was parked.

I gave him the distance he needed, but couldn't ask for. When he closed the door, I covered my mouth to keep the sound of my heart breaking from reaching his ears. His mom backed the truck out as his eyes met mine. His hand came up and he blew me a kiss, mouthing the words 'I love you.'

I don't know how I stood there and watched them leave, without running after them and begging him to stay. And I don't know how long I stood there once they were gone. It could have been minutes. It could have been hours. Nothing really meant anything to me anymore. At some point, I made it back in the house and to my room. Fell onto my bed and cried into the pillow that smelled like Ace until I fell asleep.

CHAPTER 13

J'd be by myself until my dad came home. It was a bleak existence, bumbling around the house like a ghost. Always dreading the climb up the stairs at the end of the day that took me to my bedroom. The first place Ace and I made love.

It was torture. I'd start out trying to sleep, but I could smell Ace's scent on my pillow. It made me miss him, so I'd leave my room and curl up on the couch. But on the couch, I didn't feel as close to Ace, so I'd run back up the stairs and hug my pillow against me. I was the neediest person ever, and I didn't like it. Not one bit.

Paige came by three days after Ace left, took one look at me, and cursed. "You have to pull it together, Riley. Jesus, it's not like he'll be gone forever. You're stronger than this."

Her verbal slap jarred me, making me realize how far I'd slunk into myself because Ace wasn't there. And it wasn't just Ace either. It was all of them. The Six were spread out over the globe, and all I could do was sit there, feeling sorry for myself.

Paige crossed her arms and scowled at me. "You need to

get a shower and get a hold of Dr. Anderson. He's been trying to get in touch with you since yesterday."

I forced myself to shut it off, all the thoughts, the memories, and the loneliness. Grabbing whatever my hand came into contact with for clothes, I put one foot in front of the other and walked to the bathroom, closed the door, turned on the shower, stripped down, and stepped under the hot spray. All robotically. All one step after another.

Shampoo, conditioner, soap. Turn water off. Wring out hair. Step out and dry off. One leg, the other leg, shorts up. Piece by piece, I pulled myself together. When I opened the bathroom door, a cloud of steam escaped into the hallway. I watched it billow out past me and disappear, imagining it took with it all the things that had weighted me down since the Six were gone.

When I stepped out of the bathroom, Paige pushed off the wall and looked me up and down. "Well, at least you somewhat match."

I looked down to see what she meant, realizing that I'd grabbed a pair of hot pink, jean shorts and a light purple shirt. I walked past Paige without replying. She followed me into my room and leaned against the doorframe. "Mark texted me this morning."

She pushed on, not waiting for me to reply. "He said he's settled in and starts his first class in a couple of days."

I unplugged my cell phone and gripped it in my hand, not looking at the screen. I didn't want to be disappointed if there wasn't a text there from Ace. I hadn't heard anything from him since he'd left. Not even an 'I made it safe and sound.'

Paige heaved a sigh and grabbed my phone from me. I yanked it back and slapped her hand away.

"Riley... this, whatever it is you're going through, needs to stop. You can't do this to yourself. If the Six were here, they'd kick your ass and tell you to snap out of it."

"Yeah, well, they're not here, are they? They left, and I stayed. They're moving on, and I'm stuck here. Without them. Alone and… and… just leave me the hell alone, Paige."

"I'm just trying to help you, Riley. You're my best friend, and I'm watching you suffer."

"No one asked you to help me. I certainly didn't. Thank you for stopping by to let me know Dr. Anderson wants me to call him. You can go now." I turned my back on her and cursed myself for being such a bitch. I didn't want to hurt Paige. I just didn't know how to deal with all the emotions rolling through me.

"Screw you, Riley. Do you think you're the only one who feels the loss of them leaving? Do you think you're the only one whose heart was ripped out and left to shatter alone? Do you know how many hours… seconds… I have kicked myself over and over again for finding someone, only to lose them, because life chose a different path for me?"

Paige stormed up to me and shoved my shoulder. She wasn't backing down, and neither was I.

"Paige, you can't be serious. You wanted nothing to do with Mark, or so you made it seem."

"I was protecting myself!"

"You were running away. Scared of whatever it is that made you feel something. Mark looked at you like you were everything and…" My words sputtered to a stop on my lips as the truth of my words hit me. Paige's hand clamped over her mouth, as she doubled over with her fist to her stomach. The heartbreaking cry that ripped from her broke me. I grabbed her and we crumpled to the floor, holding on to each other as we poured out our pain the only way we knew how.

I pulled back, wiping the trail of tears away and leaning

against the side of my bed. Paige's sobs hitched as she pulled her knees up to her chest.

"I'm sorry, Paige. You didn't deserve that. I had no idea… I'm… I'm sorry."

She wiped her face with the bottom of her T-shirt and blew out a long, steady breath. "We're both stronger than this, Riley. No person should let the love they feel for another tear them apart to the point of madness. Things happen for a reason. Whether we find out what that reason is or not, we can't let it rip us apart. I refuse to let this break either of us. There's a purpose to why we're being tested. Besides, nothing worth having is easy."

I bit my lip and nodded, agreeing with what she said. I took all my mixed emotions and visualized them being crumpled up and tossed out the window. "I'll try if you try."

She leaned in to me and put her head on my shoulder. "Deal. Now, call Dr. Anderson. It seemed pretty important."

I looked around for my phone. It had been in my hand until the heated argument and then our mutual breakdown. I hadn't even felt it slip from the death grip I'd had on it. I found it sticking out from the edge of the bed-skirt. No sooner did I pick it up, it rang, and I almost dropped it again. The screen lit up with Ace's name. I answered with a breathless hello as I reached out, grabbed Paige's hand, and squeezed.

"Hello, beautiful." He chuckled.

"I was wondering when I'd hear from you."

I heard him sigh softly. "Cell reception sucks here. I called my mom last night to let her know I'd made it here and then went to call you, but…"

"It's okay. I understand. I miss you."

"I miss you too. I have to make this quick, but I'll call you again as soon as I can."

"Okay,"

"I love you, Riley. Talk to you soon."

"Love you too, Jake."

The phone crackled and hissed in my ear before it went silent.

"Feel better?" Paige asked as she stood up and fixed her ponytail.

"Actually, I do." And I did. Hearing his voice made me realize I needed to suck it up and stop acting like a baby.

"Good. Listen, I gotta go. My shift starts in…" she looked down at her watch and groaned, "ten minutes. I'll call you later, okay?" She hugged me and made a beeline for the stairs.

"Okay!" I yelled just before the front door slammed closed.

I sat down on my bed, took a deep breath as I scrolled through my phone and pulled up Dr. Anderson, released the air in my lungs, and pushed send.

"Riley… thank God!" Dr. Anderson sounded frazzled.

"What's up? Paige said you needed to talk to me."

"I've had an emergency come up with my mom, and I have to leave town for a week or so. Do you think you can help me out? I know you can't take on the big stuff, but you're more than qualified to help if someone calls in and needs something. I've spoken with Dr. Jenkins, the vet over in Andalusia. He said he'd take on whatever you called him about." His sentences rolled together, never once stopping for a breath.

"Sure, I can do that."

"Thank you, you don't even know what a relief that is. Can you come to the office now?"

"Yeah, give me just a few minutes and I'll be there."

"See ya when ya get here. And thanks again, Riley. I owe you."

I set my phone down and changed into a pair of jeans and my beat-up boots.

My keys jingled in my hand, as I jogged to my truck. Having something to do would definitely help chase away the loneliness. Dr. Anderson needing me was just the thing to keep me busy.

~

Dr. Anderson was ready for me when I stepped inside the waiting room of his clinic.

"I've made a few phone calls and talked to the local ranchers. They understand that if it's an emergency, they need to call Dr. Jenkins. His number's on my desk, along with a list of numbers you might need while I'm gone. Most of the numbers are in here." He handed me the cell phone he always carried on his hip.

I slid the phone clip on the waist of my jeans, as he pulled a set of keys off his desk and handed them to me. "The keys to the kingdom," he said with a brief chuckle. "Okay, now as far as the animals in the back..."

I followed behind him as we went down the line of cages, and he rattled off what they were there for. I kept up with his speedy pace and all but stepped on him when he stopped quickly and turned around. His hand shot out and steadied me. "Sorry. Okay, now Becky will be in every Tuesday and Thursday to take care of the paperwork and stuff. Your main concern will be answering that," he pointed at the cell, "and doing what you can here before Dr. Jenkins has to be referred."

Becky had worked part time for Dr. Anderson for as long as I could remember. He'd joked that she came with the building when he'd started his practice.

"I got it, don't worry about a thing," I told him as I backed up a step and let him pass by.

"I have no idea what I'll be dealing with when I get to my mom's. She's not good, Riley, and she needs me." His face paled, and I noticed the deep lines bracketing the corners of his eyes. He was worried and trying really hard not to show it.

"You headed out now?" I asked.

"Yeah, I've got my bag in my truck, so I can leave straight from here."

"Go, I've got it from here," I said, waving him towards the front door.

He walked back to his office, grabbing a pen and paper off the desk. His hand flew along the page as he scribbled two phone numbers down. "This is my mom's house number and my personal cell number. Call me if you need anything."

I took the paper from him. "I'll program them into my cell. Don't worry about everything here, Dr. Anderson. Just go take care of your mom."

He nodded his head. "Okay, I'll call you in a week or so."

He was out the door and in his truck before I knew it.

Seconds later, the phone at my hip rang.

Four phone calls later, I sat down at Dr. Anderson's desk and rubbed my forehead. I never realized just how crazy people could be over their pets. It hadn't even been an hour since he'd left, and I was ready to bang my head against the desk. If Mrs. Snyder called one more time about Muffin's, her overweight tabby cat, bowel movements, I'd scream.

I busied myself by cleaning up the thick layer of dust that had accumulated over the years in Dr. Anderson's office. It gave me something to do as I waited for five o'clock to roll around. I'd just finished wiping down one of the three book-shelves in his office when I heard the bell over the waiting room door jingle.

"Hello?"

I wiped my grime-covered hands on my pants, and went out to meet whoever the worried male voice belonged to. When I stepped out into the waiting room, my eyes landed on a young boy who couldn't have been more than eleven or twelve. In his arms, he clutched a box against him. His eyes were pooled with tears as he rushed forward, almost shoving the box into my arms.

"My cat... she's been crying a lot and panting. Dad said to put her outside 'cause he don't wanna hear her goddamn caterwaulin' no more. I put her in there and had to close the flaps, so she wouldn't get away from me." A fat tear rolled down his cheek, and he brought his shirtsleeve up to dash it away.

I bit my tongue when he cursed. He was clearly upset. Giving him a hard time about cussing would only make him more upset. "Come on, let's go take a look at her."

He stayed in the middle of the room with his head bowed and his hands fisted at his sides. "I ain't got no money to pay you."

"What's your name?" My question made him snap his head up to look at me.

"Seth, ma'am."

"Okay, Seth, let's get..." I paused so he could tell me the cat's name.

"Sammy."

"Let's get Sammy to the back and take a look at her, okay? Then we can go from there."

He met my gaze dead on and set his shoulders. His chin came up with a brief nod, and we walked to the back where I could set Sammy down and take a look at her.

I set the box on an examining table and could hear the soft mewling noises coming from inside. I had a feeling I knew what I'd find when I opened the box.

Seth skirted the room and went to stand on the other side of the table. He crossed his arms and chewed his thumbnail as his eyes darted from me to the box. I walked over to the sink, washed my hands, and then gestured for him to do the same.

"How old is Sammy?" I asked him as I dried my hands and then crossed over to the box.

"Not very old, I don't think. I found her about a month ago. I sneak her scraps and stuff so she's been kinda hangin' around the house. My dad wasn't happy about it, but since she stayed outside, he let it go. I found her like that when I went to give her some leftover meatloaf, and I snuck her into my room. When he heard her meow, he lost it, and I put her in that... I didn't know what else to do. Can you help her? Please?"

His hand reached out to pull the flaps apart, and I put my hand on his. It trembled as he looked up at me. "It's gonna be okay, Seth. I think you're gonna find she's having kittens."

The flaps sprang free, and we peered inside. Sammy looked up at Seth briefly and went back to cleaning up the newly born kitten still covered in its sac.

"Kittens?" He stepped back and ran his hand down his face.

I reached in and ran my fingertips against Sammy's head. She purred in response. "Hey there, Momma, you have a pretty little baby."

When her breathing picked up again, I motioned for Seth to step closer. He paled, but did as I asked, and we watched as a brand-new life was brought into the world.

"Wow, that's so awesome and so disgusting at the same time," Seth said as he stared at Sammy without breaking his gaze as he spoke. "How many do you think she'll have?"

"It just depends. Sometimes, they have just a few and

sometimes, they can have a lot." I gave him a shrug. "We just have to wait it out."

He looked over my shoulder at the clock on the wall. "I have to be home soon. Can she stay here?"

"Sure." How could I tell him no? "She'll have to stay with her kittens for at least six weeks. Then you'll need to think about homes for them and getting her fixed."

His face fell, and he toed the ground. "Is it really expensive?"

I thought about it for a second. He really loved his cat, but there was no way he'd be able to come up with the money on his own. "I'll tell you what. How about if you help me out here for the next week or so, and when it's time for her to wean her kittens, then we'll work something out?"

"I'll talk to my mom and see if she'll let me come over after my chores are done." Seth leaned over the box and rubbed Sammy's nose. She purred in response and licked him. His eyes darted to the clock again, and he frowned

"Head on home. I'll take good care of her, I promise."

He stuck his hand out, and I bit the inside of my cheek to keep from chuckling. He might be young, but he had such a grown-up way about him. I shook his hand and walked him to the door.

"See ya tomorrow," he said with a wave as he jogged away.

I closed and locked the door behind me, heading back to check on my newest patient. By the time I made it back to the box, another baby was born with no signs of labor letting up. I crossed my fingers she'd only have one more and be done. I lifted the box off the table, carried her back to a cage, and slid the box inside. The last thing I wanted to happen was for her to decide to jump out and upend the box onto the floor.

Once she was settled, I checked the other three patients left into my care. My first stop was at Shelby's cage. The brown-and-white Cocker Spaniel lifted her head and wagged her tail as I spoke to her. Dr. Anderson had held her over for observation after removing a lump from her side. Nothing serious, just a fatty deposit that looked bad, but wasn't. Her stitches looked good, but she'd have to wear the cone another day or so to keep her from licking at them. I checked her food and water and then moved on to the next cage, making a mental note to take her out before I left, so I wouldn't have a mess to clean up in the morning.

The next cage down was Rodney, the chocolate lab who'd gone through a round of heartworm treatment. His owner didn't want to take him home right then. Rodney wasn't his only dog. He had two more labs at home that would want to play when they saw him, and Rodney needed to take it easy with the high dosage of heartworm medication in his system.

He stood up and pressed his nose against the door when he saw me. His tail wagged, smacking into the sides of the cage, eager to greet me. "Hey boy, you look good." I reached my hand between the bars and gave him a scratch on the ear. He sat and lifted his paw up to the door. "You gotta go outside?" He yipped at me and shifted side to side in his cage. I grabbed the leash and opened his cage, keeping a firm grip on his collar. He pulled against the leash and practically dragged me to the back door. "Okay, okay, we're going."

After he did his business, he wasn't ready to go back inside, but I made him go anyway. His head hung when I closed him back inside the cage. "I know, buddy, I'm sorry. Soon you'll be able to break outta here and run like you want to. You just have to get better first." I scratched his head when he pressed it against the door and whimpered.

I forced myself to walk away from him and check on the last patient. Inside the cage, curled up in the corner, was a baby raccoon. When he saw me, he hissed and pushed himself further back in the cage. Dr. Anderson had taken him in when he found him on the side of the road after being struck by a car. He was old enough to make it on his own as soon as his injuries had healed and he put on a little weight. I had a feeling that being stuck back with all the other animals stressed him out and kept him from packing on the pounds.

I walked back over to Shelby's cage, hooked her up to the leash, and took her outside before I went to check on Sammy and her babies. Being in the back seemed to stress her out. Her ears were pinned back, and her eyes darted everywhere. There was no way I could leave her at the office, so I flipped the lid to the box closed, carried her out to my truck, and took her home for the night.

CHAPTER 14

One day turned into another and I fell into a routine
as the days passed. Seth stopped by every day and
helped me out with whatever I had going on. When he was
done with whatever chore I gave him, he'd sit with Sammy
and her six kittens for a little bit and then head home. I'd
brought her back to the vet's office, the day after the kittens
were born, and fixed up one of the larger cages for them. The
phone didn't ring as much when word got around that Dr.
Anderson had to leave town, but people still came in and
called with non-emergency questions. Sometimes, they'd
bring their animals in to see if they needed to go to Dr.
Jenkins.

I didn't mind the slower pace.

I hadn't heard from my dad, which was weird since he
usually tried to call me a day or so before he was headed
home. I figured I'd wait one more day and if I didn't hear
from him, I'd call him.

That night when I got home, my cell phone rang. Dad's
ears must've been burning.

"Hey stranger," I said when I answered.

"How's my girl?"

"Good. Staying busy," I said, explaining to him about helping Dr. Anderson out.

"That's good, but isn't that gonna keep you from school?"

I winced and curled my hand into a fist. I hated keeping things from Dad, but I didn't want to explain it to him over the phone. I'd rather talk to him face to face, so I could gauge his reaction. My dad had an uncanny way of keeping his voice light and friendly, even when he was angry enough to spit nails. "Nah, you know me. I can do it all," I said, tossing in a laugh to keep his suspicions down.

He barked out a laugh that ended on a wheeze. "Hey, you okay, Dad?'

"I'm fine. Just caught a little cold. Hey listen, I need to renew my CDL certs, and I put it off too long to make it back to my doctor in time. Can you do me a favor?"

"Sure. What do you need?" I asked.

"In my closet, there's a lock box. The key for it is in my sock drawer. I forgot to grab my new medical card when I left, so I'll need you to take a picture of it and text me."

"Text you?" Hell had just frozen over. Of that, I was sure, because my dad would never text. He despised the whole concept. "Dad, what are you not telling me?"

"Riley, I'm fine. I just don't have my medical card on me, and I'll need it to get the physical done. Besides, aren't you the one always grumbling when I give you a hard time about texting?"

He laughed, and it sent him into a round of deep coughing.

"You sure you're all right?" I couldn't keep the concern out of my voice.

"I'll be fine. Just send that over as soon as you can, so I don't get my license pulled. Okay?"

"All right, I'm doing it right now. When will you be home?"

"Probably not for a few more weeks. They asked me to do another long haul and then a back haul that'll put me away for a while longer."

I sighed into the phone, not bothering to cover it up. "I miss you, Dad."

"I miss you too, kiddo. I'll be seeing ya. Love you. Be good. Okay?"

He never let himself sound so sad when we talked, but it was probably because he knew it would be a while before he was back home and he felt bad because of it. "Love you too, Dad. Have them check out that cough!"

When I hung up the phone, I went in search of the key in his sock drawer, pulled the box from the closet, and opened it. The medical card he'd asked for was right on top of a thick stack of envelopes. I snapped a picture and sent it to him. His reply was almost instant.

Love you, baby girl.

I made my way to the kitchen, pulled the refrigerator door open, and grumbled. I hadn't restocked on anything and a trip to the grocery store was needed. Grabbing my keys and my wallet, I slid on my flip-flops and stepped out of the house in time to see Paige pull up in my driveway.

She got out of her car and waved. "I was just coming to get you for dinner."

I walked over to the passenger side and got in. The cool air blowing from the AC vent felt good against the muggy summer air. Paige's door closed with a solid thunk, and we pulled out of the driveway. She did it so fast that I wondered if she thought I'd change my mind.

"So you've been staying pretty busy, I hear." She looked over at me and then back to the road.

"Yeah, but not as busy as it is when Dr. Anderson's there."

"When will he be back?"

I grabbed the door handle when Paige shot around an S-curve in the road. "Not sure. He should have called me by now. I hope everything's all right with his mom."

"I'm sure it's fine, Riley. He's probably just busy is all."

My hand went to my hip, and I groaned. "We have to go back to the house. I forgot his phone."

"How about we just go through a drive-thru, and we can take it back to your place?"

"That works." I could have kicked myself for not remembering to grab his phone before I left the house. What if he called to check on how I was doing? He'd think I was being irresponsible, and then he wouldn't want to ask me to help him again. Working for him was all I had left until I decided what I would do with the rest of my life. And really, that had changed over the past few weeks. I didn't want to start school only to leave when Ace was done with boot camp.

Paige pulled her car into the drive-thru lane of the only burger joint in town. The smell of greasy burgers and fries filled the confines of the car on our ride home. As soon as Paige pulled in the driveway, I shot out of the car and ran into the house. Dr. Anderson's phone was just where I'd left it on my bed. A sigh of relief washed through me. No missed calls.

I jogged back down the stairs, as Paige pulled the burgers out of the bag. "Everything okay?"

"Yeah. No missed calls, thankfully."

She unwrapped her burger and held it up to her mouth.

"Good. Now sit down and eat before the food gets colder than it already is."

I picked up a fry and twirled it in the air before sticking it in my mouth. "So what's been going on with you?"

She dusted a layer of salt off her hands and held her finger up as she took a sip of her drink. "It's been pretty busy."

"Have you heard from Mark?"

She rolled her eyes and chuckled. "He texts me all the time."

"So he's all settled in then?"

"Yeah, he's ready to start school. I think he's a little home-sick though."

"Homesick or Paige sick?"

I couldn't help the laugh that escaped when she threw a French fry at me.

"It's bad enough with him giving me a hard time, and you wanna start in, too? Geez."

"What's he giving you a hard time about?"

"Every day he asks me to come up there. Every. Single. Day."

"Paige, do you like him?"

She scoffed at my question. "Of course I like him. He's my friend, Riley."

I picked up my drink and held the straw between my teeth as I squinted at her. She had to know she wasn't fooling anyone—least of all me. "When are you going to just admit that you want to be with him?"

She pushed back from the table and crossed her arms. Her brow kicked up one side, disappearing under her hair. "You of all people should know that nothing is that easy. I have a job, Riley. I'm working towards a career, the same as everyone else. I didn't ask him to stay here and give up his dream, so why should I be asked to do that?"

I took a long sip from the straw and set the cup back down. My question had pissed her off when that wasn't my intent at all. I had to smooth things over before she stormed out. "I didn't mean it like that. I was just curious is all. I mean, I know how you both feel about each other."

She snorted. "You had no idea even when Mark demanded that I come out to the cabin."

She had me there. I'd been so wrapped up in daydreaming over Ace that I'd been in my own little bubble for a long time. "Okay, so if you aren't going to New York then what's Mark's plan? Is he coming back here after school?"

Her eyes flickered closed and when they opened, she looked down at the table. "I don't know."

"Well, nothing has to be set in stone right now. He has a few years of school. You have a few years to get your degree."

She lifted her eyes to mine. "That's what I keep telling him."

"You know as well as I do how stubborn they can all be."

She crumpled her cheeseburger wrapper up and dumped it into the garbage. "Have you heard from Jared yet?"

"No, I was waiting for him to get in touch with me. I might try to get a hold of him tonight."

"What the hell are we gonna do with these boys? They don't call, they don't write. I say we bang their heads together the next time we see them," Paige said as she stood up and pushed her chair in.

"Leaving already?" I asked.

"Yeah, gotta be back at the hospital pretty early, so I'm gonna head home and get some sleep. I've missed my bed."

"Thanks for dinner," I said, walking with her to the door.

"That wasn't dinner. That was a heart attack in a bag. Let's do it again. Next time, it's your treat," she said over her shoulder as she opened her car door.

"Sounds good. See ya later." I waved as she pulled out of the driveway.

~

I locked the front door and forced myself up the stairs. When I got to my room, I flopped down on the bed, grabbed my cell phone, and sent out texts to Josh, Jared, Mark, and Eli. I wasn't sure if I'd hear anything from Eli since I had no idea what time it was in Haiti. Josh answered me back first. We chatted for a few minutes, and he promised to call me soon. Mark replied and asked me if the burgers were any good. Clearly, he'd spoken to Paige at some point between the time she left and then. Mark seemed really excited about school, and he couldn't say enough good things about New York. No wonder Paige felt so pressured. If he could, he would have pulled me through the phone just to take me sightseeing.

I felt myself drifting off after Mark and I had wrapped up our twenty-minute text marathon. Turning over on my side, I was just about to set my phone on my nightstand when it rang. Jared's name flashed across the screen, and I answered.

"Hey, Rock God. How the hell are you?"

"Hey, Riles! Miss me already?"

I pressed the phone against my ear. Turning the volume up as far as it would go, I still had a hard time hearing him.

"Where are you? I can barely hear you."

"I'm gettin' ready for a show. When I saw your text, I figured I'd call you real quick."

"You could have just sent me a text."

"Yeah, but then I wouldn't have been able to hear your voice."

The phone cut in and out as the noise around him grew louder. "Jared?"

"I'm about to go on stage. I'll call you when the show is over. That okay?"

I looked over at my alarm clock. It was still fairly early. "Sure, maybe I'll be able to hear you then."

I heard him joking as he talked with everyone around him. "Sorry, Riley. It's getting a little crazy. I'll call you back in a little bit."

His voice all but shouted in my ear so that I could hear him over the background noise.

"Okay, bye!" I yelled, wincing at the loudness of my own voice.

The call ended. I pulled the phone away from my ear and rubbed at it furiously. I felt practically deaf in one ear after a phone call that lasted less than two minutes.

I set my phone on the nightstand and curled up. I'd hear it if I fell asleep.

~

I woke up around three in the morning and made my way to the bathroom. Jared hadn't called back. More than likely, he'd been riding on the bliss of Rock God-ism. Rubbing my eyes, I yawned as I crawled back between the sheets and felt myself falling back asleep when my phone rang, jolting me from it.

I rolled over, grabbed my phone, and answered with a thick, sleepy voice.

"Hey Riles, sorry it's so late."

He sounded drunk.

"How was the concert?"

Jared's deep laugh rumbled through the phone. "Fuckin' epic, Riles. Only thing missin' was y'all."

"Let me know when you're gonna do a concert close to here, and I'll make Paige come with me."

"We're playing the music fest in Montgomery in a couple of weeks. Think you can make that?"

"We'll be there." I could only hope Paige had the night off.

"Good. I'll have my manager get the tickets to you."

"Listen to you." I laughed. "I'll get with my manager," I said, mimicking him.

The sound of multiple voices hollering burst through the speaker on the phone. I yanked it away from my ear and winced. Jared's voice hollered over the noise so I could hear him. "The guys are back, and I can't hear a damn thing..." They shouted lewd comments at him and the next thing I heard was something sliding over the phone. His muffled voice bickered back at them. Something slammed, and silence filled the connection. I heard Jared groan before he spoke, "Sorry about that. They're really loud, which is why I waited so late to call you."

"I don't blame you. How can you even think straight with all that noise?"

"It's been an adjustment, that's for sure." He sounded a little off, and I couldn't help but wonder why.

"Is everything okay, Jared?"

He blew out a deep breath, and I could imagine him tipping his head back to look at the sky. "Yeah, I'm fine. Life on the road's been awesome. I've met some pretty epic people. People I never thought I'd meet. I'm doing what I love, so really, how can I complain?"

I would have believed him up until he let the sarcastic laugh I knew all too well slip out of him.

"Why do I feel like you're just saying that so I'll leave you alone?"

"Why do you always have to pick things apart?" He turned my wary tone back on me.

"Because I know you, Jared. And I know you're not telling me everything. But I also know not to push you. When you're ready to talk, you'll call me. Regardless of what damn time it is."

He laughed at me, and my worries slipped a little. Jared would be okay. Besides, he was like a damn cat—always landing on his feet. If the path he was on didn't go the way he wanted it to, he'd change it. It was just that simple.

"I'm gonna let you go before they follow me out here and start their shit again. I'll call you soon?"

"Why do you make it sound like it's up to me if you call?" I asked.

"Face it, Riley. Nothing about me is normal. Especially my days and nights these days."

"You're the most un-normal guy I know, Jared. Call me whenever you can."

"Night, Riles."

"Night, Jared."

When the call ended, I stared at the phone as if it had the answers to all the questions swirling around in my head. Jared was not happy. I could tell just by the tone of his voice. But he also wasn't talking about it, and I couldn't figure out what could bother him so much that he repressed his hotheaded nature and held back on saying anything. He'd crack, eventually.

I put my phone on the nightstand and pulled the covers up to my chin.

~

Sometime after four, I'd fallen into a fitful sleep. My dreams wreaked havoc on me, as they jumped all over the place. Josh, Aiden, Mark, Eli, Jared, and Ace all made appearances in blips that made no sense. It was as if my subconscious tried to gather them all up from where they were and put them in one place. My head. None of it made any sense. A room full of cots with no back wall, only the jungle, and somewhere in all of that, a rock concert that Mark took pictures of and Josh wrote a midterm paper on. Nonsense. Total and complete nonsense.

When my alarm clock went off, I slammed my hand down on top of it, silencing its aggravating noise. I needed a nap to recover from my fitful night of sleep. Unfortunately, Dr. Anderson's cell phone went off, killing any chance at going back to bed.

I rubbed at my eyes as I took a call from Old Man Willis. He needed my help with a few things. I grumbled as I dressed for the day, wondering what he needed. Trying to get an answer out of Old Man Willis was like pulling teeth on a bird. I'd hung up with him, promising I'd stop in as soon as I finished at the office. Shelby's owner was scheduled to pick her up, leaving me with one less critter to take care of. Rodney was showing signs of improvement. All he needed was Dr. Anderson's approval to head home. With any luck, that would only be a few more days.

The cell phone on my hip rang, and I answered.

"Hey, Riley. How's everything going?" Dr. Anderson's happy voice met my ears.

"Hey, Dr. Anderson. Everything's great here. How's your mom?"

"A little better, not much though. My sister will be here tomorrow, so that I can get back to work. I just wanted to let you know that I'd be home in a couple of days."

"Sounds good," I said as I pulled my truck in and parked it at the office.

Before we hung up, he asked about Rodney, Shelby, and the baby raccoon. I chewed my fingernails as I told him about Sammy and her kittens. He assured me that he'd take care of fixing them once the kittens were old enough and thanked me for not turning Seth away.

With Dr. Anderson returning, it would get back to being a little busier at the vet clinic. My days would blend themselves one into another until it was time for Jared's concert and Ace's graduation.

Since it was Saturday, Seth would be spending most of his day with me. I liked Seth; he was a good kid and a hard worker. He met me at the door of the clinic, and we walked in together.

"Mornin' Riley," he said with a grin that stretched from ear to ear.

"Good morning, Seth. So you're hangin' out with me today?"

"Yep, Momma says I've got all my chores done, and I don't have to be home 'till dinner."

"Good. You can ride over to Old Man Willis' place and help me."

He dipped his head. "I'm gonna go get Shelby ready for when she gets picked up."

"Thanks, Seth."

I walked over to Becky's desk and found Shelby's file. Everything was in order; I just needed her owner's signature and payment. My heart stuttered and then tried to stop when I realized who would be picking Shelby up. Samantha Sloan. Shit.

The bell over the door jingled. I braced myself and turned, ready for Samantha's claws to come out, but it wasn't her.

"Mrs. Sloan?"

Samantha's mom, Marcy, had come in to pick Shelby up.

"Hello, Riley. How are you?" She leaned in to look at me, as if trying to find some sort of scar or marking from the fight her daughter and I had been in.

"I'm fine, ma'am." I turned and grabbed Shelby's folder, pulling the bill out for her to sign. "If you'll just look this over and then sign it, I'll go make sure Shelby's ready to go."

The large purse she carried hit the counter with a thud, and she picked up the bill to look at it. I saw her eyes widen and chose that moment to slip into the other room. "Hey Seth? Is Shelby ready?"

Seth came out of the back with Shelby on her leash. Her tongue hung out, and her tail wagged furiously. Without the cone on, Shelby was a happy dog. "I'll take that as a yes."

When I returned to the counter, Mrs. Sloan had semi-recovered from seeing the bill. In her hand, she held a credit card. When I walked over, she winked at me. "Samantha thought that by sending me here to pick up her dog that I'd pay the bill."

I took the card from her hand and forced myself to keep a straight face. She'd handed me Samantha's credit card.

"Her dog, her responsibility. Parents really try, Riley, to make their children into the best adults they can. Sometimes, they get lucky and sometimes, they fail." She almost sounded disappointed. I kept my mouth shut. Saying anything back would backfire on me, of that I was sure.

I ran the card and waited for the receipt to print. Marcy Sloan was a genuinely nice person, with a friendly smile and a heart of gold. It made me wonder how such a nice person could have such a troll of a daughter and an asshole for a husband.

I tore the receipt from the credit card machine and slid it along the counter. Before I could pull my hand away, Marcy put her hand on mine. "I'm sorry she's been such a pain in the ass for you. Truly." Her hand squeezed mine and when she let go, I handed her a pen. With a flourish, she signed Samantha's name, winked at me, and then turned to Seth to take Shelby's leash. "Thank you, young man."

"You're welcome, ma'am. Bye, Shelby." Seth reached down

and scratched her ears. She took the opportunity to lick his face. "I'll miss you too, girl."

Marcy turned to me with a smile. "Maybe it's just having someone special in our lives that makes us better people." She darted a look from me to Seth and then back to me before she said goodbye and left.

I palmed my keys. "Is everyone all set in the back?"

"Yep, I took Rodney out and fed the raccoon. Sammy's kittens' eyes are opening!"

"Oh yeah? Guess that means we're gonna have to find a bigger area for Momma and her babies soon."

Seth followed me out to the truck as we discussed the best place to move the family of seven. When we got to Old Man Willis' place, we'd settled on cleaning out a small storage closet for Sammy and her kittens.

CHAPTER 15

Old man Willis met us in his front yard when we pulled up. He took one look at Seth, and I could almost see the gears turning in his mind. "Well, who do we have here?"

Seth walked over, shook Old Man Willis' hand, and introduced himself.

Old Man Willis tilted his hat back, scratched his chin, and looked across the yard at his barn. The old man was up to something, I could feel it.

"Well, young man, seems to me you were meant to come here with Riley."

Seth's eyes squinted as he looked up at Old Man Willis. "I was?"

Old Man Willis' hands landed on his hips, as he looked me up and down. "Riley here, she's gonna be headed off to school soon and well, she's gettin' a little 'long in the tooth'."

Rolling my eyes, I snorted and looked at Seth. "*He's* callin' *me* old…"

Old Man Willis' brought one hand off his hip and waved it out in front of him. He wore a smug look on his face, as he shot me a grin. "Now hold on there. What I mean is, I'm gettin' up there in age and, with you movin' on and all, I sure could use some help around this place. Seth here looks like a strong enough boy to help me do what needs to be done."

Old Man Willis' wife had died years ago, leaving him on his own. He never remarried and he'd never had any kids. What he did have was a huge piece of property to maintain, plus his livestock, and no family to help. Growing up, he'd gathered a few of us and put us to work with the same offer he extended to Seth. "Now mind ya, we gotta talk to your parents, but how would you like to come out here and give me a hand? I'd pay ya fair wages and all if you're interested, and your parents say it's all right."

Seth beamed at me.

"Well, come on, we ain't got all day to stand around," Old Man Willis said as he walked away from us and headed towards the barn.

Seth jogged ahead of me to stay in step with Old Man Willis. I could hear them chatting back and forth, as Seth questioned him about his farm. They disappeared inside the building when my phone rang.

I pulled the phone from my hip and went to answer it, realizing it wasn't Dr. Anderson's phone. It was mine.

Paige's name lit up my screen, confusing me. It was odd, her calling me at this time of day.

"Hey, Paige. What's up?"

"What time will you be home?" I could hear the strain in her voice.

"Are you okay?"

She snorted. "No, but I don't want to get into it right now. Call me when you're home, and I'll come over."

"Okay. I'll call you as soon as I'm headed that way."

When I hung up, I shoved the phone in my pocket and walked inside the shaded interior of the barn. Old Man

Willis leaned on the rails of a stall he'd used for storage. Inside it, Seth sorted through the junk, piling it up in a wheelbarrow so it could be hauled out.

"Finally getting rid of some junk, Willis?" I asked, walking into the stall to help Seth.

"Junk? That there is all good stuff. I just need this here space for that hardheaded calf that got tangled up a while back. Dang fool thing won't stay outta the fences."

"So you're gonna put him in here to teach him a lesson?" I looked over at Seth and winked.

He chuckled as he tipped his hat back. "Somethin' like that."

Seth and I loaded the wheelbarrow until it couldn't hold anymore. Old Man Willis pointed out where he wanted it dumped. I looked around the stall, taking note that most of the garbage had been cleared out, but there were still a few heavier pieces that needed moved. I waited for Seth to come back, so he could help me.

The heat of the day made the interior of the barn feel like a sauna, or maybe it was all the moving around I'd done. Beads of sweat slipped down over my face and ran into my eyes, making them sting. I wiped my face off on the sleeve of my shirt and leaned against the rails as I waited for Seth to come back.

"How's all them young fellars of yours doin'?" Old Man Willis asked.

"They're doing good. I don't get to talk to them too often though." I couldn't escape missing them. Even when I found myself stall deep in a pile of junk.

"How's Jake? Still at boot camp?"

My heart squeezed inside my chest. If it weren't for him being at boot camp, he'd be here with me, helping me move all of Old Man Willis' accumulated junk.

"Yeah, he'll be graduating in a couple of weeks," I

answered just as Seth came back in with the empty wheelbarrow.

I waved Seth over and together, we lifted up an old plow that at one time was used to plow the fields with a horse. Talk about horsepower. A laugh slipped out, ending on a squeal as a rat shot out from the back of the stall and ran between my feet.

"I was afraid of that," Old Man Willis said as he looked across the barn to where the rat had made its escape. "Guess I'm gonna need me some mousers soon." He wiped his face with a handkerchief on a sigh.

"I think I know just where you can get some of those. You'll just have to wait a few weeks for them to get big enough," I said, giving Seth a smirk.

"Yeah, they'll be the best mousers you've ever had!" Seth chimed in.

Old Man Willis squinted his eyes as he looked at Seth. "Huh, the best you say?"

"Best in 'Bama," Seth answered with a grin that all but swallowed his face.

"Well, than that settles that, I'd say."

Seth nodded along as we carried the old plow out and set it in front of the barn. I looked up in time to catch Old Man Willis' smile. He winked at me with a shrug.

I mouthed the word 'softie' at him, and he wagged his finger at me. For an old man who looked as mean as a rattlesnake and as tough as leather, he was one of the most gentle-hearted people around these parts. Seth would love working for him.

Two tires, one plow, and several crates later, the stall was clean and ready for use. Old Man Willis had snuck off to the house, but I knew he'd be back before we left.

I rubbed my filthy hands down the front of my jeans. "I need a shower and about a gallon of water."

I looked over at the sink to the back of the barn. At one point, it worked, but something had happened to the waterline coming into the sink, putting it out of commission.

Seth hiked his shirt up and wiped his face. There wasn't a spot on that kid that was clean. "Ready to head out?"

Seth closed the stall and rolled the wheelbarrow back over to where he'd gotten it from, and we left the barn. The breeze had picked up, and the clouds darkened above us.

When I got to the truck, Old Man Willis came out of his house, carrying two bottles of water. When he got to us, he handed over the waters and went to slip me some money like he'd always done. I shook my head no at him and tilted it in Seth's direction. Old Man Willis never missed a beat. He reached out to shake Seth's hand. "For your hard work today."

The look on Seth's face was almost comical when he realized what the old man had done. "Sir, I can't accept this."

Old Man Willis pegged him with a hardened stare. "And why not?"

Seth's eyes were cast downward, looking anywhere but up at the man standing in front of him. His shoulder hitched with a shrug, but he didn't answer.

"Well, the way I see it, is if you put in a hard day's work, you deserve a hard day's pay." Old Man Willis put his hand on Seth's shoulder and leaned down so he would look at him. "You earned it. Now put it in your pocket and save it."

Old Man Willis stepped back from Seth and turned his attention on me. "Talk with his momma, would ya? I could use a good worker 'round here."

"Will do," I said, opening the passenger side door for Seth. "Let's get you home before your mom wonders where you're at."

Seth walked past Old Man Willis and stopped. He lifted

his head and turned with his hand outstretched. "Thank you, sir."

Old Man Willis laughed. "Don't thank me just yet, son. There's plenty more work here to do. Hard work. By the end of summer, you'll look like you've been to one of them yuppie gyms."

That brought a chuckle out of Seth.

I slid behind the steering wheel, started the truck, and kicked on the AC. When Seth's door slammed closed, I put the truck in gear and with a wave, we left Old Man Willis' place.

Seth was quiet on the ride to his house, and I left him to his thoughts. Things had changed a lot for him since that fateful day he brought Sammy into the office. He'd grown. Day by day, he gained a little more confidence, a little more self-worth. The opportunity that Old Man Willis extended to him was the same sort of offer he'd made to Ace and me when we were younger. It was how I bought the truck I drove.

Seth piped up enough to give me directions to his house. When I pulled up in the yard, a woman stepped out onto the porch. Her hair was pulled up out of her face. From where I sat, I could tell she was tired. Her face split into a grin when she saw Seth.

"You coming?" he asked when he opened his door.

I shook my head to clear it and shut the truck off. Seeing Seth's mom's face transform at the sight of her son made me realized how lucky he was. He had a mom that loved him so much that the sight of him made her face go from worn and tired to happy and proud.

I got out of the truck and climbed the porch steps, introducing myself to her.

For as dirty as Seth was, his mom still put her arm around his shoulder and held him close.

"It's nice to meet you, Riley. I'm Cindy. Seth talks about you all the time."

I watched as a tinge of red touched his cheeks. "It's nice to meet you, Cindy. If you have a few minutes, I'd like to talk to you."

"Sure. Seth, why don't you head on in and get cleaned up while Riley and I talk?"

Seth shoved his hand in his pocket as he stepped forward and pulled out the money Old Man Willis had given him. He gestured for me to take it. "That way she knows where it came from," he explained before he headed inside to get cleaned up.

Cindy gave me an odd look, but she waited for me to explain to her why Seth had money.

"I hope you don't mind, but I took him out to Old Man Willis' today to help me."

Understanding dawned on her face. "Well, that sure explains why he's covered in dirt from head to toe."

"He's a hard worker, your son. Old Man Willis offered him a job on the farm. It wouldn't be all the time, but it would give Seth a chance at earning some money. If it's okay with you, that is."

Cindy worried her lip between her teeth. "He's had a rough time of it lately. Schools been... tough, and he's been trying to find his place, I guess is the best way to put it. But you, Riley, you've made such a difference in him in these last couple of weeks. I can't tell you how much that means to me."

Seth was probably one of the easiest kids to be around. Knowing he'd had trouble with school made me feel an even deeper connection with him. It was like watching myself when I was younger, before the Six. Before I knew what friendship and loyalty meant. I could only hope Seth found the same kind of friends I had.

"Seth's a great kid. I'm glad to have him around," I held

my hand out and placed the folded bills in her hand. "He made some money today. I guess he wanted me to give it to you."

Her hand closed around the bills, and a look of happiness lit up her face. "Well, I guess that means he'll need a bank account."

"Looks that way. I'll give Seth Old Man Willis' number. That way you can speak to him if you'd like," I said, turning to leave.

"Would you like to stay for dinner?" Cindy called out to me as I stepped off the porch.

I appreciated the offer, but I promised Paige I'd call her as soon as I was on my way home. From the sound of her voice earlier, I didn't want to make her wait any longer. "Thank you, but I promised a friend I'd meet up with them. Tell Seth I'll see him tomorrow."

I waved as I fired up my truck and headed home.

My thoughts lingered back to what Seth's mom had said about school being tough for him, and an idea hit me. Josh's little brother was about the same age as Seth. I picked up the phone and called Paige, leaving her a message that I was on my way home, but I had to pop into Josh's for a minute.

I was in luck. Josh's brother was outside when I pulled into my driveway.

"Hey, Aaron!"

He picked up his hand and waved as he walked across the yard. "Hey, Riles."

He favored his brother and if he continued growing like he had, he'd be the same size as Josh, if not taller. "Hey, what do you have planned for tomorrow?"

He kicked at the ground and sighed. "Nothing. This summer blows already."

I couldn't help but laugh at him. He gave me a dirty look

and grumbled, "It's not funny. Everyone is doing something, and I get to sit at home."

Perfect. "How about helping me out at Dr. Anderson's office and maybe even out at Old Man Willis' place when he needs a hand?"

He scrunched his eyes up at me. "I'm not stickin' my hand up no cows butt."

I swatted him. "You sound just like Josh."

His hands went to his hips, and his head tipped back on a laugh.

"So how 'bout it?"

"Sure. I got nuthin' better to do."

"Awesome. I'll be ready to go at seven tomorrow morning. You think you can get your lazy self outta bed that early?"

He rolled his eyes. "I'm up at that time all school year. I think I can handle it."

His hand came up to shade his eyes, and he pointed at Paige's car as it rolled to a stop in my driveway. "You got company. See ya tomorrow."

He took off across his yard before I could reply.

I waited for Paige to get out of her car. When she just sat there, I walked over and opened her door. Her head was resting on the steering wheel, and silent sobs shook her shoulders. "Holy shit, Paige. What's wrong?"

She pushed away from the steering wheel and swiped at her tears. Her anger was evident with each jerky movement. "Everything, Riley. Every. Fuckin'. Thing."

I stepped back, so she could get out of the car. I'd seen Paige upset before. I'd seen her fighting mad, but I'd never seen her like that. Her entire body trembled. Each movement she made seemed measured, as if it were the only thing keeping her from exploding.

"Let's go inside and you can tell me what's got you so upset."

She walked beside me in silence, and I feared when she finally let go, it would be impressive.

Inside the kitchen, she pulled out a chair and sat with her hands clasped on the table. Her knuckles turned white from the pressure she put on them.

"Spill it. What's got you so angry?" I said, sitting down to face her.

"Angry? Oh, I'm so much more than angry right now."

"I can see that. What happened?"

"They're not hiring me. I worked," her words caught on a sob, "so hard. So many hours, just wasted. And they hired some girl who's been on the floor for a week. A fuckin' *week*!"

I had no idea what to say, but I was right there with Paige. The hospital hiring someone brand new over her was complete bullshit.

I shot up from my chair and took off towards the stairs.

"Where the hell are you going?" Paige shouted after me.

My hand wrapped around the wooden baseball bat I kept behind my door. I slapped it against my palm as I came down the stairs and stopped a few feet from her. "Let's go break her legs or fuck up her car. I don't care which one. You pick, and I'll swing."

She was out the door before me and jumped in my truck. I peeled out of my driveway and took off down the road.

We passed by the hospital, and she laughed. "Ice cream, huh?"

"Duh, neither of us is going to jail tonight. We can break her legs tomorrow or something."

Paige laughed at me and rested her head against the seat. "I'd be so lost without you, Riley. Thanks for at least pretending that we'd give her the beat down of her life."

I turned into the parking lot of the local ice cream stand,

Twisters, and shut my truck off. "Maybe you weren't meant to stay there. Maybe this is just a sign that this isn't the right path for you."

She turned on the bench seat and dropped her hands in her lap. "Being a nurse is all that I know, Riley. I'm not letting this stop me. I just have to figure out what's next."

We got out of the truck and placed our orders at the window. As we waited, I thought about how to bring up Mark.

The kid behind the counter handed us our dishes loaded with every topping available, and we sat down at one of the tables.

Paige dove in, and I patted myself on the back for being such a good friend. The thought of the girl who stole Paige's dream out from under her still made me want to take my baseball bat to her, but the reality of it was I just wasn't that type of person, and Paige knew it.

I licked my spoon clean and groaned as I clutched at my stomach. "I can't eat another bite."

Paige scraped the bottom of her plastic dish as if it would reveal more. "Dang, Paige. Where do you put it all?"

She jabbed at the dish with a frown. "I'm angry, and food helps."

"It's a good thing you don't get angry very often. I'd have to tote you around in a wheelbarrow from all the ice cream you'd consume."

She dropped the bowl and spoon on the table. "What the hell am I supposed to do, Riley?"

I grabbed both our bowls, got up from the table, and dumped them in the garbage. "Well, for starters, you need to decide if staying here in Opp is what you want."

She pushed herself from the table, and we walked back to my truck. "I feel like this place is sucking out my soul."

It was the answer I'd been waiting for. "So get out of here.

Maybe you should take Mark up on his offer." I said it in an easygoing tone. One she couldn't get mad at me for.

She didn't answer me until we'd pulled out of the parking lot of Twisters. "You don't think that makes me look weak? Like I can't do it on my own, and I need him?"

Her questions were valid. I could understand what she meant, because Paige always counted on herself for things. No one ever had to hold her hand or help her. She preferred it that way.

"Weak? No, not in the least bit. If anything, it makes you smart. Use the opportunity to do something better for you. Having Mark around would just be a bonus."

She turned her head and looked out the window. "That's what scares me the most. I've never felt so drawn to a person before."

I rolled my window down, letting the warm air rush through the cab of the truck. "Sometimes the things that scare us most are the things that make us stronger."

That brought a jittery laugh from her. "Yeah, we'll see."

At least she wasn't ready to fly apart anymore. And if she weren't working day in and day out at the hospital, she'd be free to go with me to Jared's concert. "I guess that means you'll be free next week?"

She huffed at me. "I guess so."

I turned the radio on, turning the volume low enough to talk. "Good, because you and I are going to a concert next week in Montgomery."

"What concert?" she asked, rolling her head along the back of the seat to look at me.

I shot her a grin. "Jared's band is playing at the Montgomery Music Fest, and we're going." I wouldn't take no for an answer.

"Great. I'll break out the hooker heels and goth makeup."

Her tone was snarky, but I knew deep down, she wanted to go see Jared play just as much as I did.

∼

When we got back to my house, Paige walked over to her car. "I'm gonna head home and get some sleep."

I kept my thoughts to myself. The chances of Paige going home and sleeping were about the same chances of me sprouting wings to fly. I could almost guarantee she'd be getting in touch with Mark. Paige was a driven person. She wanted decisions made and then carried out. Cut and dry. Over and done. If anything could be said about Paige, it was that she wasn't a wishy-washy person.

I let myself into the house, locked the door behind me, and trudged up the stairs. I'd eaten way too much ice cream, and my stomach protested against me for it.

My thoughts flipped back over the conversation I'd had with Paige, and it hit me. If Paige decided to move to New York with Mark, I'd be the only one that stayed in Opp. Did that mean I was the small-town girl trapped in the small-town life? After boot camp, would Ace still feel the same about me? About us? Surely, his experiences away from home would change how he looked at things. And what if he missed out on a chance to see the world, like Aiden? Was I that selfish to hold him back?

Sitting down on the edge of my bed, I toed my boots off. I hadn't even taken a shower. My clothes were filthy and stained with sweat. I grabbed the bottom of my shirt, tugged it over my head, and tossed it in my hamper. Shucking my jeans, I grabbed a change of clothes and headed for the shower.

∼

I was so excited to get out of the rut I'd found myself in. When Dr. Anderson made it back, I gladly handed over his phone and keys. It didn't take long before his phone rang off the hook, and it was back to business as usual for him. Most days, I tagged along, and other days, I stopped out at Old Man Willis' house to check in on how things were going.

More often than not, Aaron and Seth could be found working on something together. Old Man Willis' farm hadn't looked that good in years. It was nice to see a younger generation picking up the reins and carrying on where Ace and I left off.

I missed Ace. I missed the way life was before adulthood had swept us all in different directions.

Each day rolled into the next until Jared's concert.

My bags had been packed for three days, and I booked a hotel room close to where the music fest would take place. We'd be able to walk to the concert and not have to fight with traffic. In only a handful of hours, I'd get to see Jared.

"We're taking my car." Paige's voice snapped me out of my wayward thoughts.

"Of course we're taking your car. My truck probably wouldn't make it," I said, lifting up my duffel bag when Paige popped her trunk open.

CHAPTER 16

"*H*oly shit can you believe the people here?" Paige's mouth hung open, as she took in the crowd of people around us.

I grabbed her by the hand and pulled her along behind me, as I searched for the best spot to watch the concert. I hadn't heard anything from Jared since we'd talked the last time, and he'd told me that he'd be there. It wasn't for lack of trying. I'd called him the last three days, but he never picked up.

Paige tugged against the tight hold I had on her. "Where are you going? You've led us in so many circles that even the drunk people think we're crazy!"

I came to an abrupt stop, and Paige bounced off me. "I'm looking for a spot that Jared will be able to see us when he comes on stage!"

"Seriously, Riles," she groaned as she leaned in closer to me, so that I could hear her without her having to shout. "Just pick a spot! It's a sea of damn people. There's no way he'd pick us out of this crowd."

I sighed. She was right.

"Oh, look! Over there seems to have enough room, and they don't look completely wasted yet. Perfect." Paige latched onto my wrist and pulled me through a gap in the crowd until we reached a spot where we could stand side by side without the fear of being crushed.

In moving us, she'd put us left of center stage. The band playing was one I hadn't heard before, but the crowd seemed to love them. Even Paige nodded her head along to the beat.

The band closed their set with a newly released song that made the crowd go insane, shifting closer to the stage, carrying Paige and me closer as they moved in behind us. This massive guy slopped his drink down Paige's back because of the surge of people shifting around us.

"Hey!" Paige's arm flew back as she gut-checked the guy behind her.

"Oh shit, I'm so sorry!" He actually looked embarrassed.

Paige bared her teeth at him, and he chuckled. "I'll make it up to you, I swear! Next band—my shoulders. Sound good?"

Paige laughed in his face. "Are you for real? Why would I want my crotch up close and personal with the back of your neck?" He blushed all the way to the tips of his crew cut. The red was so deep on his pale skin that it looked like a sunburn. He rubbed his hand against the back of his neck and looked down at the ground.

I jabbed Paige with my elbow.

"What?" she snapped at me.

"Jeez, he was just trying to be nice. At least it was just soda and you're not covered in beer," I said as I flicked a gaze over at him. "Think about it. If he lifted you up, you could get Jared's attention."

She looked at me in total disbelief. "My entire back is soaked! You want Jared's attention, then you get up on his shoulders."

She turned her back on me, facing forward, ignoring both me and the blushing man behind her.

"I'm really sorry," he said, flicking his eyes at Paige's ramrod-straight back.

"No harm done. She's just not good with crowds. They make her testy," I said, giving him a reassuring smile.

He tilted his head and squinted. "If she doesn't like this type of crowd, why did she come? I mean, wow... that sounded harsh. What I meant is…"

I held my hand up and waved off the explanation. "A good friend of ours is playing next. She came with me, so that I wouldn't be alone."

"No shit, you know one of the guys from Destroying Doubt?"

I couldn't hold back the huge grin spreading across my face. "Yeah, I went to school with Jared. He's one of my best friends."

He leaned down and shouted to be heard over the screaming when Jared's band was introduced. "Does he know you're here?"

"Yeah, but there's no way he'd be able to find us in this," I said, gesturing to the press of bodies around us.

"He will if you stand on my shoulders! It'll put you higher up than anyone here." He was a tall man and standing on his shoulders would be a long fall. I wasn't coordinated enough to do that.

"Thanks, but I think I'll pass."

He flexed his arm, patting it with a smirk on his face. "Do you honestly think these would drop you?"

I swallowed the constricted feeling in my throat.

"Trust me…" He leaned in, waiting for me to tell him my name.

I leaned back, and he laughed. "I'm Oliver, and you're a

smart girl. I didn't mean to scare you. The offer's there if you want. Just let me know."

Before he could turn away from me, I held my hand out. "Riley."

He enveloped my hand in his. "Nice to meet you, Riley."

The crowd around us exploded, and Paige turned to look back at me. When she saw my hand in Oliver's, she shot me a dirty look and pointed at the stage.

Jared and his bandmates were taking up their places. He scanned the crowd as the bass guitarist leaned over and spoke in his ear.

Oliver leaned towards me. "Looks like he's looking for someone."

Before I could say anything back, Oliver lifted me up and my feet were planted on his shoulders. His hands linked with mine to keep me balanced. When Jared saw me, he waved and walked over to the edge of the stage. Leaning down, he spoke to a security guard. They both looked my way as he pointed me out. Jared watched the security guard push his way through the crowd for a second, and then he took his place at the middle of the stage.

Oliver jiggled my arm to get my attention. "Ready to get down?"

I peered down at him and felt myself tilting to the left, feeling myself falling. Oliver let go of my hands and grabbed my thighs, as he moved his feet apart and braced himself. "Just trust me, okay?"

At least that was what I thought he said as he held on and balanced me in front of him. I didn't even have time to blink before my back slammed into his chest and his hands held the back of my thighs, as if I were sitting on a chair. He lowered me further and let go of one of my legs and then the other as he steadied me until I could stand.

"See? I told you to trust me. I've never dropped a girl yet."

My hand fisted the front of his shirt, as my knees wobbled. "What are you, a damn gymnast?"

That brought a deep chuckle from him. "Nah. Special Ops."

"Military?"

"Something like that." His head jerked to someone standing behind me. "I think the security guy wants to talk to you."

I looked over my shoulder and saw the same guy Jared had talked to earlier, pushing his way through the crowd to get to me.

"Excuse me, Miss, but Jared has asked for you to meet him after the show. Just head up to the stage when it's over, and I'll take you back to where the band is."

I nodded at the Mr. Clean look-alike and he turned away, pushing back through the crowd.

The strum of an electric guitar belted out of the speakers, as Jared spoke to the crowd.

All the noise rushed into my ears, and time sort of stalled out for me. Jared was on stage like he'd always talked about. He stood center stage as people screamed around him. We'd all joked about it over the years, giving him a hard time about his need to be a celebrity, and all I could do was stare in awe at what he'd become.

The band kicked off one of their original songs, before Jared had joined, and rocked the crowd. After that, they played a few more cover songs from other bands. Songs I'd never heard before, but I screamed along with the crowd anyway.

By the time the band was done, Jared was covered in sweat. His chest heaved as he gripped the microphone. He brought his thumb and forefinger up in the symbol of the Six and winked at me. The crowed roared for more, surging forward until bodies were pressed so tight against me, I felt like I couldn't breathe. Jared turned to the drummer, and they closed their set out with a song that made everyone lose their damn minds.

Someone shoved in between Paige and me. She cried out, flailing her arm in my direction. An elbow caught me in the chin, and I slammed into a girl behind me. She shoved me forward, and I couldn't catch myself as I fell. I knew if I couldn't get up, I'd be crushed by the crowd. My hand splayed against the trampled grass as I caught myself from hitting the ground face first. The crowd kept surging forward. I was forced to drop to the ground and roll to get away from the shoes coming at me. I came to a sudden stop when I rolled into the feet of the people in front of me. My arm went around my head to protect myself as best as I could as I curled my legs up to my stomach, making myself as small as possible. Getting to my knees would be a fight. Standing was impossible.

I peeked out from between my arms, looking for a small spot I could try to pop up in, when I saw Oliver picking people up and moving them. His massive shoulders cut a path directly in front of me, clearing enough room for Paige to get to me.

Paige put her arm around me and helped me up, as Oliver shoved people out of the way, making enough room for us to get out of the crowd.

Security met us halfway and stepped in beside Paige and me until we made it out of the thickest part of the crowd. They ushered us back behind the fenced-in area where the bands had parked their tour buses. Behind the stage was so much quieter than being in front. I felt my anxiety drop, and I pulled Paige close. "Are you okay?"

When she looked at me, I saw the panic she'd kept contained. "That is the craziest thing you've ever put me through. Never again, Riley. Do you hear me? Never.

Again." She was angry, but she hugged me until my ribs protested.

I pulled against her tight hold. "Ouch, Paige. You're crushing my lungs."

She loosened her arms and looped her arm through mine. "I thought you'd been trampled. Thank God that guy helped us." She pointed over at Oliver, who stood talking to a security guard. It was then I noticed a small wire running up behind Oliver's ear to a fitted earpiece. He looked over at me. I pointed at my ear and scowled at him. He shrugged as he finished his conversation with the security guard, and then walked over to where Paige and I waited.

"I thought you were just here for the concert," I said, leaning over to get a better look at the black earpiece he wore.

He looked past me as he scanned the area. "I am, but as crowd control."

Paige squared her shoulders and tossed her hair back. "Well, I'm glad he was there. If not, they'd be hauling your corpse out at the end of the night. What the hell is wrong with these people anyway?"

Oliver chuckled. "I ask myself the same question at every concert." His eyes squinted as he looked around Paige. "Looks like Jared is coming to get you. If you ladies will excuse me, I need to get back out there."

I put my hand on his arm to stop him. "Wait!" He partially turned so that he could look over his shoulder at me. "Thank you, Oliver. I really appreciate your help."

He dipped his head. "Anytime, although maybe not again today. Okay?"

My legs trembled at the thought. "Maybe not ever."

His laugh was deep as he shook his head. "Maybe you should just stick to the radio," he said as he walked away.

I turned back in Jared's direction as he picked me up and

spun me around. "How awesome was that?" he shouted with his face lit up like a kid on Christmas morning. He hooted and spun me until I wanted to throw up.

"Put her down, Jared. Jesus, between you and the crowd that almost crushed her, she's not gonna make it through today," Paige said as she grabbed Jared's arm and forced him to stop spinning me in circles.

When he set me down on my feet, I leaned my head on his shoulder to keep from falling over.

Jared put his arm around me. "The crowd almost crushed her?"

Paige pointed in the vicinity of the stage. Another band had started up and the sea of people was going crazy. "It's complete madness out there."

I picked my head up, and Jared smiled at me. "You guys were really good. Is it like that at every concert?"

"Jared!" His name was screamed loud enough to be heard over the music pumping out of the stacked speakers. Before I had a chance to turn around to see who the voice belonged to, I was shoved into Paige. She caught me, and we stood, slack-jawed, as a girl wrapped her entire body around Jared, yanking his head to hers and kissing him like she planned on sucking his tongue out through his mouth. Jared's arms flailed, and he staggered. Her grip on him was so firm that he had to grab her arms and push her back, which did nothing about the leg lock she had on him.

Paige busted out with a laugh that irritated me. She slapped her leg and shot me a look that said *'can you believe that shit?'*

I crossed my arms and turned away, not wanting to make a scene. Jared had a psycho girl on his hands, and he needed to deal with her. I'd had enough of his crazy fans.

Out of the corner of my eye, I could see him struggling.

"Damn it, can you *please* stop trying to stick your tongue down my throat?"

The girl giggled as she rubbed herself against him. "You and me. Your bus, your band. I don't care, just…"

I snapped and stormed over to stand behind Jared, where she had no choice but to look at me. "Oh my god! Seriously? Could you be more of whore?"

Jared's hands were planted against her shoulders, as he locked his arms out straight to push her off him. "Can one of you wave down security before she gets pregnant by osmosis?"

Paige stopped laughing and turned in a full circle, looking for help. "Be right back!" she shouted over her shoulder as she took off.

The girl cackled and threw herself backwards, giving Jared no choice but to grab her arms before she slammed her head into the ground.

When I snorted at his heroics, he made the mistake of turning his head to look at me. The female octopus took advantage of the distraction I'd caused and wrapped her arms around the back of his neck.

Jared didn't even try to keep her from falling. He kept his head turned to face me, putting his hand up in front of his face so she couldn't get to his mouth. No matter how hard she tugged on his face, she couldn't get him to turn it back towards her.

"Can you get the fuck off me? I'm not interested." I could see the anger dancing in his eyes. His patience was a fine thread away from snapping.

My eyes darted around the fenced-off area. There were people milling about, but no one seemed concerned about the situation Jared was in. They grinned and looked away, making no offer to assist him. Paige only had another minute to come through with help, or I'd pull that bitch's hair out strand by strand and then feed it to her.

I scanned the area again and saw Paige jogging towards us. She waved at me when I noticed her. Behind her was a golf cart. When I waved back at her, the golf cart picked up speed and swerved around her, sliding to a stop beside us. The lone security guard appraised the situation and pulled out a handheld radio.

The girl attached to Jared laughed when the security guard tried to pull her off him. At that point, Jared was tired from the concert and then having to hold off the girl who'd become his own personal ornament. I could see it in his eyes when he all but silently begged me to help him.

The security guard took a step back to answer his radio, and I made my move. I gave Jared a slight tip of my head and he craned his neck as far as he could to the side. Pulling my arm back, my fist connected with her jaw, and she went limp in Jared's arms. He lowered her, none to carefully, to the ground and walked backwards until he bumped into me.

The security guard looked down at the unconscious girl and up at me. "You shouldn't have done that."

"I better not go to jail for this, Jared," I whispered against his shoulder.

I felt his body sag a little. "What was she supposed to do? That girl has been hanging off my damn neck for the past ten minutes. No one else stepped in, and even you couldn't pry her off."

The security guard's hands settled on his hips, as he looked down at the girl again. When he looked back up, he seemed confused. "You mean to tell me she was assaulting you?"

Paige stepped in front of Jared. "She ran at him, knocked over Riley, and launched herself at him. He asked her several times to let him go, and she ignored him." When she was done speaking, she crossed her arms and planted her feet. When the security guard made no move towards Jared and me, Paige looked over her shoulder. "Are you all right, Jared?"

I felt him straighten up. "Yeah, I'm good, but she needs to go." He nodded his head slightly at the girl still sprawled on the ground.

The security guard rolled the girl over and looped what looked like zip-ties over her wrists. When he was done, a second golf cart rolled to a stop and Oliver darted over to where we stood. "Can't even leave you on your own for an hour, Riley." He shook his head as a smile stretched across his face.

I shrugged my shoulder and looked away.

"A friend of yours?" Jared's eyebrow rose up and disappeared under his hair.

When Paige heard him, she spun around and shoved her finger into his chest. "He saved her from your crazy ass fans when they shoved her to the ground and almost made her a part of it."

Jared sucked in a sharp breath. "I thought you were kidding... just being dramatic... Shit, Riles. I'm sorry." His chin hit his chest, and Paige snatched her hand away.

Oliver and the other security guard put the unconscious girl in the security guard's golf cart, and he drove away. Oliver watched him leave and then walked over to where we stood.

"So you have a pretty good right hook. Tom, the security guard, was impressed anyway."

I chewed my lip, cowering behind Jared, as I waited for him to ask me to put my hands behind my back.

When I looked up, he winked at me. "Might I suggest you take that bodyguard idea seriously, Mr. Jackson? This concert is milder than most, but you and your friends could have been seriously injured today. Thankfully, you only had to face a horny groupie. Next time, you might not get so lucky."

Jared face went into a sneer. "Shut up, Oliver. My parents had no right hiring you. I don't need your help. Just go."

Paige's mouth dropped open, and she glared at Jared when Oliver shook his head and walked away. "Are you serious? All of that could have been eliminated if you'd stop being so damn stubborn!"

"I don't need a shadow babysitting my every move!" Jared roared back at her.

"No, you fucking idiot. You're right. You don't need a babysitter. You need a fucking savior!" Her arms fell beside her into clenched fists. "Riley, I'm done here. Can we go?"

Before I could step in and calm the situation down, Paige stormed off. I took off after her. When I caught up with her, I was almost at a jog to keep pace. "Paige, wait!"

She never broke stride. "No, Riley. I won't wait. And you shouldn't either. This is no place for us. We need to go home."

"But, we just got here… We haven't even had a chance to see Jared."

"You can stay as long as you like today. I'm heading back to the hotel. We're leaving tomorrow, even if I have to knock you out and stuff you in my car."

I let her go. She was beyond hearing anything I had to say.

Jared jogged up to me. "Is she okay?"

My eyes filled with tears. I'd just wanted today to be a good day. I hadn't seen Jared in weeks. Hadn't seen any of the Six in weeks, and I missed them. When he saw the first tear fall, he pulled me into a hug.

"I'm sorry, Riley. Maybe being here wasn't a smart idea. You should go back to the hotel with Paige."

I pulled back from him, wiping the wetness from my

cheeks. "And then what, Jared? Forget I know you? Forget we're friends?"

He grabbed my hands and held them tight. "No, Riles. Never that. I couldn't live with myself if you weren't my friend. I just think that concerts aren't a good idea. We'll see each other in between my concerts. I can fly you and Paige out when I have a few days between gigs. We can hang out in a safe place where you don't get shoved to the ground, and I don't get attacked."

"I'm not ready to say good-bye. I just barely got to say hello," I said, kicking my foot against the grass.

"Hey," he said, lifting my chin, "it's okay. Besides, the bands packing up and heading out in like thirty minutes."

A sigh slipped past my lips. I braced myself to argue with him, as he lifted his hand and waved at someone behind me. "Jared…"

A golf cart rolled up beside us. When I turned, Oliver patted the seat beside him. "Come on; let's go find your friend so she doesn't have to walk back to the hotel alone."

Jared hugged me tight and then ushered me into the golf cart. "I'll call you!" he shouted as he turned and jogged away.

"What the hell?" Jared had handed me off without even looking back.

"Where to?" Oliver asked as he turned the golf cart around.

CHAPTER 17

When we pulled into my driveway the next day, things were tense between Paige and me. She'd been furious over what happened at Jared's concert, and I really didn't blame her, but there was nothing we could do about it. How was Jared to know that would happen? I couldn't stay mad at him for things that were out of his control. Paige, on the other hand, was ready to beat the shit out of him the next time she saw him. I don't know how many times she repeated the fact that I could have died, been trampled to death in the crowd, all because of his need to be some sort of rock-n-roll god. It didn't do any good to fight back with her. She needed time to process it and then get over it. I'd wait it out, and things would be fine. Besides, it was highly unlikely Jared would invite us back to one of his concerts anyway. It would probably be months before I saw him again.

The silver lining in all of it was the fact that Ace's graduation was fast approaching, and I'd get to see him again. Hold him again. My fingers came into contact with the pendant they'd given me. Each one of them had a little piece of my heart. Each one of them was a link to who I was. Each one was living their lives while I stood in a sort of stasis of my own making. I picked up the phone and called Dr. Anderson. I wasn't going to sit around and feel sorry for myself. I had a life too, damn it, and I needed to start living it.

As I pulled up Dr. Anderson's number, my phone rang. The unknown number flashed on my screen, making me curious as to who it could be. There weren't that many people I talked to, and those I did were programmed in my phone. Instead of answering it, I let it go to voice mail and called Dr. Anderson. If it were important, they'd leave me a message.

~

Dr. Anderson put me right to work and, over the next couple of days, I got up with the sun and worked until well after it set. There had been a higher rate of emergencies than normal for the vet's office, and I tagged along with Dr. Anderson to gain as much experience as I could. Once Ace graduated, I planned to go back to school. I just wasn't sure which one yet. His graduation was in just a couple of days, and my stomach danced nervously as the hours passed by. I'd checked in with his mom, and we were all set to leave the day before he graduated. We were staying at a hotel close to Fort Benning.

My phone had rang a couple of times while I'd been armpit deep in a cow while helping Dr. Anderson, and I wasn't able to answer it. By midday, I'd missed four calls from the same unknown number that had called me a few days before. When we got back to the clinic, I scrubbed my hands again with antimicrobial soap and changed my cow shit-stained shirt with a T-shirt Dr. Anderson gave me. When I stepped out of the bathroom, my phone went off again.

"Riley?" Dr. Anderson called to me from the back where he kept all his overnight patients. "I need your help."

I dismissed the phone call and ran towards the sound of his concerned voice.

We were a flurry of activity over the next hour, trying to save the twelve-year-old Australian Shepard that belonged to a little boy named Sam. Nothing we did worked. It was as if the dog was ready. It was his time. We had to let him go with a little peace and a whole lot of tears.

I swiped at my face and bit my lip to keep from sounding like a blubbering baby.

"I wish I could say it gets easier, Riley. But it really doesn't. We just have to comfort ourselves in knowing that we did everything we could. It was just his time. Why don't you head on home and get some rest while I talk to the family? You've worked your ass off these last few days with me. Now I need you to rest. Okay?"

I nodded and backed out of the room. Could I really handle a job where no matter what I did, I could never save them all?

I left out the back door, more like escaped, and drove home, not remembering even getting in my truck, let alone starting it. Letting myself into the house, I made my way to the stairs, and my phone rang. It was that unknown number again, and whoever it was—they were persistent. I slid my finger across the screen and answered.

"Ms. Clifton?" I'd never heard the person on the other end of the line before.

"Yes, this is Riley Clifton." My mind raced as I waited for what he said next.

"This is Dr. Steiner. I'm the head Cardiologist at Houston General. I'm calling because your father was a patient of mine for the last couple of weeks."

I lowered myself to sit on the stairs. My hand gripped the phone, as dread settled into my stomach.

"Miss, are you still there?" The soft-spoken voice he used made me break into a cold sweat.

"Is everything okay with my dad?" I gripped the phone in my hands until I heard the plastic crack.

"I'm very sorry to have to do this over the phone, Ms. Clifton, but it was your dad's last instructions."

"Last instructions?" There had to be some sort of mistake.

"Your father was admitted into Houston General after coming in with the compliant of having chest pains. Upon his admittance, he had a mild heart attack. He underwent surgery to clear the blockage we'd found in an MRI. Unfortunately, his heart became weakened, and we were unable to save him on the operating table."

My hand clamped over my mouth, as my keening cries ripped from my throat. How could my dad have not told me? Why would he keep it from me? I could have been there. I could have...

"Ms. Clifton? Once again, I'm very sorry to have to tell you like this. However, I need to inform you of the rest before we hang up." He never paused, probably knowing he'd shocked me and wrecked me all at the same time. "Your father insisted on a Living Will before he underwent surgery. In his will, it asked us to only contact you in the chance he did not survive the surgery. All of the medical costs have been covered by his insurance provider. If you receive any bills, please contact the insurance company and they can help you sort it out. I know this is a lot to take in. Please understand he only wanted to make this process as easy as possible for you. I just need you to know that before I tell you what his last and final instructions were."

I swallowed the acid crawling up my throat and pushed myself to say something in reply. "I under—I understand."

"Thank you, Ms. Clifton. In his last instructions, he has listed the following. I am to remind you of the locked box in his closet. In it will be all the paperwork you'll need for the house and his life insurance policies. Your father chose to be cremated. His remains have been sent off, and I'm waiting for the cremains to be shipped back here to the hospital, or to you if you prefer."

I bit my cheek until I tasted blood. "Me... I want him sent to me."

"Of course. I'll get the paperwork submitted and have your father's cremains sent to you. Please know that I personally wish you the best. I had the honor of speaking with your father before his surgery. He was a very nice man who loved you very much."

That angered me a little. How dare he tell me how my father felt? How dare he be the one that spent my father's final days with him? It should have been me. Not him. "Don't act like you knew anything about him. Don't tell me how good he was when he couldn't even bother telling me what was going on. He kept himself from me. He kept me from being able to tell him I loved him... from being able to say goodbye!"

I hurled my phone across the room and it hit the wall, flying apart in pieces.

I shot off the stairs. Oh God... Oh God... I shouldn't have done that! Why did I do that? I slammed my hands against my head as I buckled to the floor, rocking my body as I let go and wrapped my arms around my legs. How was I supposed to know when they'd ship what was left of my dad? How would I get back in touch with the doctor? My phone was shattered. Would they be able to retrieve the number he'd called from? I had to get to the store I'd bought my phone from. I needed a new phone. I needed the doctor's number. I needed to get up off the floor and stand up. I just couldn't. My arms wouldn't unlock from my legs, because if they did, and I stood up and grabbed my keys, it meant I had to buy a new phone because I'd smashed my old one. I'd smashed it because the doctor on the other end of the phone had said my dad was dead. My dad couldn't be dead. He was all I had left of my family.

My sobs strangled me. I couldn't breathe past them. It had to be a bad dream. I'd just fallen asleep. I'd wake up, and it would all have just been a nightmare brought on from losing a patient. A beautiful Australian Sheppard that belonged to a little boy named Sam.

~

"Riley!" My shoulder wobbled, and I lifted my head. Mary, Ace's mom, looked down at me. Concern etched the corners of her eye and bracketed her mouth, as she slipped her hand under my chin. "What happened?"

My arms were locked around my legs. My back ached, and my ass was numb all the way to my feet. My eyes darted around as I tried to figure out why I was sitting on the floor. Pieces of my phone were strewn across the tile as if it had exploded. In that moment, it all rushed back at me. My dad was dead.

Ace's mom pulled me into her arms and ran her hands along my hair, as she used her other hand to pull my locked fingers apart. When my arms dropped into her lap, she picked one hand up and rubbed the circulation back into it. "Talk to me, Riley. What's wrong?"

I pushed the explanation out between hitched breaths and what felt like a closed-off windpipe. "...dad. His doctor called... heart attack. Shipping his remains."

I broke, and she held on to me. My arms and legs were useless until the circulation came back. When it did, pinpoints of pain raced along almost the entire length of my body, making breathing in and out send live wires through me, until the blood flowed through my veins properly.

Ace's mom stayed right there with me, moving me to the couch when she knew I could stand up with her assistance. She draped a blanket over me to help with the chill that wracked my body and slid a pillow under my head to give me some sort of comfort. I could see her every so often as she floated in and out of my fixed stare. The worry on her face made me feel even worse. I just didn't have the inner strength to convey to her that I'd be okay. I had to be okay. My dad would be coming home... coming home in a box soon, and I needed to be able to meet him at the door.

I heard her hushed tone as she made phone calls from another room. The sound of her moving around in the kitchen. The doorbell when it rang and she opened it for whoever was on the other side. It wouldn't be my dad yet.

I felt Paige's hand on my shoulder, saw her hovering in front of me. Staring at me, willing me to say something. Anything. I just couldn't. If I did, it would make me force myself back to reality. I wasn't ready for reality; I needed the numbness I'd wrapped around me.

My eyes closed and opened. Each long blink blended one day into the next, blissfully cutting me off from the sorrow and hurt that had taken me in its talons and ripped me open.

Paige and Mary stayed by my side. I heard them talk to pass the time. Ace's graduation had come and gone. Where was he? He'd said he had leave after he graduated, but he hadn't shown up. And I hadn't asked. Was he mad that I didn't make it to his graduation? Was he angry with me because his mom had stayed to watch over my still form, while everyone else around me carried on about their days?

The doorbell rang, and I knew who it was before Paige or Mary could announce them. I shoved the blankets off me and stood up on shaky legs. They fell in behind me, ready to catch me should I lose my balance. I'd be damned if I couldn't make it to the door to greet my dad.

I turned the doorknob and jerked the door open, not looking at the man standing there, only at the box he held in his hands with a clipboard resting on top of it. "If I could get you to sign here, ma'am?" He went to set the box down, and I grabbed his arm.

He stopped and shifted uncomfortably.

Paige reached past me, grabbed the clipboard, and handed it, and the pen, to me. I scribbled my name and she took it back, so that I could take the box from the stranger's hands. It was heavy as I wrapped my arm around it and carried it to the couch. When I sat down, I placed the box beside me and put my hand over the top of it. My dad was finally home where he belonged.

Paige slid a wooden TV table in front of me and set a glass of orange juice down on it. "I'll bring you some soup."

I looked up at her when she stepped back. I wasn't sick. I didn't need orange juice or soup. I needed my dad. Not a box of what remained of him.

"Please, Riley. Drink the juice," Mary said as she handed Paige some crackers and walked back to the kitchen.

I picked the glass up. It was the least I could do for all she'd done for me.

Sweetness exploded on my taste buds, and my mouth watered from the small sip I'd taken.

Paige sat down across from me in the recliner my dad

always sat in when he watched the news. I put the glass back down and pressed my hands together in my lap.

"I talked to the guys," Paige said. I darted a look at her, and she gave me a pained smile. "They said they'd come home if you want them too."

My shoulder hitched up in an attempt at a shrug.

"Don't do that, Riley." Paige's voice came out as a hiss, and I shrank back against the couch. "No, don't you dare sink back into whatever had a hold of you until the doorbell rang. Do you hear me? I won't let you do this to yourself! Cry, yell, throw things, but damn it, don't you dare slip off to some place I can't reach you."

Paige had moved the table from in front of me and fell to her knees, grabbing my hands. She squeezed our hands together and pulled me towards her. Warmth crept into my fingertips as she anchored me in the present. Anchored me to her. A low, keening wail worked its way through me, and I fell against her.

I have no idea how long I cried. It seemed like the tears were endless until they were just gone.

My body shuddered in spasms that made my chest heave as I caught my breath. When Paige got up, I saw a pained look on her face as she stood and stretched her legs and back.

"How about some soup?" she asked me.

I rubbed my thumb under my swollen eyes to wipe what was left of my tears away. Blowing out a ragged breath, I straightened my shoulders. "Sure."

Paige propped pillows behind me, sliding the wooden TV table in front of me as Mary set down a bowl with steam rising from it.

"It's my homemade chicken soup," she said as she stretched out her hand and tucked a wayward strand of hair behind my ear. "Eat some of that and then you can go take a shower and change into more comfortable clothes."

I did as she asked and put a spoonful of broth in my mouth, swallowing and repeating until the spoon scraped against the bottom of the empty bowl. I'd been hungrier than I thought.

Paige helped me up the stairs and led me into the bathroom. She turned the shower on and stepped back. "I'm gonna get you some clean clothes. Leave the door unlocked. Okay?"

"I'm fine, Paige."

She scowled at me. "Don't push it with me right now, Riley. I'm on two hours of sleep, and I'm about to break myself. Just get in the damn shower, and I'll be back with your clothes."

I grumbled as I pulled my T-shirt off and tossed it at her. "I hope your bedside manner was better with your patients."

Tears fell from her eyes, and she put her hand to her mouth to muffle her sob. "There you are. I thought I'd never reach you. You scared the hell out of me, Riley."

I looked down and shuffled my feet against the worn linoleum. "I'm sorry."

"You shouldn't be sorry. I'm just glad you found your way back to me." She wiped her eyes and waved her hand at her face to stem off the flow of tears as she backed out of the bathroom, closing the door.

I stripped the rest of my clothes off and stood underneath the hot water, letting in run down my face as I absorbed the heat. When I finally felt warm, I scrubbed my skin red and washed my hair twice. Anything to clean off whatever heaviness pulled at me, wanting to weigh me down.

The bathroom door opened, and Paige called out to me. "Your clean clothes are on the sink counter. I'll be downstairs with Mary. Yell if you need me."

I pulled a corner of the shower curtain back. "Thanks. I'll be down in a few minutes."

My muscles protested when I moved too fast. I guess that was what happened when you lost yourself so entirely that you didn't even have it in you to move for days at a time.

Paige had found me my comfiest sweatpants and a soft, cotton T-shirt. I pulled on my clothes, ran a comb through my hair, and then brushed my teeth. When I opened the bathroom door, the doorbell rang. As I made my way down the stairs, I noticed a deliveryman holding a flower arrangement. Mary signed for it and closed the door. When she turned, she saw me. "More flowers. Where would you like them?"

"More?" I allowed myself to look further past her and around the living room. Every available open spot had a vase or basket. "What am I supposed to do with all of these?"

"If you don't want all of them, you could send them to the hospital. There are lots of people there that might get some enjoyment out of them," Paige said as she swept her hand in an arch at the floral shop that had taken over my living room.

I made my way down the last two steps and went over to the first arrangement on my left. "Yeah, that would be great."

"I left the cards on them so that we can send thank-you notes to everyone. If you want, we can mark what they sent on the back of the cards before you donate the flowers."

Paige grabbed a pen and I pulled each card out, to read who the flowers came from, and then handed it to her, so she could make a small note of what it came off. Aiden, Mark, Josh, Eli, and Jared's parents all sent beautiful plants. They knew me well enough to send something I could keep.

"Paige?" I rubbed the petal of a white carnation between my fingers, focusing on the satiny feel of it.

Paige's hand stilled mid-scribble, and she turned to look at me. "Yeah?"

I let go of the flower petal, moved to the next arrangement, and plucked the card from its holder. I handed it to her, not really reading it. "Can you tell the guys… tell 'em I'm okay and that I appreciate them wanting to come, but it's not necessary?"

She tried to scoff at me. "No, really, that's the way I want it. Dad wasn't into funerals, so I don't plan on doing anything. Besides, they all have things they're doing right now. Knowing they'd drop everything to be here is enough."

Paige reached out, putting her hand on my arm. "Are you sure, Riley?"

I gave a sharp nod. I'd made my decision, and I'd stick by it. Paige knew it too, because she pulled her hand away and went back to filling out the back of each card I handed her.

When we were finished, a majority of the flower arrangements were loaded into Paige's car, minus the beautiful wreath of white roses with gold ribbon from Dr. Anderson. I hung that on the outside of the front door, as Paige grabbed her keys.

Something tugged at the back of my mind—something having to do with Paige and the hospital. I rubbed my temple, trying to remember what it was.

"Riley, don't worry about it. Going back there doesn't bother me anymore."

When she pulled out of the driveway, I remembered why. Paige no longer worked there because they hired someone else. I felt awful that she'd just driven away with a carload of flowers to a place she probably never wanted to see again.

Mary came up beside me and wrapped her arm around my waist. I leaned into her, taking the comfort she gave. "I'm really sorry you missed Ace's graduation."

She squeezed me tighter and stepped back, so we could go inside the house. "You needed me here."

"And Ace needed you there."

"Jake understands, Riley. He was so upset when he found out and couldn't be here for you. He asked me to stay here."

I walked over, pulled a cup down from the cupboard, and filled it with water. "What happened to him coming here on leave?"

Mary followed me into the living room and sat down on the couch, next to the box that hadn't been moved since I'd set it there. "His team received some sort of orders. He couldn't talk about it with me, but he promised he'd call us as soon as he could. I don't even know how long he'll be away for." Her lips curved into a smile. The sort of smile you fake when you were trying your hardest not to cry.

I poured the last bit of water out into the soil of a pink-colored Hydrangea and gathered my thoughts. Mary needed me just as much as I needed her. I kept her mind off Ace and she kept me close, stepping in like a mom would do when your life fell apart. It was hard to hate a woman who hadn't been around for a very long time, but at that moment, I detested my mother and hoped she'd never find her way back to me.

"I think you should find a nice spot to put your um, the box—your dad." She winced as she struggled with what to say.

Breathe in, breathe out.

Pick a spot.

Any spot that placed what was left of my dad in my line of vision.

Across the room, mounted to the wall, was a shelf my dad built when he was younger. It had hung on the wall ever since I could remember. That was the place.

I used my nail to break the tape and opened the flaps, revealing a dark Mahogany box inside. Engraved in the wood was his name, date of birth, and date of death. I pinched my lips together and pulled the box to my chest, wrapping my arms around the satiny feel of the polished wood. "I think up there would be nice."

Mary walked up beside me and looked at the shelf. We'd have to move a few things, but that was no big deal. She left my side long enough to grab a rag and some furniture polish. In just minutes, a spot was cleared. I lifted the box up and slid it on the shelf. It fit like it was meant to be there.

CHAPTER 18

6 **Months Later:**
Life to the living carried on after the death of someone you loved. There was nothing you could do to change it. You were forced to accept it—or not to accept it. I did my fair share of 'what ifs' after the death of my dad. I wandered the house like a ghost myself most days, waiting for a sign that it was okay to move on with my life. Waiting on a phone call from Ace. Waiting.

Mary stopped by at least three times a week to check on me. Paige forced me out of the house until I started doing it on my own. It was then when I knew I'd chosen to continue on. It was then I knew I needed to focus on myself and let everything else happen the way it was supposed to. Waiting for Ace to call only made me fall further into a depression that seeped the colors from my world. I couldn't let anyone have that much power over me. I loved him. I'd wait for him. But I damned sure wasn't going to stop living because he wasn't around. He was at least still alive.

Dr. Anderson hired me on as his part-time assistant with

the stipulation that I had to sign up for college. So I did. When I wasn't in the cab of Dr. Anderson's truck, bouncing around on a back road, I was sitting in front of a college professor, taking notes.

Mark, Eli, Josh, Jared, and even Aiden called me from time to time. And Mark sent the picture of all seven of us that he'd taken at the cabin. It was one of his best photos, I thought. I'd hung it on the opposite wall of the living room from where my dad's ashes were, surrounding me with the reminders of those I loved.

Paige decided to take Mark's offer and move to New York, on the condition that I'd come and visit her every year. She told me that the first year I missed would be the year she moved back home and then kicked my ass. Not that she'd do either one of those things, but it was nice hearing the threatening tone in her voice when she'd said it. It made me fully understand what our friendship meant to her. I helped her pack and waved to her when she pulled out of her driveway. Tears slid down her cheeks when she stopped, rolled down the window, and blew me a kiss. It took everything in me not to call her back and make her stay, so that I wouldn't be alone.

When Josh found out that Paige had left, he called me, asking me if I wanted him to come home. He told me he didn't like the thought that I was on my own without any of my friends around. It took a while to convince him that I was fine. That I was where I wanted to be, and I damned sure didn't want anyone to give up their lives so they could hold my hand, as if I couldn't do it without someone constantly beside me.

I had to do it. I had to prove to myself that life could be lived on my own. Without the crutch of someone hovering over me like I was fragile. Someone ready to splinter apart because of all of the cracks. I wasn't porcelain. I was flesh and blood. Bones and skin. All working together. All healing together. Every day reinforced it. Every day made me stronger, as the cracks fused together a little more. A patch-worked me that could stand resilient, no matter what life threw at me.

And I'd done so well.

~

It'd been a long day. First class, and then a call from Dr. Anderson asking me to come assist him with an emergency call because someone had dropped off a dog that had been hit by a car. It'd been bad. Four hours of surgery later, and then it was a wait-and-see game. If he were strong enough, he might make it. Chances were, though, he wouldn't last through the night. I'd numbed myself from it. I couldn't allow the bitterness of the negligent driver, that left him on the side of the road, swallow me whole. I pushed back the tears that rimmed my eyes and threatened to spill. The closed-off feeling in my throat when I tried to swallow. I pushed all of it back and drove home.

Mary's car sat in my driveway, and I couldn't help but wonder why she was there. I never saw her on Thursdays because she usually worked a double shift. I jammed the truck in park and cut the ignition. Before my imagination could get out of control, she stepped outside with a wave. My shoulders sagged in relief, as I palmed the keys and got out of the truck.

I met her at the door, and she pulled me into a hug. "How was your day?"

I shook my head with a snort of disgust. "Long. And it ended really shitty. How come you're here?" I felt awful after I said it. Mary didn't need a reason to come to the house.

She chewed on her bottom lip, clasping her hands in front of her. "I wanted to talk to you about something."

My stomach clenched, as I watched her face for a hint as to what was wrong. "It can't be that bad. Can it?" A nervous laugh attached itself to my question.

Mary crossed her arms and hugged them against her chest. "The diner cut my hours and, to add insult to injury, my landlord passed away some time ago. Now his kids want to take all of his properties and sell them. They've given me a month to 'clear out' is how they put it."

I walked over to the couch and sat with a heavy plop. My dad would have given me hell for it. 'The couch is not a trampoline, Riley,' he would have said. I felt a flicker of a smile crawl across my lips and looked around. Being here on my own was lonely. Not that my house was huge, but it felt lifeless with only me bumbling around in it most days. In fact, the only time it felt like a home was when Mary was there, fluttering around the kitchen. Her laugh made the walls seem less like a cage and more like a shelter.

"I've started looking at apartments…" Her voice cut into my wandering thoughts.

"No. You're coming here. This is where you belong." I said it with such finality that she jumped.

She closed her eyes and took a deep breath. When she released it, she crossed the room and sat down beside me on the couch. "Riley, I really appreciate the offer, but this is your home. Maybe when Jake gets back, it'll be your home together. You don't need me here… in the way."

What she said confused me. How could she ever think she'd be in the way?

"Do you even know when Jake will be back? And what about when he leaves again? You have work. I have school. We both have things to do and not enough money between the two of us to live on our own. It's the best thing for both of us."

What I'd said wasn't entirely true. The life insurance policy my dad had taken out covered everything. The house was paid for. All I had to do was keep up with the other bills and taxes. There was even enough money left over for a comfortable savings account. But there was no reason to tell her that. It would only make her think she'd be taking advantage of me. The truth of it was... I selfishly needed her. If she got an apartment, she'd probably have to get a second job to pay for everything, and she wouldn't be around much. There was no way I'd let her do that.

"Riley, it wasn't my intention for you to offer up your home. I just wanted you to know I'd be moving. And to see if you'd help me since I know I can't move the entire house on my own," she said, picking up my hand and squeezing it.

My head fell back against the couch cushion, and I heaved a sigh. She wasn't just going to give in. "Mary, I want you to stay here. I don't like living on my own, and there's plenty of room for the both of us. You'd be doing me a favor if you came here to live."

Silence filled the space between us, as she worried her lip and looked away from me. "I'll think about it."

I nudged her with my knee. "Don't think too long about it. There's a lot we need to do to get you ready to move in here."

Her laugh sounded a little off and I leaned forward, getting a good look at her face. She dashed the tears away and nodded. "Fine. Since you're not giving me much of a choice, I suppose the best thing to do is agree with you. But, Riley? The minute it gets to be too much or you want to be on your own, you have to promise me that you'll tell me. Okay?"

I felt like a bobble head with the way my head dipped and

swayed. She'd agreed to stay. Neither of us would be alone anymore.

~

Over the next week, we'd packed up her house during the day and then went back home to sort through what I had. Converging two houses together was time consuming and a little overwhelming, but Mary made it sort of fun.

We'd started with the hardest part first. Cleaning out my dad's room. Mary had insisted I take the master bedroom so that we could just move my stuff and Ace's in at the same time. I'd blushed when she said it, but she continued as if it were no big deal.

When it came time to move the heavy furniture, I enlisted Dr. Anderson, Seth, and Aaron to help us. By the end of the day, all the big furniture was moved and set up. All that was left was to finish packing up the rest of whatever Mary wanted to keep. She didn't have a whole lot to pack and yet, she still managed to have several boxes of things she'd planned to donate to the Red Cross.

Between the two of us, we put a huge dent in all the extra stuff in my house to make room. It was the first time in a long time that my house had a feminine touch. Gone were the dark curtains, replaced by sheer panels that allowed the sun to light up the room. Soft, fluffy towels were stacked inside the linen closet that had a hinted scent of lavender that escaped when you opened the door. The windows were so clean that you could see your reflection when you passed by them.

My chest didn't ache anymore on the ride home at the end of the day. I felt liberated and whole again, knowing my home was filled with laughter and love. She and I, we'd make it. And when Ace came home, it would only get better.

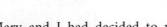

Mary and I had decided to paint the living room a soft, buttery yellow, so all the furniture was pulled to the middle of the room. We were almost done when my cell phone rang. I'd taken to keeping it in my back pocket, so I didn't miss any calls. Not hearing from Ace for so long had weighed heavy on me. Would it always be like that? Could I just pick up and move off to wherever he was, only to sit around wondering when the phone would ring? I shook my head and set the paint roller in its tray. Pulling the phone out of my back pocket, I glanced at the screen and a moment of panic shot through me. Unknown Caller. I swiped my finger across the screen and answered.

"Hello." The line was static filled, but I swear I could hear someone breathing on the other end.

I pushed the phone against my ear as hard as I could, hoping to hear better.

"Riley... so sorry..." I knew that voice. I could pick it out of a crowd of a hundred people.

"Ace!" The connection hummed and popped in my ear. Garbled noised scratched at my eardrum, but he never answered. It sounded as if he stood in the middle of a crowd, and the noise drowned out all else. "Ace, can you hear me?" Nothing. Absolute silence. "Jake?" He didn't answer. I pulled the phone away from my ear and saw that the call had been dropped. I pushed the number and tried to redial it, but all I got was a weird tone, and then it disconnected.

"Is everything okay, Riley?" Mary asked, putting her hand on my arm.

I looked at her and slipped the phone into my back pocket. "I don't know. That was Jake. I'm sure of it, but the call dropped, and I can't call it back."

She nodded her head and plastered a smile on her face.

"I'm sure he'll call you back as soon as he gets a better connection."

She was right. She had to be. There was no way Ace called just to tell me he was sorry. What the hell did he have to be sorry for, and why call just to say that? I'd rather he'd said 'I'm coming home'. I shook my head to keep the bitterness from setting in. There was a reasonable explanation, and I wasn't going to get angry with him. That he'd called would be enough until the next time I spoke to him. When I did, I'd tell him his phone conversations were severely lacking.

No matter how much I wanted to push it aside, it nagged at me for the rest of the day.

After all the furniture was moved back into place, I jogged up the stairs and grabbed a shower. I was probably the worst painter in the world. There was more on me than the walls.

Mary and I ordered pizza for dinner. Neither one of us had it in us to cook. Between moving, cleaning, and work, both of us were exhausted. It was a good kind of tired though. The type where you fall into bed, have a dreamless sleep, and wake up refreshed enough to tackle a new day.

It had been two days since Ace's mysterious call. He hadn't called back, and a niggling sense of worry danced on my nerves. When Mary and I packed his stuff up, we'd put the boxes in my closet. I decided that I'd put them away when I got home from class. My English Lit professor was long winded, and I found myself drifting off as he spoke. Most days, I fought just to keep my eyes open, and my grades reflected it. I couldn't wait for class to be over with. I just needed to get through twenty more minutes, then I'd be able to jump in my truck and head home. I had to pass the class, so I forced myself to pay attention.

When the hour was up, I all but ran out of the room and to the parking lot. My truck roared to life and I rolled my window down, letting the fresh air wake me up. Ten minutes later, I pulled into the driveway and parked. A car I'd never seen before sat in front of the house, making me wonder if maybe Mary had company that stopped by.

Upon closer inspection, I could see someone sitting inside the car. I slammed my truck door shut and took a step towards the other vehicle, when the driver's side door opened and a man dressed in uniform got out. He closed his door with a soft thunk and pulled his cap onto his head. Confused as to why he was there, I waited for him to walk up to me.

"Excuse me, Miss, but does Mary Aceton live here?" he asked, looking from me to the house.

I felt myself stiffen. "She does. May I ask why you're here?"

"I need to speak to her, please." He wasn't giving an inch, but neither was I.

The front door opened, and Mary called out. "Riley? Who's here?"

The man in front of me spun on his heels and walked over to where Mary stood in the open doorway. "Are you Mary Aceton?"

Her hand flew to her throat. "Yes."

The man gestured to the doorway. "May I come in for a moment?"

Mary stepped back, disappearing inside the house, and I found myself moving forward without even thinking about it. That man dressed in uniform wasn't welcome here. He had bad news. I could feel it.

I made it into the house, as Mary dropped into a kitchen

chair. The sharply dressed soldier had removed his hat and held it in front of him with a hand that clutched it tight.

I walked over, stood behind Mary's chair, and put my hand on her shoulder. Her hand shot up and grasped at mine.

"Ms. Aceton, my name is Sergeant Phillip McKinney. I served in the same special ops team as your son, Jake. Ma'am, there's no easy way to say this, so I'll just…" He paused for a second, and I watched his Adam's apple bob up and down. "Jake's team was sent in on a mission. The mission was compromised. The transport carrying part of my team was taken out. Jake was one of the men who didn't make it."

I felt my knees giving out on me, and I swayed behind Mary. Her sob cracked something that I thought I had a hold on wide open. I shook from head to toe and forced my legs to hold me. "There has to be a misunderstanding. Ace just called me the other day."

Sergeant Phillip's lips pulled flat along his teeth. "That's impossible, ma'am. The attack happened last week." He shoved his hand inside his pants pocket and pulled out a long chain. It dangled from his fingers in a flash of silver. "This is the only thing that we could find."

I reached out, snatched the dog tags from his fingers, and ran my thumb over Jake's name. "I think you better look into this a little more. Jake called me two days ago. I know it was him!" I shook the dog tags in the air between us. "How can you say this is all that's left? He wore these, correct?"

Sergeant Phillip's stance never changed. He remained calm and kept a steady eye on me. "I understand it's hard to believe, ma'am. Trust me, I know."

I snorted at what he said and rolled my eyes. "You claim he was under attack wearing these. I find it odd that there isn't even a single black mark or scratch on them. You're lying, and I want to know why! And I want to know where Ace is!"

Mary shot up from her seat and grabbed a hold of me, catching me before I shoved the man standing in front of me. It was like she knew I was at the end of my rope and about to snap.

Sergeant Phillip's stance changed. He relaxed and slapped his hat against his leg. "Ace said you were a spitfire." One side of his mouth kicked up at the corner. Not quite a smile, not quite a grimace, and I wanted to scratch it off his face with both hands.

"Ms. Aceton, I'm truly sorry for your loss. I know it in no way brings back your son, but I'm sorry all the same. You'll be contacted by personal later in the week with routine paperwork that will have to be filled out. Until then, here's my number if you need anything."

Mary's hand shook so hard that Sergeant Phillip had to steady it with one hand and put the card between her fingers with his other. He didn't let her go right away. "I considered him a friend and am honored to have served with him."

Mary nodded and clutched the card in her hand. I looked between the two of them in shock. "That's it? Here's my card, sorry for your loss?"

"Riley…" Mary went to put her hand on my arm.

"*No!* I refuse to believe this lie! Get out of my house. Ace is not dead! Do you hear me? *He's not dead!*" I shoved him, and I kept shoving him, until he was out the door and I'd slammed it, locking it between us. Nothing bad could happen when you closed the door and locked it. No more lies could be spread to your ears if you couldn't hear them. I caught myself as I teetered forward against the door, sliding until my forehead pressed against the wood and clutched at the silver chain still wrapped around my fingers.

He was not dead. He couldn't be. He called me… told me he was… told me he was sorry! Sorry for what? For pretending he was dead? For allowing someone to come to his mother and say he'd died while on a mission?

Why would he lie like that? He had to be in trouble. That had to be the reason for the farce going on around us. I refused to accept it. I refused to let Mary accept it. I pushed myself off the door and watched as Mary crumpled to the ground.

I pulled her into my lap, and she wrapped her arms around me. Her heart-wrenching sobs shook both of us, and I let her cry. She needed to cry because she believed Sergeant Phillip. She believed the lies he so easily gave us.

I held her until her soft, keening wails were further and further apart. I made her stand and walked her to the couch. Pulled a blanket over her and shifted a pillow under her head. The same thing she'd done for me the day she found me on the floor, when I'd found out that my father had died. I watched her eyes flutter closed, as she breathed though the choppy breaths that crying leaves you with. When I knew she was asleep, I went upstairs and pulled my cell phone out of my pocket. Who could I call? Who could help me uncover the lies given to us by a uniformed man who claimed to be Ace's friend?

I rubbed at my head and took a long, deep breath, blowing it out on a sigh as my eyes pricked with unshed tears. I would not mourn him. I refused to let myself feel that pain because deep down in my heart, I knew he was alive. He had to be alive. I couldn't lose another person I loved.

I blinked, clearing my wavered vision, and went to the recent call list, selecting the number that I'd repeatedly tried to get through to. It didn't even ring as it went to an annoying, steady beep that told me the number was no longer any good. Lies and deception. How the hell was I supposed to fight against the government? Who would believe me? Who would stand up and fight with me?

Aiden was military. He might be able to look into it, but then again, he might just accept what they said too. I didn't need to be told to accept what they'd told me, and I had a feeling that Aiden would say just that. Eli was halfway around the world, and I couldn't ask him to come home early for me. Josh was in no place to help me; he had a hard enough time helping himself most days. Paige and Mark? They were finally happy together, both on the fast track with their careers. No, they were out. That left Jared. Could I call him and ask him for help? Would he help me without it jeopardizing his rock-n-roll lifestyle? Maybe he could help me hire a lawyer or a private investigator... somebody to help me figure out just what the hell had happened. Maybe he could ask his parents to help me. I knew I was reaching at straws, but it was all I had.

I pulled his number up and put the phone to my ear, as I chewed on my thumbnail. When he answered, all I could hear was what sounded like an argument. Jared yelled at someone and then something scratched across my eardrum. I pulled the phone away and was about to hang up when I heard Jared's voice again. He let out one final string of curse words before he answered with a sigh.

"Hey, Riles."

My throat closed up. My words died on my lips. I'd never been so scared to speak about something in my life and Jared, he'd want all the details.

"Riley... you there?" I could hear the concern in his voice.

I shuddered as I forced myself to answer. "Jared..." My voice came out sounding like a scared child, and I heard him suck in a deep breath.

"What happened? What's wrong?"

"Jared... it's Ace."

"Just stay put, Riley. I'll be there as soon as I can." The phone disconnected, and I dropped it on the bed. Jared was coming home. He'd know what to do. The tears I'd tried so hard to keep at bay broke free and I curled into a ball on my bed, crying until I couldn't breathe.

Jared was on his way. Jared would know what to do. Ace was not dead. We'd move heaven and hell to prove it.

DID YOU ENJOY THE SUMMER I FELL?

If you enjoyed this book, please take a few seconds to review, rate, and/or share on any social media platform that you've finished and loved it. Just a couple seconds and a few words make all the difference to the work authors put into their writing and promoting.

It is for you that I write, and it is to you that I am indebted.

♥ **Sonya Loveday**

ACKNOWLEDGMENTS

To my betas…Megan and Candice, thank you for your input and being just as excited as I was about this new series. You ladies ROCK!

Lovena West, thank you for allowing me to use your amazing photos.

A huge thank you to my editor, Cynthia Shepp for keeping me in check, and calling me to the carpet when things 'wouldn't work that way'.

To Rebecca Gaskill, thank you for being the last set of eyes. Your help means more than you know!

As always, I thank my family for being so supportive and encouraging. My bestest Candace, for being the bestest. *I squish you*

And last, but not least, my sincerest thanks to my readers. I hope you enjoyed the first book in The Six Series!

DEDICATION

Mom & Dad
As always, much love.

Mom & Dad P.
You're the best in-laws a girl could ask for.

Taylor
Enjoy the next four years!

Will
Keep rockin' that beanie!

Billy
Some people spend their entire lives searching for what we have.

Sonya Loveday is a full time author. Mother of two teenagers. Wife to an amazing man for 19 years. Dog lover. Cat lover.

coffee addict. Night Owl. She's a sucker for a good book. Loves the quiet life. Has the bestest best friend in the whole world.

Her imagination never shuts off which makes it hard to sleep. The worst cook. Seriously.

www.sonyaloveday.com
sonya.loveday@gmail.com

Being a **Newsletter** Subscriber has it's *perks*!

Want to keep up to date with all things Sonya Loveday?

Being a subscriber means you get:

- First look at covers
- Free ebooks
- Exclusive Giveaways
- Early announcements
- & More

www.sonyaloveday.com

TITLES BY SONYA LOVEDAY

THE CASTED SERIES

Casted

Spelled

THE SIX SERIES

The Summer I Fell (Book 1)

End Note (Book 2)

Relevance (Book 2.5)

If Ever I Fall (Book 3)

The Vows We Make (Book 4)

All We Are (Book 5)

Under Northern Lights (Book 6 - Coming Nov 16th, 2017)

GAME OF HEARTS NOVELS

BY SONYA LOVEDAY & CANDACE KNOEBEL

Love Always

Runaway Heart

When Two Hearts Collide

SWOONWORTHY STANDALONES

What It Takes

Made in the USA
Middletown, DE
07 December 2017